DIA COULDN'T HELP WONDERING
IF HE WOULD PENETRATE HER DISGUISE.

She had just opened her mouth to give an excuse for their presence when Unknown leveled his gun over her shoulder and fired, drilling a small, silent hole in the young man's face. Before Dia could react, he had pushed her aside and sprung forward to catch the sagging body before it could strike the desk.

At Talley's signal, the rest of the team came in. By gesture, they reported the corridor quiet. Softly, they shut the anteroom door. The locksmith knelt at the inner door, tested it, found it locked, and began to manipulate her equipment. Unknown took Dia's arm in a crushing grip and drew her to one side, away from any line of sight from the inner office. Talley and the other team member stood over the locksmith, waiting tensely, their guns drawn. At the locksmith's nod, Unknown slammed his hand over Dia's mouth and gave his own nod. Dia was too angry to struggle against the sudden restraint as she watched the door slide open.

Phyllis Eisenstein

IN THE HANDS
OF GLORY

A TIMESCAPE BOOK
PUBLISHED BY POCKET BOOKS NEW YORK

This novel is a work of fiction. Names, characters, places and incidents are either the product of the author's imagination or are used fictitiously, and any resemblance to actual persons, living or dead, events or locales is entirely coincidental.

Another *Original* publication of TIMESCAPE BOOKS

 A Timescape Book published by
POCKET BOOKS, a Simon & Schuster division of
GULF & WESTERN CORPORATION
1230 Avenue of the Americas, New York, N.Y. 10020

Copyright © 1981 by Phyllis Eisenstein

ISBN: 0-671-83335-9

First Timescape Books printing November, 1981

10 9 8 7 6 5 4 3 2 1

POCKET and colophon are trademarks of Simon & Schuster.

Use of the TIMESCAPE trademark under exclusive license from trademark owner.

Printed in the U.S.A.

for Lynne Aronson,
best of friends

PART ONE
PRISONER

We were orbiting Beta Corvi, engaged in routine maintenance, when the courier arrived. I suspected the contents even before unsealing the cannister—for years rumors had been circulating from world to world and throughout the fleets: the Congress of Planets, in secret session, was debating the fate of the Federation; already the organization was breaking down as farflung members ignored the central authority. I had heard those rumors and tried to quell them, never believing that the end would come in my lifetime. Yet now I held the recall order in my hands:

> The 36th Tactical Strike Force will report immediately to Patrol HQ to participate in ceremonies marking the dissolution of the Stellar Federation.

There followed a directive on the disposition of my ships subsequent to the ceremonies—some to be distributed among planets near HQ, some to be turned over for auction, the majority to be retired to "permanent storage." The message ended:

> After the Federation Patrol is disbanded, every effort will be made by the independent planetary governments to find alternative employment for Patrol personnel.

Like our ships, we were going to be junked.

> —from the *Memoirs of Brigadier General
> Marcus Bohannon, Commander,
> 36th Tactical Strike Force,
> Stellar Federation Patrol*

ONE

An instant frozen in memory: above, beside, before, behind—the placid sky; below—the sculptured carpet of summer-green forest, with rivulets like silver wire sparkling under the high sun. The aircraft rode an electromagnetic jetstream across the winds of Amphora; in the cockpit, Dia opened her mouth to ask her companion some trivial question. . . .

The instant melted in chaos: a flash too brilliant for the eyes, leaving darkness in its wake; a sound too loud for the ears, ringing through flesh and blood and bone; a breath-snatching concussion, as if a giant hand had batted the craft aside.

Blind, deaf, numb, she screamed the pilot's name even as she reached for her own controls.

Vision came back slowly, black and gold, a narrow corridor set with burnished bits of brass. The sky was a shimmering clockface, the horizon a spinning sweep hand. Her fingers tugged at the steering grips, flicked switches, rapped dials, pushed, pulled . . . but Dia felt none of it—they were someone else's fingers, directed at a distance by her will.

Fighting the sluggish controls, she chanced a sidelong glance at Michael. His pilot's console was a wreckage, and fragments of the shattered windscreen glittered among the ruins. His chair was cracked and smoldering. He slumped in the seat, held there by only one strap, his body blackened, bloody, ripped from groin to neck, his skull showing sudden white where the face was peeled away.

Dia's own blood blurred the horrid vision, closing her eyes when she could not; smearing it away with one crimson sleeve, she was able to wrench her attention back to her own half of the cockpit. The horizon had slowed its mad reeling, but now the forest loomed close. Wind screamed past her cheeks as she cursed the failing grips, the gutted fusilage, the dying engines, but her skin was numb to the blast, and her ears were filled with the discordant toll of bells. Heeling the craft around, she sought an open landing space; there was none. The forest changed with proximity: the nubbly carpet became an endless expanse of green-fringed pikes. Branches scoured the bottom of the craft, and it bucked and twisted like a living mount. A series of jolts swung it right, left, right again, and then its nose caught and the great metal bird heaved tail upward in a ponderous somersault. Shuddering, it came to rest upside down among the broken trees.

She dangled from her chair, its harness preventing her from falling to the canopy. Feebly, her fingers scrabbled at the buckles. Her head felt near bursting, and her lungs struggled against a great weight. The last thing she saw before consciousness slipped away was Michael's skull-face, staring at her, blood dripping from it in a steady rhythm.

TWO

Once more she stands at attention in the graduation line, one of thirty shiny-new third lieutenants waiting for the Brigadier to set gold bars upon their shoulders. Once more she hears the anthem of the Patrol, all brass and drums, vibrating the ground beneath her boots. She hardly notices the Brigadier himself—he is merely a tall shape moving slowly toward her, pausing at the man on her left, then abruptly blocking her field of vision. She perceives the tug at each shoulder as the insignia slips into place, feels the firm grip on her proffered hand; when it is released, she snaps an automatic salute, and the Brigadier answers briefly before sliding onward. . . .

Now she sees that face in the crowd once more. A single face in the front row, vignetted by the gray blur of a hundred other faces. A dark-haired face with trim mustache, shaggy brows, a high-bridged nose, eyes black as space. Those eyes have followed her from the moment she climbed to the dais, from the moment her own gaze made chance contact with them. Who is he? she wonders again—the face seems familiar, but her memory has no name to give it. He smiles, and in that smile she can read a message, a question . . . a promise. She smiles in return, a mere quirk of the lips, nothing unbecoming a newly minted officer; and they smile together until the time when the new officers must turn and march off, eyes front, arms and legs swinging in unison.

Evening and the celebration: each graduate on the arm of a parent, women with their fathers, men with their mothers, leading the Grand Parade. Many are the great names represented here; many the high ranks and the decorations, to match the aspirations of the young. Resplendent in dress uniform, they strut around the floor like exotic birds, be-

12

decked with plumes and gold and flashing gems, a circle of royal blue and white. Dia walks with her father, her fingers light upon his arm, her eyes searching for a face in the throng.

Then a hand touches her shoulder, and she turns, knowing that he has been watching her all along.

Music whirls them away, rushes about them like a riptide, drenches them. Locked together, they swoop, they sail, they soar, as if they have been dancing partners all their lives. They circle the room, weaving among the other dancers like gold threads highlighting a tapestry. There are no words between them, not while the music makes its demands, but their eyes speak. And then they are through the great double doors and outside, on the wide balcony of this tallest spire of the Citadel. The clean wind snatches at their breath as they cling to the balustrade and each other.

"So," he says, and he holds her at arm's length and looks at her afresh. For the first time she sees his full-major's leaves, and the four marksmanship medals on his chest. He is tall, and his hands are strong on her shoulders. "You," he says. "I want you."

She catches his wrists, clamping her fingers hard to still their shaking. His eyes loom, dark and deep. She cannot tear her own away from them. "I don't even know your name," she whispers.

"Michael Drew."

"I know that name."

He smiles again, that selfsame smile. "Of course you do."

She touches the row of medals, senses the muscles beneath them, fancies she can even feel the pulsing heart, though the pounding she hears is her own heart, racing wildly. "I know that name."

His lips are warm, and his breath is sweet, and his arms are too strong to push away, even if she wanted to.

Michael.

Michael.

Michael.

She woke to dimness, to silence, and to pain. Her first conscious breath was a needle in her left side, echoing in her shoulder and neck, rippling down her arm. Clenching her teeth, she tried to exhale slowly. Her whole body ached as if she had been beaten with steel bars. Except

her legs—those she could not feel at all. Her mouth tasted
of blood. She moaned softly, his name.

"Don't move, Lieutenant," said a high-pitched, childlike voice near her head. A shape bent over her, a shadow
among shadows; she could not make out features or clothing. "You are in pain?"

"My side," she whispered.

A slight pressure of fingers at her temples brought a
and body had immensely lengthened. Her eyelids drooped,
but at a distance, as if the connections between her mind
and body and immensely lengthened. Her eyelids drooped,
and taut muscles relaxed. She could think now, though her
mind seemed encased in gel. Her ribs were cracked, she
knew, and worse—from the hips down she had no sensation. *I'm smashed to pieces. I should be dead. Like Michael.*
The memory of his corpse cut through her stupor; she
opened her eyes against it, against the tears that struggled
in her chest and throat. Desperately, she searched for something else to focus on. She lay upon her back, on a hard
surface, a blanket pulled up to her chin. If there were
walls or ceiling anywhere about, they were lost in the
gloom; only the faintest illumination, as from a distant
candle, relieved the darkness. Cool, damp air assailed her
nostrils.

To her unknown companion, she whispered, "Who are
you?"

"Rest, Lieutenant. Conserve your strength."

"Are you loyal? Or a rebel?"

Only silence answered her question.

Far off, a light appeared—it bobbed and flashed like a
firefly, brightening until it became a lantern carried by a
slow-walking man. In the growing radiance, Dia could begin to see her surroundings—a wall of pale stone rose on
her right, its surface glinting with moisture. Her bed was
a thin med-evac pallet, resting on a floor of hard-packed
earth some few meters broad. Beyond this lay a wilderness
of rubble—massive slabs of limestone, piled man-high,
tumbled or tilted in ragged rows, like dominoes rudely
dumped from their boxes. Among these scattered mega-
liths wound a narrow path, along which came the man. Entering the clear space, he set the lantern near Dia's hip and
knelt beside it. He was a lean, hollow-cheeked fellow, with
hair so blond that his brows and lashes were nearly invisible against his pale skin. Dark clothing lent him a

spectral quality, as if his hands and head floated in the shadowy air.

"Lieutenant Catlin? I'm your doctor." His voice was deep and resonant. He touched her forehead gently, and now she realized that her face was heavily bandaged. "So you're having some pain? Well, that's not surprising. You're lucky to be alive."

"How bad is it?" she murmured.

His gaze shifted to her lower left thigh; she perceived faint, colored lights dancing across his face and surmised that he was consulting a medical display. "I don't think you want to know that right now. Don't worry—you're young, you'll heal quickly. I don't expect any permanent damage."

"My legs . . ."

"Nerve blocks. You won't be doing much walking in the near future." He climbed to his feet and picked up the lantern. "Relax, Lieutenant—you're going to be all right." He turned away, his body shielding the glow, casting vaulting shadows on the rock wall.

"Please, Doctor," she whispered, "leave me a light."

He glanced back. "Tomorrow. You won't be needing it today."

She felt a touch above her nose, the fingers of the unseen companion, who must have been sitting behind her head. Almost immediately, bone-weariness crept down her body, and her vision blurred. Her last waking thought was of Michael.

THREE

Around the parallel bars, up and over and around again,
flight without wings, swooping, soaring, twisting; left hand,
right hand, knees straight, up and over one last time, then
double somersault down! The mat jars beneath her feet,
and then Michael scoops her into his arms and swings her
around; centrifugal force flings her ankles up and away.

"Beautiful!" he shouts, his voice loud in her ears. "Beau-
tiful," he whispers, nuzzling her neck.

Limp, she hangs on him like a cloth doll, her breath
ragged. Every muscle aches; her arms shake, her wrists
feel like jelly. Her head lolls back as he lowers her to
the mat and begins a slow massage. Her back, her shoul-
ders, her arms. . . . As he works, he speaks of the future,
of competitions and awards, of his pride, and her parents'.
She sighs in pain and pleasure, hardly listening, but feeling,
feeling the smooth pressure of his hands on her sweat-
slick flesh. Gradually, his touch lightens, massage blending
into caress, and his voice sinks to a wordless murmur. He
leans close, his body brushing hers; she turns and reaches
out for him, for the whole of his weight. Tortured muscles
cry for her attention, but she ignores them. Michael is all;
Michael is everything; nothing else matters.

For an instant, when she opened her eyes, she thought
he lay beside her, that the crash and the pain and his death
were only a nightmare. A mellow glow and the sounds of
shuffling cards dragged her back to reality. An experimental breath told her the pain had returned. "Help me," she
gasped, and a delicate pressure at her temples immersed
her in a pool of euphoria. She lay shuddering for a long
moment and then murmured, "Thank you, whoever you
are."

A riffle of cards answered her.

Dia turned her face toward the sound and saw, on the floor beside her, illuminated by a small lantern, a plump, furry creature about one-half human size. A harness of black leather crossed its chest, supporting a holstered gun of unfamiliar design; and its eyes were hidden behind thick, dark goggles. It held a stack of playing cards in five-fingered paws, and its bewhiskered muzzle twitched as it turned over the top card and added it to the array on the floor. The animal was playing solitaire.

"What the hell . . . ?" said Dia.

The creature inclined its head in her direction, and a small pink tongue flicked out of its mouth. "My name," it said in a familiar, high voice, "is Strux. I am an adult male and your nurse. Do you play cribbage?"

"You're . . . not human," said Dia.

"No, indeed. I am, however, quite skilled in medical matters, and you may repose your utmost confidence in me."

Regaining her composure, Dia said, "I was not aware that any members of a nonhuman intelligent race were currently on Amphora." She delved into memories of the trading ships that occasionally touched down on her world: sometimes their crews were human, sometimes not. At a distance, she had seen saffron-skinned giants and feathered midgets; she knew, from holographs, of others that no one on Amphora had ever viewed in the flesh—scaly, chitinous, betentacled, they bore little resemblance to this sleek, brown-furred individual. "What planet are you from?"

Strux laid a red queen on a black king. "I apologize for not being allowed to answer that question, Lieutenant." Turning toward her, he said, "Am I to understand that you do not play cribbage?"

"No, I don't."

"A pity." His teeth were small, pointed; his nose was moist and black and mobile. "Would you care to learn?"

Cautiously, she moved her arms, found them stiff and awkward—the left would not bend at all, the right made only a shallow arc. Dragging at the blanket with weak fingers, she exposed her upper body. A loose, sleeveless gray tunic swaddled her, and the unbending arm was encased in a white tube from shoulder to knuckles; the other arm was bandaged with a flexible joint at the elbow. She could not lift either. "I don't think I could handle the cards right now."

His attention on the deck once more, Strux turned up the ace of hearts. "I know many games. Perhaps when you have mended somewhat, we will find one that is mutually suitable."

She gazed upward, along the glistening wall. "You give me the impression that I'll be here quite a long time."

"So you may," he replied.

She glanced at him sidelong. "And where is *here?*"

His nose twitched, whiskers bobbing. "Again, I am not allowed to answer."

"This is a cavern, isn't it?"

He gathered the cards together. "I am sure you will find cribbage a much more rewarding endeavor, Lieutenant, than this interrogation." He shuffled with swift precision. "Would you care for a drink of water?"

Thoughtfully, she tested her mouth with her tongue. "I don't seem to be thirsty."

Strux leaned over her, opened the collar of the tunic and prodded her left shoulder. By tucking her chin almost against her chest, Dia was able to see a small whitish hemisphere cradled in the hollow of her neck. "This will last perhaps an hour longer," he said. "After that, should you become thirsty I have been instructed to administer fluids orally." He settled back on his haunches, and Dia glimpsed a fat tail curving around the far side of his body.

"Am I allowed to sit up?"

"Not until the doctor gives his approval."

"When do I see him?"

"Soon. He sent orders to wake you for his visit." He dealt a pyramid of cards. "Otherwise, it is simpler and safer to keep you unconscious until your injuries have healed somewhat."

"Safer?"

"Excessive movement at this stage could delay your recovery."

Dia sighed. "And I don't ask questions while I'm unconscious."

Strux inclined his head, but whether that was a nod of agreement or merely a closer perusal of the cards, she could not tell.

In a matter of moments, the doctor arrived. In addition to a lantern, he carried a large cushion, which he dropped beside the pallet for a seat. Strux swept the cards aside to make room for him.

"Good morning," he said. "How are you feeling?"

"A little better. Not enough."

His fingers touched her cheek, turned her face toward him. "You heal quickly. We can take the tape off those lacerations soon."

She frowned, feeling the tug of bandages across her nose and forehead. "Was I badly cut? Will my face be scarred?"

"You were badly cut in a number of places," he replied. "But there's no reason to expect any scarring. You won't want to look at yourself in a mirror for a while, though."

"I *do* want to look at myself," she said firmly.

"You're bruised and swollen; you won't recognize yourself."

"I want to know about my condition, Doctor."

He smiled slightly. "You Patrollers are so damned stubborn." Reaching into his breast pocket, he pulled out a packet that unfolded into a large mirror. "I had the feeling I wouldn't be able to talk you out of it." He held the mirror above her face.

Dia stared at a stranger—an ugly stranger: a bulbous beak, a bloated travesty of her own narrow nose; bloodshot eyes sunk deep in puffy, discolored flesh; cheeks and forehead marred by scab-crusted lines visible beneath transparent dressings. Her stomach quivered at the sight. "How can you stand to look at me?" she murmured.

"I've seen worse," he said. "Had enough?"

"Wait." Under a veil of tangled hair, a thick metal band crossed her forehead; a red light glowed like a baleful eye in its center, and on either side were rows of studs marked with incised numbers. "What's the red light?"

"The Inducer. It keeps you feeling good."

"And puts me to sleep whenever you like?"

"Yes."

"All right, you can take the mirror away."

He folded it up and replaced it in his pocket. "Your face *looks* terrible, but the injuries are really minor— lacerations, contusions, a hairline fracture of the nose. You were apparently struck by flying debris."

Her lips tightened. "Yes, quite a lot of debris is generated when an antiaircraft beam hits its target. Very messy. What other injuries?"

"Are you sure you feel up to discussing them?"

"I'll never feel more up to it than I do now, thanks to your little Inducer. Let's not play games, Doctor."

"Very well," he said, meeting her stare. "Starting at the bottom—both of your legs were smashed; your left arm was just about torn off at the elbow, your right was ripped open to the bone, your ribs were crushed, your collarbone snapped . . . and you've seen your face. If your head had been as badly damaged as the rest, I wouldn't have been able to save you."

She shut her eyes and swallowed with difficulty. The catalog of damage made her stomach crawl, yet at the same time she could scarcely connect it with herself. How could she be so mangled, she marveled, and still live? She was glad they were all covered, the smashed and ripped parts; thinking about them only brought back the vision of Michael. She pushed away that memory, or tried to. "Thank you," she said at last. "I appreciate your honesty."

When he spoke next, his voice was muted, distant. "Damned stubborn Patrollers."

Opening her eyes, Dia saw that he had stepped back onto the path, lantern in hand. "Doctor? *You* put me back together?"

"Yes."

"Will I . . . will I work? My arms, my legs?"

He scowled and turned away. "Of course you'll work. I'm a damn good doctor."

"I owe you my life," she murmured, more to herself than to him.

Glancing back over his shoulder, he said, "Yes, you do." Lit from below, his face was cadaverous, the hollows of his cheeks deep, his eyes heavy-lidded. Fine lines seemed to drag at the corners of his mouth. His shoulders slumped, as if too weary to straighten. "You'd be quite dead now if they hadn't brought you to me."

Her throat tight, she said, "I wish . . . I owed you *his* life as well."

He hesitated a bare instant. "The pilot?"

"Yes."

"There was nothing I could do."

She stared upward, at empty air. "We were lovers."

Sometime in the vast silence that followed, small dark fingers touched her temples, and she gave in gratefully to the Inducer's power.

FOUR

She sees a line of targets stretching from one infinity to another, and a matching line of men and women in blue Patrol uniform, their right arms raised to shoulder height, their beamers leveled at the targets. Beside her, Michael fires shot after shot, the target chiming a clear, high note with every strike; then he switches hands and repeats the action. He shrugs—this is child's play to him. Dia's aim is not so accurate, and he stands behind her to guide her arm. She says, I don't need your help, but he only smiles and kisses her cheek. He says, think of it as a man; the bull's-eye is his heart; if you don't kill him, he'll kill you. Her aim improves. Her target rings steadily, and at the final shot it begins to tip over backward. She shouts, and as if her voice is the impetus, all the targets fall, one after the other, tumbling. . . . They strike the floor with a sound like distant thunder.

When she woke, the doctor and Strux were sitting nearby, and somewhere far away, the thunders of her dream echoed on. Her very pallet seemed to shake faintly in sympathy.

"What's happening?" she muttered, blinking sleep away.

The doctor laid a hand on her shoulder. "Nothing to worry about, Lieutenant."

"That can't be a storm."

"It isn't."

"What is it then?"

His lips curved in a slow smile. "You must be feeling better."

Startled, she said, "I am." Searching within herself, she found the pain a weak thing, a background against which she could feel her heartbeat, her breath, and the diffuse itch of healing flesh. The euphoria was missing, and she felt no need of it. She sighed deeply, and knitting ribs creaked in protest—a small discomfort, easy to accept. "I can hardly believe it. I don't need the Inducer."

"Good. The euphoria can be addictive, and I wouldn't want to keep you on it any longer than necessary. Now, how about sitting up for breakfast?"

"Is it morning?"

"Close enough."

"So what's that noise?"

"You're going to have breakfast," he said, plucking the white hemisphere from her shoulder and tossing it to Strux. He touched something above Dia's head, and the back of the bed lifted till she sat upright.

"It sounds like an avalanche," she said, her head swimming for a moment in the new posture.

He shrugged.

Strux placed a tray over her lap, securing it to two metal arms that swung up from the pallet. The tray bore a bowl of red, rather soupy gel and a long flexible straw.

"Here," said the doctor, inserting the straw between her lips. "You won't be able to ask questions while you eat."

She sucked at the fruit-flavored gel for a time and then let the straw droop. "Are you afraid to answer questions because I'm going to be sent back to my own side? Are you afraid we'll be able to find this place if I know what the sound is?"

"Well, we can't take any chances, can we?" he replied, reinserting the straw in her mouth. "Finish your meal."

"I'm not really hungry," she mumbled.

"Eat anyway. Your digestive system needs the stimulation."

She ate, glancing around sharply, trying to pierce the blackness that lay beyond their oasis of light. From her left came a faint rattle, as of pebbles bouncing on a hard pavement. Some fragments, she thought, breaking loose from the ceiling.

Finishing the gel, she spat away the straw. "This cave is under a mountain that's a rebel stronghold, and the Patrol is tearing it apart rock by rock."

The doctor shrugged. "I wouldn't know."

She looked at him through narrowed eyes. "I think you know."

He met her gaze. "Whatever I may know, I can't tell you."

"Nothing?"

"You're alive. You're going to be all right. That ought to be enough for you, after what you've been through."

"But why, Doctor?" She tried to read his face, to find some truth behind those pale eyes. "Why am I alive? Why didn't you let me die back there in the wreck?"

"Doctors try not to let their patients die."

"Not you-the-doctor. *You*—all of you." She glanced at Strux, sitting placidly by the lantern, his tail curled about his feet. "You and the others responsible for hiding me down here." Exasperation crept into her voice. "Do you think I'm a fool and don't know who's got me? If you weren't rebels, you'd have sent me back to the Citadel before this!"

The doctor smiled slightly. "Well, I suppose I can't deny it."

"Answer me then—why am I here?"

"Why not? Why should we have let you die when there was a chance you'd survive?"

She shook her head. "That's nonsense, and we both know it. You've been killing us and we've been killing you for years. Why save me? What do I have that you want? Information? You're in trouble if you think so, believe me. You'll find that a transport co-pilot doesn't have any worth knowing. I'm a *very* junior officer, Doctor; the Patrol doesn't reveal many secrets to third lieutenants." She felt herself frowning, an ache lacing through her cheeks and nose. Her voice hardened. "The *pilot* would have been more useful."

"Ah, yes," said the doctor. "Major Drew."

She didn't look at his face now, but at the lantern; she stared into its pale glow, let it wash through her, over her. "He was an experienced field commander. Headed for a Staff job. He knew the people, the places. The secrets." Her voice was growing ragged, the words muffled by the tightness of her throat. "You saved the wrong one, Doctor . . . if you wanted information. You should have let me die instead."

"I didn't have a choice, Lieutenant. He was killed by the beam; he was dead before you hit the ground."

"The beam . . ." she said, her throat constricting, and for a moment she could not draw another breath. A great

weight seemed to press down on her as she thought of
Michael, as she saw once more the skull that had been
his head, stark and bloody against the lantern light. Dizzily,
she fought the pressure, and the tremors that followed. Before her eyes, the lantern shrank and grew, like a pulsat-
ing sun, brighter, dimmer, brighter.

Someone touched her, gripped her shoulders firmly. The
doctor. "Easy now. Easy. Strux, get this tray away and
bring another blanket. Quickly."

She shook her head as she felt the extra weight of the
cover, but she could not speak. She was not cold—the
tremors didn't come from that. They came from something
else, inside. From grief, a beast with claws. Never before
had she known anyone killed by the rebels. Known *of*
them, yes, heard reports, seen pictures. But her family was
mainly administrative, and her friends were too young to
have seen much combat. And Michael had always been
lucky. Always . . . before.

Grief shrieked in her vitals, had been shrieking all along,
but the Inducer had kept her from hearing. She knew her
former self-control now for a sham. With a little euphoric
aid, she had kept her grief at bay, and now, without that
shield, it engulfed her. Desperately, she embraced it, struggled, transformed it into hot fury and turned it on the
nearest enemy.

"If I had the strength," she gasped, "I'd rip you apart."

"Easy, Lieutenant. Just relax." His hands still held her,
and as her vision cleared, she saw him leaning close, his
eyes focused on a spot above her left ear, reading some
indicator on the Inducer. "You're all right. You felt faint
there, didn't you? But it's passing. Nothing to be alarmed
about."

"So efficient, Doctor," she whispered. "You couldn't
have been at the beam controls. You'd surely have killed
us both with one efficient shot."

"I'm not a soldier, Lieutenant. I don't kill people."

"You're a rebel."

"But I'm a doctor, and you're my patient. We don't
have to fight each other."

"You're the enemy. If I had a weapon, I'd use it."

"That would be foolish. Strux and I aren't exactly alone
here. Even if you killed both of us, you couldn't escape;
the rest would come and kill you and all my work would
be wasted."

"It wouldn't matter. I'd owe it to the Patrol. And to *him*."

His hands dropped away. He stood up and looked down at her; he seemed vastly tall. There was no smile on his lips. "How many rebels have you killed, Lieutenant Catlin?"

"None," she said, feeling the tears on her face, warm as blood. "None. Yet."

"And your beloved Major Drew?"

"He was a credit to the Patrol."

His hands curled into fists. "That he was. Oh, yes. We know his name quite well. We know of his medals, and his bravery. They'll surely raise a statue to him in the Citadel Square. The model Patroller." Turning, he yanked his lantern from the ground and strode away.

Strux called after him, "Shall I put her back to sleep, Doctor?"

His shout echoed against the far walls. "No! Let her cry for the bastard!"

She shut her eyes and clenched her teeth and wept till patches of color danced behind her eyelids, till she strangled on the tears and the pain of coughing forced her to calm herself. Exhausted, she lay limp. With the soft riffle of cards for lullaby, she finally slid into sleep.

FIVE

The arena resounds with applause, and the crowd surges to its feet cheering like a million trumpets sounding fanfare. Michael's hand is warm and strong in hers; the championship medals gleam sun-bright on their chests. Drunk on delight, they leap from the dais, bound for their own private celebration—they leap . . . and the world blurs around them, rippling like reflections in a pool of windblown water. Vibration lances through the unfocused air, a high-pitched note almost beyond the range of human hearing, part sound, part shiver. Michael's hand melts away, and Dia tumbles, clutching for balance at nothingness, while the distant line of the horizon spins like a pinwheel. . . .

She woke, her fingers clutching convulsively at the blanket. She lay prone once more. The world was steady, rockbound, gently lit by a small lantern, and Strux sat nearby playing solitaire. Dia glanced around—the moisture-studded stone was gone; there were no walls in sight, just piles of rubble beyond the bedside clearing, and three fat stalagmites standing sentry by an open footpath. Somewhere above, she thought, there must be matching stalactites, but she could not see them.

"Where are we? We've moved," she said, peering into the darkness. "I know we've moved."

"Yes," replied Strux.

"Why?"

He adjusted the cards, straightening rows that needed none. He said nothing.

"So they were getting too close. Was it a narrow escape?"

His whiskers twitched, and he brushed at them with one

paw, as a human being might smooth his mustache. "There was no danger."

She frowned at him. "Who are you, Strux? Why are you here? Why are you helping the rebels?"

"I am in sympathy with their views."

"In sympathy? I can't believe it! Their cause is lost: It's just a matter of time before they're crushed, and you'll be crushed along with them. Don't you think you should belong to the *winning* side?"

His pale pink tongue flicked from the corner of his mouth. "I *am* on the winning side, Lieutenant."

"You can't be serious! They haven't the weapons, the training, the organization, the technological base. . . ."

He played a last card, then leaned back on his haunches, scanning the array. "I have won." He smeared the cards together. "An admirable feat, succeeding after ninety-one attempts—I shall always remember that statistic. Are you hungry, Lieutenant?"

She sighed in exasperation. "Yes, I am hungry." She became aware of a gnawing sensation in the pit of her stomach. "In fact, I'm ravenous. And thirsty, too."

"Ah, the gastrointestinal system approaches normality. A good sign." Tray and gel were packed in a large rucksack beside the lantern; he set them up and tipped Dia into a sitting position. "You are substantially improved today, are you not? I can tell by your lively conversation."

Lifting her right arm with great effort, she was able to clutch the straw with weak fingers. Ignoring the pains that shot up to her elbow, she sampled the gel. Meaty this time, it soothed her clamoring stomach. "When do I get solid food?" she asked.

"Soon enough. These transitions must be carefully gauged."

"And when do I start excreting normally? I presume I'm hooked up to some clever device for that."

"Oh, yes," said Strux, unclamping the tray. "The convenience of such apparatus makes nursing a simple task. Later, we will convert to the bedpan—primitive, but necessary for the sake of your gastrointestinal system."

"My gastrointestinal system thanks you," she muttered.

Strux picked up his cards. "The doctor will see you soon."

Dia looked away, into the darkness. "I'd rather not

speak to him today. Can't you tell him I'm improved, and let it go at that?"

"You are the patient, Lieutenant, not I."

She bit her lip. "I behaved poorly yesterday. I had no right to talk to a noncombatant like that. My commanding officer would have censured me."

"I can understand your desire for revenge. If someone killed my mate, I, too, would wish to strike out at anyone who called that individual ally."

Pressure built up behind her eyes till she thought they would start from their sockets; she had to let a few tears leak out to relieve the agony. "Revenge won't bring him back," she whispered. Breathing shallowly, she was able to dam the threatening flood, and her voice only shook slightly when she sighed his name. Turning her gaze back to Strux, she said, "He earned the love and respect of his fellow officers. He won't be forgotten in the Citadel."

"He will not be forgotten," Strux agreed, laying cards down methodically. "He is responsible for many deaths among the independence-seeking colonists."

"The *rebels*," she said sharply, "are responsible for many deaths in the Patrol. *No* one would be getting killed now if the rebels hadn't started all the shooting, at the so-called conference at Meachum's Hill. If they had been able to compromise, we'd all be working together today, instead of wasting our resources fighting each other."

"That is certainly true." Strux flipped a card over, scrutinizing it intently. "I have no desire to engage in an ideological argument, Lieutenant. The doctor may feel otherwise—his parents were killed in a Patrol raid some years ago. No one knows who led that raid, but if it was not the well-known Major Michael Drew, it was another just like him. Thus you may understand the emotions behind his words." He peered up at her, his goggles glinting in the lantern light. "Have you never seen combat?"

She shook her head. "Not yet. Michael was on leave of absence, and neither of us was due to join an active unit until next month. We were . . . combining supply transport with a vacation . . . when it happened." She stared into the light, drowning memory with its glow; and this time that brightness did not overwhelm her but seemed to seep into her mind, parch her, evaporate all her tears, to leave her shriveled and dusty. Half to herself, she said, "I don't know why I wasn't killed, too."

"Because you're a hell of a pilot." The doctor's voice snapped her out of her reverie. "I watched you bring that transport down. I never saw anything like it." He stood beyond the lamp, fists on his hips. "An interesting thing about these caves—if you stand in the proper spot, you can listen in on far-off conversations." He looked down at Strux. "Red five on the black four." He walked past the solitaire game and squatted by Dia's pallet. "We said harsh words yesterday—words that came from the gut, not the head. We're enemies, yes, and there's nothing we can do about that; but my job is to get you on your feet, and your job is to help me do that." He reached into his breast pocket. "I thought you might want these back." Her gold third lieutenant's bars gleamed on his palm. "We had to cut your uniform off—what was left of it."

She took a deep, steadying breath. "It was very kind of you to bring them, Doctor." She tried to scoop them up, but her fingers could not grasp the light, metal-coated plastic. "Will you clip them to my shirt?"

He hesitated. "It's not a uniform, just one of my casuals."

"You don't want it desecrated? I promise you, Doctor, they won't leave any mark."

"All right." He set them on her shoulders.

"And Major Drew's insignia?"

"Buried with him."

Her mouth compressed. "They belong to his next of kin. He has a brother—"

"Lieutenant . . . we couldn't deliver them."

"You could have given them to me."

His eyes went hard. "Our courtesy is limited . . . where Major Drew is concerned."

"How you hate him! He's dead, and you still hate him!"

"I don't give the orders, Lieutenant Catlin; my hatreds have no effect on our operations. I wasn't there when he was buried; I didn't make that decision. I'm sorry if it offends you, but we are not obliged to follow Patrol etiquette."

She turned her face away from him. "It's a matter of emotional comfort, Doctor. Surely you can understand that."

"I understand it quite well," he replied, his voice brittle. "When the Patrol hit my parents' home, everything was destroyed. Everything. I don't have a stick of wood to remember them by."

Dia bowed her head and said softly, "I suppose it doesn't really matter. The thing can't replace the person." She took a slow breath. "If your parents were rebels . . . well, they took their chances, just as Major Drew and I did. But I'm sorry about them. I'm sorry that anyone has to die in this crazy conflict."

Gently, he touched her shoulder, covering the insignia with his closed fingers. "And I'm sorry . . . that Michael Drew meant so much to you."

She shook her head. "I won't defend him; he doesn't need any defense. He lived up to the highest standards of the Patrol."

"And you hero-worshipped him," he muttered.

"I admired him . . . and loved him."

"In that order?"

"I admired him before I ever met him. And after I met him . . . I came to love him soon enough. I don't expect you to understand that. He was just a reputation to you. But to me he was a real human being, and the finest officer I knew." In her mind's eye she saw him again, whole and strong and vital. "I was proud to be his lover."

The doctor stood abruptly. "You're looking very well, Lieutenant. I think we can take those nerve blocks off your legs tomorrow. Give those fingers a little exercise—I'd recommend a game of cards with Strux, if you don't mind losing."

"I've lost before."

His lips pursed and then he smiled slightly. "I'll bet you didn't like it."

She looked up at him. "I'm usually a good sport, where games are concerned. I don't believe cribbage is generally played to the death."

"You'll have to discuss that with Strux. I'll see you tomorrow, Lieutenant." He walked off toward the stalagmites, passed between two of them, and vanished into the darkness.

"He doesn't have a lantern," Dia observed. "He must know the route well . . . or his destination isn't far."

"Sorry, Lieutenant," said Strux. "I am not allowed to acknowledge either of those guesses."

Her eyebrows lifted. "Can't I worm *any* information out of you, Strux?"

"If you wish to learn cribbage," he said, "I have been given a complete security clearance as regards the rules, which are quite simple. When only two players are involved, I deal six cards to each—"

Without realizing it, she had surrendered. Strux set the tray up, arranged the cards on top of it, and kept score in his head. The hardest part of the play for Dia was holding the cards—they tended to slip out of her fingers and land face-up in her lap. Strux retrieved them, pretending not to see their values, but soon they were falling too frequently, and Dia had to call a halt. She was losing by a wide margin.

"I will remember the score," said Strux, "and tomorrow we will continue."

Dia sighed, lowering her aching arms to her lap. "Doctor's orders," she muttered.

"Indeed," replied Strux. "I am gratified that the doctor considers cribbage a worthwhile therapy."

"Couldn't we try some poker next time? Surely you play poker?"

Rummaging in his bag, he found a container of gel, opened it and added a straw. "I play poker, though I do not consider it my game. Poker, however, is nothing without a wager, and you, Lieutenant Catlin, possess nothing worth wagering."

She opened her mouth to the straw. Fruit-flavored again. After one sip, she said, "You wouldn't take my IOU, I suppose."

Strux's nose and whiskers twitched. "It would be difficult to collect . . . and I, personally, have no use for money."

She leaned back, staring pensively at the three stalagmites, pulling occasionally at the straw; eventually the gel was consumed. Dia yawned and felt the tape on her cheeks crackle. "Strux?" she murmured. "What's his name?"

Strux took the tray away and gently lowered the back of her pallet. "To whose name do you refer?"

"The doctor's, of course."

"Ah . . . I am not allowed to answer that, Lieutenant."

"But you told me your name."

He tucked the coverlet around her shoulders. "The possibility that I would appear in Citadel records is vanishingly small. I cannot say the same of any human being."

"I can't go on calling him 'Doctor.' "

"Lieutenant, no amount of feigned naivete will draw information from me." His small fingers, furred about the knuckles but naked and black-skinned at the pads, moved toward her forehead.

"No," she said. "Don't put me to sleep with the Inducer. I'm tired enough to do it on my own."

"Very well." He sat back on his haunches watching her.

She closed her eyes, wondering if, after she had drifted off by herself, the Inducer would be employed to guarantee her slumber.

SIX

Awaiting their turn in the exhibition match, she and Michael stand side by side, shoulders touching; confidence sings between them like electricity. She checks the charge in her beamer and then, acknowledging the judges' signal, steps to the target range, raises the gun, aims. The target is a playing card—the ace of diamonds, red, tiny, at the extreme limit of human vision. As the beam strikes it once and then again, the diamond shape melts and runs, contorting, fragmenting, coalescing into a human face. She wonders how she can possibly discern the features at this great distance, but she recognizes the hollow cheeks, the blue eyes, the hair so blond that brows and lashes are almost invisible. Her finger slips off the trigger for a moment. "Michael?" she whispers. "Fire," he says, somewhere behind her. She fires.

The doctor was standing over her when she woke. "Good morning."

She squinted up at him. "I think I killed you in my dream. It was your face, anyway."

"That's a macabre prelude to breakfast." Kneeling, he raised the pallet and attached the tray. Strux passed him gel and a straw. "You'll be switching to real food for tomorrow if you tolerate this meal as well as you did the last two. A shame—this stuff is so much simpler."

"I am an excellent cook," said Strux.

"Limited . . . but excellent."

"Yours would be the first complaint, Doctor."

Dia reached for the straw but found she could barely lift her arms, and when she flexed her fingers, the ache in the muscles of her forearms was terrible.

"Don't push yourself," said the doctor. He thrust the

33

straw into her mouth. "Relax. You're not ready for hand-stands yet."

She smiled a little, wondering if he knew that she had trophies for gymnastics. When he answered her smile with one of his own, she dropped her eyes and concentrated on the gel.

When the container was empty, he tossed it aside. "You've probably gotten used to not having legs by this time."

"I wouldn't say that," Dia murmured. "But if they're as badly damaged as you claim, I guess I haven't missed them."

He lifted the blanket, revealing the two rigid white tubes that encased Dia's legs. At the top of each tube, encircling her thigh just below the shirt, was a metal band embossed with studs and glowing red jewels. "Lie still," said the doctor, and he played a brief pattern on the studs. The red lights dimmed and, simultaneously, Dia felt sensation returning to her legs, first at the hips and then oozing ankleward like heavy syrup. There was no pins-and-needles feeling, as of returning circulation; there was simply a bone-deep ache crawling down her legs. She groaned softly.

"Is the pain too intense?" he asked, his fingers hovering over the studs.

"No, no, I can take it."

He studied her face a moment. "You're sure?"

She nodded. "I'll be all right. I just . . . wasn't expecting it. I'll be all right."

"We've speeded up your healing time, but broken bones and torn muscles only respond so fast. The skin heals more quickly." He touched her cheek with one finger. "Those tapes can probably come off tomorrow." He glanced at her feet. "Wiggle your toes."

Her toes twitched slightly. "That hurts."

"Then everything is fine." He tucked the blanket around her legs. "You're lucky to have such a terrific surgeon."

"It's nice that you have so much confidence in your abilities, Doctor . . ." She left the title hanging, unfinished, and she looked at him quizzically. "Doctor, what *is* your name?"

He smiled. "Strux told me you'd been asking that. Do they give a course at the Patrol Academy on prisoners of war interrogating their captors?"

"No, it's something I picked up on my own. Look, if you don't want me to know your name, and I don't feel comfortable just calling you 'Doctor,' why don't you make up a name and let me use that? Be creative."

"That's a possibility." He looked at Strux. "What shall I call myself?"

Strux shrugged his furry shoulders.

"No imagination, that's your problem, my friend," said the doctor. "No room in your life for anything but facts and figures."

"I would not presume to choose a name for another sapient being," Strux replied imperturbably. "That is an individual's own prerogative. I would suggest, however, something easy to remember. Perhaps 'John' or 'Sam' would suit you."

The doctor shook his head. "Too common. Neither suits me at all." He turned back to Dia. "How about . . . Talley?"

"Talley *what?*"

"Oh, no need for last names among us. Just Talley; and I shall call you Dia."

"That's friendly of you," she said.

"It's a pretty name."

"My mother picked it; I'll tell her you liked it."

"And you might even be a pretty girl, under all that mess."

"I am, if I heal as well as you say I will."

"Ah—no false modesty for you, I see."

She met his eyes. "I like to think that I'm a realist, Doctor."

"Talley. After all, it was your idea."

"Talley."

"I hope this change in our relationship means you'll stop killing me in your dreams."

"I'm afraid I don't have any control over my dreams. And you're still . . . the enemy. You're not going to win me over by being charming. If that *is* what you're trying to be."

He glanced toward Strux. "I believe the lady impugns my motives."

Dia sighed. "If you intend to interrogate me, please get on with it. In my present condition, I haven't much patience with babble."

"I'm not a very good interrogator," said Talley.

"Are they going to send someone better?"

"Maybe. If I can't get any answers."

"What will *he* do? Torture me?" She laughed weakly. "I'm sure I don't know any more than you do. At the moment, I'm Transport personnel—Command tells me to fly somewhere. I do it. You saw the cargo, which was more than I did; it was already loaded and sealed by the time I came aboard."

"Where were you taking it?"

"North. You could see that for yourselves."

"To the garrison at Pelham's Woods?"

"Is there another garrison in that direction?"

"How many Patrollers are stationed there?"

"A bunch."

"Is that all you can tell me?"

"I never got there, so I couldn't count them."

"You must have known something about the place—you chose it for a vacation."

"My brother Paul was up there. He and Major Drew had never met. I thought they'd like each other." She frowned. "He's probably been recalled to the Citadel by this time—for my memorial service."

Surprise showed on the doctor's face. "Will they assume you're dead without the evidence of a body?"

"Was there any Patrol investigation of the crash site?"

He nodded. "A scouting party looked it over the next day, but we hadn't left anything worth salvaging by that time."

"Including corpses. I suppose you didn't . . . mark his grave."

"No."

"Then no one knows if we're alive or dead. But they'll assume the worst. The rebels are well-known for their ruthlessness."

"As is the Patrol. But you're still alive."

She shook her head slowly. "I still can't imagine why."

"Perhaps because we're not nearly as ruthless as you think—as you've been taught to think. After all, it's the Patrol that's the aggressor; we're only fighting to regain our freedom."

"You have a small mind, Doctor Talley," she said softly. "A small, provincial, unrealistic mind. All you Amphorans—your naivete would be touching if it weren't so senseless. I almost believe you'd be glad to be conquered by Outsiders, if only it meant the end of the Patrol." She glanced toward Strux, her eyes narrowed. "Or maybe you've *already* been conquered . . . though I can't exactly envision Strux as an overlord. . . ."

"I am not an overlord," said Strux. "I am merely a sympathetic friend."

"The first of many sympathetic friends?" inquired Dia.

"We've only been conquered *once*," Talley said firmly, "and that was eighty years ago, when the Patrol landed. And if it takes another eighty years, we'll win this planet back from you!"

Dia sighed in exasperation. "It's our planet, too. I was born on Amphora, and so were my parents."

Talley shook his head. "No, I won't argue birthright with you, not after eighty years. But we had a nice little world once, pretty far off the beaten track; our own world. And then the Patrol dropped in, with its big guns and bigger ideas."

"It was a period of confusion. You were weak, unarmed, open to invasion."

"Yes, and we got it, too."

She sat up a little straighter, in spite of the ache it caused her. "We made an honest bargain. We've protected you. No one would dare attack this planet while we were here."

"And in return, we were set to work for you. We built your city and your factories and your weapons. We grew your food, we even made your uniforms. We worked for you till we didn't belong to ourselves any more. Thousands of us—tens of thousands—became your technicians, never mind what our parents wanted, never mind what *we* wanted."

"You had a low-level technology. You couldn't manufacture what was needed without some sacrifice."

"Sacrifice? That's the word all right, Lieutenant. A whole world sacrificed to the greater glory of the Patrol!"

"Don't be foolish, Doctor. We can't protect the planet without weapons, ships—"

"The only protection this planet needs is from you!"

"I can't *believe* you rebels have so little foresight. Without us, you'd be vulnerable again. What would you do if a fleet of Outsiders arrived?"

"Exactly what we're doing now." His lips curved in a humorless smile. "Don't be so holy-holy, Lieutenant. The Patrol isn't here for *our* sake. It hasn't turned this planet into a munitions factory for *us*. You're the ones who are afraid. You're the ones who need to be armed. We only wish you had picked some other world to play your military games on."

Her eyes blazed at his words, and her lips tightened into a thin line. "Your mind is earthbound, Doctor. You had peace here for a century under the Federation's wings, and you think you can go back to that. Well, those wings are gone; it's everyone for himself out there where the Federation *used* to be. Dreamer! There's no law out there but strength. Even in the Federation's heyday, what do you think the Patrol did? It didn't spend all its time chasing a few isolated renegades. It kept the peace on the frontiers, arbitrated disputes, prevented military aggression by its very existence. Now there's no more Federation, and no Patrol but what's on this planet. You're lucky to have us, Doctor!"

He stood, looked down at her coolly. "There's a touch of paranoia about you Patrollers."

"Justified caution, not paranoia. We know what's out there; you don't."

Now his face and voice displayed his annoyance. "Most worlds back then were too busy with internal affairs, and with their own developing commerce, to engage in interstellar warfare. The Federation was disbanded because it was too large. Distances between stars were too great, communication was time consuming. Even back then, Amphora only got a ship from the capital once a year." He moved to the foot of her pallet, gazed at her down the length of her body. "If we'd been attacked even then, say by pirates, the Patrol could never have gotten to us in time to help. We relied on local defenses, local militia, and we *thought* we were well enough organized to turn away any enemy. Of course, we didn't count on the enemy being a squadron of Patrol ships, armed to the teeth with the latest equipment!" He turned away from her to stare into the dark, his hands clasped tightly behind his back. "I doubt," he added at last, "that any ordinary aggressor would be as formidable."

Dia leaned back, exhausted by the effort of argument. "After eighty years without Federation law—I don't doubt any possibility."

"You?" He glared at her over one shoulder. "What can *you* know, Lieutenant—a mere transport co-pilot? You've been *told* by your superior officers, by your Council and your Brigadier, but *you* don't know."

"I respect their judgment."

"Well, I don't."

"Fortunately, the majority of Amphorans agree with me."

"Do you really think so?"

She smiled slightly. "Work in the shipyards goes on."

"That's fear, Lieutenant Catlin, not agreement. The Patrol has some very potent means of coercion."

"Who's paranoid now, Doctor?"

"It's not paranoia when the threat is real."

Dia chuckled softly, ignoring the ache it brought to her ribs. "Really, Doctor—using my own argument against me! This is a hell of an interrogation. We've even forgotten we're on a first-name basis."

Talley shook his head. "I told you I wasn't a very good interrogator."

"Why don't you just ask the questions and be done with them, instead of getting us embroiled in a dispute over . . . politics?"

"No more questions for today."

"Well, I have a few of my own."

He looked away from her. "Don't ask them."

"Why do you go on, Talley?" Her voice was tired—the effort of speaking had caught up with her. "It just means more bloodshed. You won't win. You can't."

His hands clenched into fists. "Why did you come here? Why didn't you all go back to Patrol Headquarters and get yourselves decommissioned?"

"We were needed," she said quietly. "We couldn't just quit. We couldn't."

"Damn you all," he said and, passing the stalagmites, vanished into the gloom.

Dia turned her face toward Strux, who sat quietly with the cards clutched in his hands. "And why are you here?" she murmured. "What do you want from the rebels? From any of us?"

His moist nose twitched, and the whiskers bobbed, gleaming like metal filaments in the lanternlight. "I want peace, Lieutenant Catlin, and flowers in the spring."

"You want Amphora."

He cocked his head to one side, seemed to consider her

statement, and then he said, "Yes, I do want Amphora. I do."

She was too exhausted to question him further, felt sleep creeping close, her eyes filming over. Gazing at his furry head, his little pink tongue showing now between his lips as the cards skipped from his hands one by one, she could see nothing sinister: a well-groomed animal with dextrous fingers, nothing more. Even his small, pointed teeth, occasionally glimpsed, were hardly threatening. Could this really be the invader that the Patrol was waiting to combat? She wanted to stroke his sleek pelt, as if he were an overgrown cat; she wondered, as slumber claimed her, if he could purr.

SEVEN

A distant voice.
Michael.
*Far away, she can see him beckoning, but between them
lies an invisible barrier, unyielding as diamond. She beats
upon it with her fists until she can feel the impact of every
blow in her bones; the very air shivers from her effort, but
the unseen wall does not crack. She calls his name, and
he waves in return but cannot approach, can only shout,
the cry echoing as from the bottom of a deep well. Now
strange hands try to pluck her from the barrier, and she
wrenches free of them and leans against the wall, as if her
weight could force it aside; the obstruction is cool against
her cheek and mouth, against her groping, aching hands.
From behind, she is drawn away, steel claws locked about
her elbows—she cannot pry them loose. Violently, she
twists to face her captor; if her arms were free, she would
strangle that smile from his familiar pale face.*

"Wake up, Dia! Wake up!"

Groggy, she opened her eyes, but her vision was filmed
over, blurred with sleep. Hands clutched at her shoulders,
shook her till her head rocked on the pillow. "Let go of
me!" she growled, her words running together. The hands
gripped her still. Talley and Strux came into slow focus
above her, leaning close. With her right arm, she pushed
Talley's hands away.

"I thought you'd want to be wakened," he said. "It
looked pretty bad."

She nodded, too exhausted by the dream-struggle to
speak.

"You were rolling around—you might have hurt yourself."

41

Her lips were dry, her breathing dusty, as if the damp cave were a desert. "Water?" she whispered, her throat aching from silent screams. Talley held the straw to her mouth, and she sucked greedily at the cool liquid.

"Take it easy," he said. "You'll choke."

She relaxed, gasping, let the straw slip away. "Is it morning already?"

"No, it's the middle of the night."

"Not time to wake up?"

"No."

"Then what are you doing here?"

"Taking my turn at watching the patient. Strux needs sleep, too, you know."

"You've been here . . . every night?"

"Yes."

She raised an eyebrow. "Hoping I'll talk in my sleep?"

"You do."

"What?"

"You call his name."

She shut her eyes tight. "I assume . . . that will pass."

He touched her left hand, squeezed it gently. "Go back to sleep, Dia. You've only had a few hours."

"Go back to dreams, you mean." She looked up into the darkness. "I'd rather not."

"Do you want to talk about it?"

"I don't think so."

"I'll stay here. If you get restless, I'll wake you again."

Dia shook her head. "Waking or sleeping, I can't seem to get away from you."

"Do you mean . . . that I was in the nightmare?"

"Yes."

"Not in a very positive role, I suppose."

"Not positive at all."

He glanced at Strux. "Maybe you'd better stay with her, then." He drew his hand away from hers. "I'm sorry you still see me as your enemy. I wish we could deal with each other on different terms."

"I think we're just going to have to resign ourselves, Doctor."

"I suppose so." He straightened up with a sigh. "I'll see you in the morning," he said and walked off into the dark.

Strux smoothed Dia's blanket, fluffed her pillow. "You are tired," he said quietly. "I see that in your face. You should try to sleep again."

"I'm tired, but I don't want to sleep. Talk to me, Strux. Tell me about yourself. Do you have a mate? Children?"

He settled back on his haunches, picked up his deck of cards and held them, fingering the topmost card without turning it over. "I believe I may speak of such things. Yes, I have a single mate and six cubs."

"Do you miss them?"

"When I am far away from them, I miss them."

"How long has it been since you've seen them, Strux?"

Delicately, he began shuffling the cards. "Ah, Lieutenant, your voice sounds so sympathetic. You feel for me, do you not, so far from my family? You could not possibly wish to trick me into revealing that which I must keep secret—the distance to my home." His goggled eyes turned toward her, but she could not read the unhuman expression on his half-hidden face. "Conversation being so dangerous, would you perhaps prefer to continue our game of cribbage?"

"I'm sorry, Strux."

"I understand, Lieutenant. You look to the day when you will return home with valuable information. I cannot blame you for trying whatever ploy may come to hand. But I am compelled to evade those attempts, and I hope you will not take my evasions as personal affronts."

"No, of course not."

"Then . . . cribbage?"

"We might as well finish that game."

Strux played sharply, taking most of the points. Dia played to pass the time and didn't care that she lost. The muscles of her arms and shoulders ached as she manipulated the cards, and when Strux suggested an additional game Dia declined.

"I can't seem to concentrate any more." She stifled a yawn. "My brain is all foggy, and my eyes feel like they're a meter behind my head. I feel . . . as if I've been awake for hours, but it hasn't been that long, has it?"

"Accelerated healing commonly requires all the patient's strength," Strux replied. "One sleeps, eats, and sleeps again, even though the diet is extremely high in all vital nutrients. I am certain, however, that you would not wish to spend one third of a year healing at your natural pace."

"My legs will be healed, but I'll be too tired to stand up."

"There will be some debilitation, but the doctor assures

me that you are young and healthy enough to regain your former level of activity."

"Then you'll have to chain me to the wall, because the two of you won't be enough to keep me here against my will."

"I presume the doctor has taken that into consideration, Lieutenant. If necessary, chains are easy enough to procure."

She had to smile. "Has anyone ever told you that you're a trifle pedantic, Strux?"

He smoothed his whiskers with two small fingers. "Often," he said. "My people have a certain desire for precision of thought and language that is not shared by other species. Humans find us . . . stuffy."

"You're an incongruous creature—covered with fur like a child's toy, but speaking human language like a college professor."

"That is a rather anthropocentric view, Lieutenant."

"Yes." She yawned uncontrollably, and her eyes began to water. "Yes, I guess I'm exposing my own deficiencies . . . but I have this yearning to pet you. I suppose you'd be insulted."

"Not at all. I am proud of my fur, as a human would be proud of glossy, abundant hair." He sidled closer. "If you wish to touch it, feel free to do so."

His pelt was silky smooth. "I'd be proud, too," she murmured, and languor overcame her, shutting her eyes and slowing her breathing. She dozed, too near the threshold of waking to dream. She heard Strux move about, heard the cards riffling, but let herself drift with those sounds as if they were a river current rocking her bed. She knew morning arrived when Strux brushed his furry hand across her cheek.

She yawned away the shreds of slumber. "No nightmares this time."

He set up her tray. "After breakfast, I intend to disconnect you from the excretory circuits and then to bathe you. The doctor has agreed to stay away until I call him; I shall put that off until you are quite comfortable."

"Thank you."

"You will have to see him, Lieutenant. You will have to make some adjustment to his presence."

Dia lifted both arms to the tray, rested them there. "It's very good tactics, Strux, to seem to be on my side, to be kind and sympathetic to win my trust. But how could anyone who looks so much like a stuffed toy not be trustworthy? You're perfect!" She watched him rummage in the rucksack. "What are you doing?"

He came up with a squat cylinder, which he sat on end and linked to the lantern with a short length of cable. When the top of the cylinder began to glow a dull red, he set a frying pan on it, spooned grease into the pan and dropped grayish slices of a dense, breadlike substance into the grease. Sizzling and fragrant, breakfast began to brown at the edges.

"This," said Strux, "is the manner in which I continue to solicit your trust. I think you will find it a tasty meal."

"What is it?" Dia asked.

"Perhaps you had best eat first and ask its identity afterward. I would not wish to prejudice you."

"It *smells* good."

"In my modest opinion, it is delicious. Your first solid meal, Lieutenant. You will need a fork this time." Deftly, he flipped the slices, browned them on the second side, and slid them onto a small plate. "I do not believe you require my assistance in feeding yourself."

She picked up the fork and held it firmly in her right hand. The aroma of breakfast made her mouth water, and she swallowed several times before touching it. The fork easily cut the yielding slices, the crisp outer layer and the soft white interior. On her tongue, the substance was heavy with the flavor of sweet, browned butter, and beneath that was a faint hint of aged beef.

"Delicious," she said, when all the slices were gone.

Strux pulled a gnarled, roundish object the size of a man's fist from his sack. "You have eaten of this fungus," he said, holding it close for her inspection. "It is quite high in protein—an admirable food."

"I have nothing against fungi," said Dia.

He packed it away in his bag. "Some humans find such things repellent. I have never understood that attitude, and I am pleased that you do not share it."

"And now for today's excitement." She pushed the tray into his hands.

"It is a simple matter," said Strux, lowering the pallet to the horizontal position, "but it may feel a trifle peculiar." He folded the blanket aside and pushed her shirt up, and Dia felt the cool damp cave air on her naked belly for the first time; goose bumps climbed toward her shoulders. His fingers brushed the insides of her thighs and slid under her hips, lifting; a brief tickling sensation in her groin signaled the removal of apparatus she had not even been aware of, and then her body rested firmly on the pallet once more. Strux smoothed the shirt down over her hips and replaced the blanket.

"I'd call that simple," said Dia.

"The machine removes waste before it leaves the body, powders it, stores it inside the bed. The bedpan is far less efficient, but it does allow freedom of movement, and because you are going outside today, that must be an important consideration."

"Outside?"

"Yes. Fresh air and sunshine have certain salutary qualities; although our lantern is an excellent source of all wavelengths, it does not offer the psychological benefits of sunlight." He dipped into his bag and found a large square of green fabric. Starting with her neck, he scrubbed vigorously with the dry, smooth cloth, leaving the skin tingling in its wake. "I'm sure you would prefer a hot bath, but our facilities are rather limited."

"I don't really mind."

He eased the loose gray shirt up to her armpits, cleansed her shoulders, swabbed her breasts and stomach, dipped down into her crotch. Then he raised the pallet and leaned her forward to scrub her back. "I have a pair of trousers for your outing, Lieutenant. I fear they will not fit well, but with a tight belt they will not fall off."

The trousers were baggy, faded and blue. With a little difficulty he worked them over the casts on her legs. Their waist was far too wide, but he produced a belt to snug it up. "I will call the doctor now."

She sighed. "If you must."

"I must." He whistled then, a sweet, high-pitched melody, and in a few moments Talley passed between two of the stalagmites and greeted his patient.

"I hope you're feeling better this morning."

"I'm all right."

"You *look* better."

She shrugged. "I always look better after a good breakfast."

"I see Strux has gotten you ready for our jaunt outside, but I'd like to take the tapes off your face before we go."

"Fine."

He knelt beside the pallet. "Give me the solvent, Strux." His furry assistant proffered a bowl of greenish liquid and a small sponge. Talley wet the sponge and dabbed gently at Dia's cheek. Slowly the tape dissolved, leaving her face flexible but tender, as though with new-peeled sunburn.

"I think you'll see an improvement," Talley said, and he unfolded his mirror to let her view herself.

She inspected her face carefully. The swelling had gone down, and the scabs were gone, leaving only faint pink lines in their place; the pouches around her eyes were pale yellow rather than black. Her short hair hung in shaggy elflocks over her ears and forehead.

"You wouldn't have a comb, would you, Doctor?"

He handed her a comb. "Keep it."

Awkwardly, she tugged at her hair one-handed. "Strux should have cleaned my hair, too," she muttered, and he immediately obliged with another bath-cloth. Then he took over the combing. "I look gorgeous," she said when he had finished. "Now if only I could walk . . ."

Talley shook his head. "I don't think you'd be able to handle crutches."

"I'm willing to try."

"No. The floor isn't soft enough for that kind of experimentation. Are you ready to go outside?"

She nodded.

Still kneeling, he slid his hands under her back and legs. "Put your right arm around my neck."

She recoiled from his touch, slipping sideways on the pallet, which only made him clutch her more firmly. She wanted to push him away, to peel those arms off her body, their pressure too intimate even through a layer of clothing—more intimate, somehow, than Strux's hands had been. "You're not going to *carry* me?"

"You're not heavy."

"But I'm . . . awkward. You'll have trouble. A stretcher would be better."

"We don't need a stretcher, Dia. Come on."

She hesitated still, not wanting the heat of his body against her, that heat so evident now that, blanketless, she was keenly aware of the ambient coolness. As a doctor he could be a disembodied pair of hands; as an enemy, an argumentative voice. But holding her in his arms, with their faces so close that their breaths mingled . . . seemed too large a shift in their relationship. It was not the efficient doctor who wanted this, she thought, but the calculating interrogator.

"Come on," he said. "It'll be easier this way. You'll see."

Sighing deeply, she crooked her arm about his neck. But she held herself stiff, aloof, looking away from him, even when he cradled her close. He lifted her smoothly, carried her as if she weighed no more than a child, and strode swiftly toward the stalagmites, while Strux scurried after with blanket and lantern.

Their private pool of light splashed about them, flowing just ahead of their footsteps, illuminating the mouth and then the interior of a narrow tunnel. Talley walked sideways through it, and even so Dia's toes nearly brushed the wall once or twice. The floor rose in a series of broad steps, and the ceiling followed suit more slowly, till stone like rough white stucco was bare centimeters above Talley's head. Then the tunnel forked, one branch turning sharply, the other descending in a jumble of broken rock; Talley chose the latter and stepped, surefooted, along the steep decline.

Gazing ahead, Dia saw daylight. The lantern radiance became a pale ghost as the three travelers emerged from the cavern. Dia shut her eyes against the outer glare.

Strux spread the blanket a few steps from the tunnel mouth, and Talley set his patient down there; he was not even breathing hard from the journey. Removed from the cool draft of the depths, Dia shivered once in the penetrating heat of the sun, and then she leaned back against warm rocks to bask in its rays. Free of his grasp, she felt her muscles relax slowly, achingly. Presently her eyes had adjusted enough to open, and she surveyed her surroundings.

Her perch was a precarious one on a ledge among woody bushes. Almost at her feet was a precipice, a steep drop of some hundred meters to deceptively soft-looking foliage. At her back rose a hill clothed in greenery, treetops like so many stiff soldiers against the sky. To east and west the land rolled with similar eminences, and southward it dropped away to a smooth, forested plain.

"Are these the Veil Hills?" she asked.

"Sunlight and fresh air," said Talley, looking up toward the clouds, "but no answers." He was standing close beside her, hands on his hips. Strux had retreated to the far end of the ledge, perhaps five meters away, and was looking westward, skyward.

"We've traveled quite a distance, then, from the crash site, and Pelham's Woods is that way." Dia indicated the slope behind her back with her bendable arm.

He caught her elbow. "I'm glad to see you using this arm so freely. Does it still hurt?"

"It itches a bit."

"That's all right." He turned, scanned the sky again.

"What are you looking for?" Dia asked.

"Enemies."

"I hope you're not expecting any."

He glanced sidewise at her. "The possibility of rescue doesn't appeal to you?"

"They wouldn't be here to rescue me since they think I'm dead; and I'm not really spry enough to dodge the shooting."

"Well, it's unlikely that any Patrol craft would be passing this way," he said, sitting down beside her. "We're off the usual air routes. Still, we can't take any chances."

Dia scraped at the surface on which they rested, and her fingers came up black with moist soil. "Unless they know where to look, they'll hardly see us here."

He touched her elbow. "I can't trust you not to make some attempt to signal your fellow Patrollers."

"What—in semaphore? With my white casts as flags? Come on, Doctor—these hills aren't much, but they're big enough to make us look like insects from the air."

He smiled slightly. "You're dismissing the vaunted Patrol ingenuity?"

"Oh, sure; I'll start a fire by rubbing two sticks together while your back is turned; the Brigadier himself will leap into your cave and arrest you."

The smile disappeared. "You might find a way. We can't afford that."

The sound of a footstep made them both turn toward the mouth of the tunnel. A man of middling height emerged, his green clothing smudged with dirt, his head covered by a dark hood, only the eyes showing brilliant blue through round holes. His muffled voice issued from behind the cloth: "And if you don't cooperate with us, we might decide we can't afford to let you live."

Dia glanced at Talley as the newcomer spoke, saw his

mouth tighten; it gave her the instant impression that he would play the nice-guy role against the masked man's menace. She smiled grimly and clasped her hands atop one thigh in preparation for a siege.

"Hello .there," she said. "I like your costume. Is it the latest fashion in rebel circles?"

Talley frowned at her.

"Our doctor," the masked man declared, "does not worry that he might be identified through Citadel files. I am not so foolish."

"What difference would it make—if you kill me?" Her eyebrows lifted. "Or are you just uglier than he is?"

Talley nudged her arm.

"Careless talk from a prisoner of war," said the masked man. "But of course such taunts will never persuade me to unmask, so you can keep your cute Patroller tricks to yourself."

"Let's have some rebel tricks instead. What kind of co-operation do you want, and do you really expect me to co-operate with someone whose face I can't see and whose name I don't know? I assume you have a face under that. Do you have a name, too?"

"No names, Lieutenant Catlin."

"Well, *there's* a name. Mine."

"You don't need to know mine."

"Oh, on the contrary, I do. How else can I carry on a proper conversation with you. Just ask the doctor if you don't believe me."

He shot a glance at Talley. "Call me whatever you like. It doesn't matter."

"Well, then . . . how about John X. Unknown?" She smiled broadly at him. "It fits the mask nicely, don't you think?"

"That will do." He moved till he stood above her, and his shadow engulfed her. She had to look up to his mask, and the sun glowed behind his head like an unbearable halo; she looked at his boots instead—fine black boots of Kyrlian leather. Her brother Paul had a similar pair, though much more worn; they were expensive. Dia filed that fact with the other minutiae she had gleaned from Strux and Talley—it didn't add up to much, but the Citadel computer might be able to make something of it.

"Lieutenant Catlin, you have been cooperative so far . . . in your sleep." He waited for some reaction, and when none but a level stare at his kneecaps was forthcoming, he continued. "The Inducer has many uses, the greatest of which—for our purposes—is its induction of a certain . . . looseness of the tongue. The mind relaxes in sleep, defenses go down. There are no inhibitions. No code of honor." He shifted one foot, and pebbles rolled beneath his boot. "Although you have not seen me before, I have seen you. And heard you."

"So I talk in my sleep," she said, shrugging. "I hope you found it entertaining."

"Most entertaining. But there are things we'd like clarified. The sleeping mind is not well-organized; it mixes conjecture with actuality, value judgment with fact. It has little discrimination."

"It doesn't have much information, either. I presume the doctor told you that I've never been in the field before."

"An unfortunate circumstance," said Unknown, "but not entirely without compensations. Your mother is on the Council, your father is a chief of Materiel. You've had access to certain kinds of information. You might be surprised at the knowledge we'd find useful; troop movements aren't everything."

"I suppose not."

"You've betrayed the Patrol, Lieutenant. How does it feel to be a traitor?"

She laughed, a short, sharp bark. "I'm hardly responsible for babbling in my sleep while half-dead and drugged."

"Even so, you gave us valuable information."

"If you say so. But not willingly."

"Would that matter to a court-martial?"

She squinted up at him, saw his head as a black hump before the dazzling sun. "Just what are you getting at?"

"That you can't very well go back now. That you have only two alternatives."

"Which are?"

"You can join us and give us whatever other knowledge you have, freely and in an organized fashion . . . or you can kill yourself to prevent us from getting it."

"Kill myself? With what? A fork? That is, if Doctor Talley ever lets me have another one, now that I've mentioned it. Or maybe I should pick up a rock and bash myself with it."

Unknown swept a hand outward, to encompass the precipice and the empty air beyond. "You could throw your self off this mountain. It wouldn't be hard, even with your . . . disabilities. I wouldn't stand in your way."

"Stop it!" shouted Talley, scrambling to his feet. He grabbed Unknown by the arm and shook him. "What the hell are you trying to accomplish?"

Right on time, Dia mused. *Talley to the defense of the fair damsel.*

Unknown stripped the doctor's hand away. "How much longer do you think we can spend on her? You're needed back at HQ, Doctor."

"They can get along without me. Or we can take her there."

"Not on your life. She's not going anywhere near HQ."

"Unless, of course, I throw my lot in with you gentlemen," Dia said sweetly. "Won't that make everything jolly —an ex-Patroller in your fine rebellion."

Talley glared down at her. "Be quiet, Dia."

She ignored him. "You're not fooling me, Mr. Unknown. You don't trust me and I don't trust you. If I stay with you, it'll be as prisoner, not comrade—I don't doubt that for a moment. Now, if you want to know all about the Academy graduation ceremonies, I'd be glad to oblige, but I don't think you'd find that too useful."

The masked man drew himself up. "I don't really want to stoop to *forcible* persuasion."

Dia took a deep breath. "I knew we'd get there eventually." To Talley, she said, "He's going to mess up all your work."

"Answer his questions, Dia. You'll see it's really minor stuff."

"Then why is he so eager to know it?"

"We'll take the casts off your legs first," said Unknown, "and then I'll smash the bones with a sledgehammer. Slowly, of course. A small sledgehammer will do."

"Dia!"

Her fingers worked against each other smoothly, the moist soil as lubricant. "I'm a Patroller, and we have a standing oath never to aid or inform the enemy. So I guess I'm just in for a bad time."

"You'll break," growled Unknown. "Pain is the great leveler."

She glanced up at him one last time and then away, toward the furthest hills. "I don't know. Could be."

"Come over here," Talley said to the masked man. "I

want to talk to you." They stepped inside the tunnel, and Strux moved closer to Dia.

"He will hurt you," he said.

"It's called torture."

"I do not wish to see it. I do not wish to tend you afterward. You are weak, Lieutenant Catlin, with no reserves to sustain you."

She leaned back against the warm rocks. "It's a funny place to talk about dying, out in the sunlight. When we came out of the cave, I felt like we were climbing out of Hades." Her eyes closed. "I guess I really died in the crash—this is just the epilogue of the story."

Loud noises issued from the cave mouth—two men shouting at each other.

"First time I ever had a pair of bucks fighting over me," she muttered. "What are they arguing about—who gets in the first whack?"

Strux rose on his hind legs, stretched to his full height, his nose up, twitching. His small hands worked on the empty air as if kneading dough and then tucked in tight against his chest. His fur bristled, smudging the lines of his plump body till he was just a mass of fluff, only the tip of his muzzle undistorted. Surrounded by fur, the goggles peered out, turned to Dia. "We must return to the interior," he said, and he scuttled toward the tunnel mouth, calling to the doctor.

Talley emerged and looked skyward, his gaze following the line of Strux's pointing finger. Then he scooped Dia up into his arms and ducked into the tunnel. The masked man was gone. Strux came up with the lantern, and Talley strode forward then, as if trying to trample his hurrying shadow. In spite of his burden, his footsteps were light, almost silent. Following him, Strux made no sound at all.

Dia had seen nothing in the sky. But she presumed that her companions had better eyes, or perhaps were better used to detecting Patrol craft in spite of their sky-blue camouflage. "I thought we were off the usual air routes," she said.

"We were," Talley replied. "Maybe we're not any more."

"What happened to our loathsome friend with the sledgehammer fetish?"

"He had a report to make."

"About me or the aircraft?"

"Both."

"You mean he has superiors to consult before he can start tenderizing me?"

His arms tightened. "You're very cool about it all."

"I just try to see the humor in the situation."

They entered the room of the three stalagmites, and Strux hurried ahead to lay the lantern in its customary place. "I wouldn't be so humorous if it were me about to be . . . persuaded," Talley said, setting her down gently. He eased her shoulders, her head to the pallet. He straightened the legs of her trousers, the sleeves of her shirt, her collar. He seemed not to want to take his hands away from her. "Why don't you just tell him whatever he wants to know? You're never going back to face a court-martial."

She gazed at him levelly. "No?"

Taking the blanket from Strux, he tucked it under her feet, around her legs and torso. He kept his eyes on the task, avoiding hers. "Would you *want* to?"

"I'd want to go back, of course. I'm not too excited by the prospect of a court-martial."

"What would they do to you?"

"If I talked? Shoot me, probably."

"After torture . . . ?"

"That wouldn't make any difference."

"At least you'd be safe with us . . . alive, anyway."

"Under perpetual arrest?" She smoothed a wrinkle in the coverlet. "Of course, you might find it more convenient to dispose of me once you exhausted me as a resource."

He shook his head.

"Be realistic, Doctor. I'm a casualty. I was a casualty the moment your friends cut me out of my harness. It's just taking me a little longer to die . . . than it did Michael."

"Damned stubborn Patroller," he growled. He started to turn away, but her voice stopped him.

"Tell me, Doctor . . . did I *really* talk in my sleep?"

He nodded stiffly. "How else could we have found out all that personal information about your family?"

"Oh, I'm sure there are ways. My parents' ranks and assignments are on file in the Citadel."

"You're assuming we have spies in the Citadel."

"Don't you?"

"No answers, Dia. No information to the enemy."

"Right. Absolutely right."

He walked away into the darkness.

Strux puttered with lunch, but Dia hardly noticed the food, eating mechanically. The specter of Michael floated in her mind—she had done what he would have done, said what he would have said, thought what he would have thought. So far, she was a worthy acolyte, but she wondered how worthy she would be when the sledgehammer struck her legs. *What now, dear love? Tell them nonsense to gain a few days or weeks of life?* Michael, she knew, would despise her for it. She pounded angrily on her left thigh, on the cast that immobilized it. Better than chains, her legs imprisoned her, sealed her fate. She couldn't even kick at her captors.

She dozed, and Michael came to swear her to silence with his hands on her forehead, and she woke, protesting that she had sworn, she had sworn, and nothing could make her break that oath. She woke, and the hands on her forehead were cool, familiar. Talley's. She reached up with her right arm to push him away, for she felt the hard metal of the Inducer against her skin; but his hands were stronger, far stronger than hers.

"It's better this way, Dia. Sleep," he said, and she had to obey.

EIGHT

She lies spread-eagled on the rack—a simple rectangular structure, a pole at each corner, a steel cuff riveted to the pole; locking snugly about a wrist or ankle, the cuff is padded to protect the tender flesh from unrelenting metal. A huge wheel, its knobby spokes extending well beyond the rim, rests upright at her feet; the masked man, the Unknown, leans upon it, and through the mask—as if it were made of cheesecloth—she sees his face, a skull with toothy grin and gaping sockets.

"Answers!" he cries in sepulchral tones. "Answers!" The voice rumbles across the room and rebounds from the walls with cyclopean force; her flesh chills beneath the echoes of its passage. "Answers!"

She stares at the ceiling, which unfolds into a mirror, and sees herself blink.

"Answers!" he cackles, and under his eager, black-gloved hands the wheel begins to turn, grating, groaning, as if it were moving the world. He laughs on a rising note, and the laugh becomes a wolf-howl lifted to a moon that floats, misty, in the mirror above her eyes.

She watches her reflection elongate, the limbs stretch till bone and muscle creak. And then the flesh, strained beyond endurance, parts, thin strands drawing away from each other like fresh-spun silk from a falling spider. Her arms and legs give way at the joints, white cartilage showing at every breach, and blood is spraying from her body, geysering, spattering the mirror with a multitude of red stars. From deep in her throat, a hoarse cry spews forth to meet the laughing wolf, to wrestle it upward toward the pale blond moon.

"No answers!" she shrieks, and the pale moon himself

*reaches down with warm and ghostly arms to boost her
on her way.*

She woke to a crackling sound and, for a moment,
thought it the rack of her dream and pulled her limbs in,
fetal-wise, to protect them. Then she came awake fully and
realized that both her arms had bent. Bandages and cast
were gone; new pink flesh cloaked her bones from wrist to
shoulder.

"Lie still!" Talley commanded. With a great effort, she
raised her head, which now seemed to weigh as much as
the mountain above her. She saw him cutting the cast off
her left leg; her right was bare already. The cutting tool
crackled as it moved toward her hip. Over his eyes, Talley
wore goggles, although there were no sparks or fragments
of debris flying off.

A low rumble, less a sound than a bone-shaking vibration, pulsed through the cave; the darkness was filled with
the snap and rattle of stalactites breaking free and shat-
tering against the floor.

"What's happening?" Dia raised herself on one elbow,
and the arm trembled under the stress.

"You've been unconscious for a long time," he said. He
dropped the tool and jerked the two halves of the cast
apart. "I pushed your healing rate to the limit. Can you
stand?"

"Stand?" She blinked at her new legs. They were thin,
wandlike. Below the gray shirt, her pelvis showed through
her flesh in bold relief. With shaking hands she touched her
neck, her shoulders, her face.

"You won't like the way you look—healing burned up a
lot of your protein." He slipped the trousers over her legs,
notched the belt securely about her waist. "Can you stand?"

Again, the floor of the cave quivered.

"Is it an earthquake?"

For answer, he jerked her to her feet. "You're weak, I
know you're weak, but surely you're strong enough to
stand!"

Swaying, she stood, one arm about his shoulders. He
seemed so solid, like some deep-rooted tree. Her legs were
like water, her arms little better. "I don't think I'm ready
for a long march."

"Take a couple of steps. You can do it."

Using his body as a crutch, she took a step, then another. On the third, her knees buckled.

He caught her as she fell, lifted her easily in his arms. "No, you're not ready," he muttered, and he kicked at the lantern. It went out as it fell over, and darkness engulfed them.

Her grip on his shoulders tightened reflexively. Her world had suddenly shrunk to him, her only anchor in emptiness. She could feel his heart pounding against her own ribs, could hear the breath whispering through his nostrils. Once more, the cave shook, and she felt the vibration transmitted through his body. "What's going on? Is it the Patrol?"

"Good guess." He strode forward, oblivious of the pitch-black air. Dia understood the nature of the goggles now: they transformed the heat of the human body into visible light. He had two living lanterns to guide him, though she thought that her radiance must be feeble beside his. She shrank into his warmth, feeling chilled to the bone by the coolness of the cave.

She asked, "Where's Strux?"

"I sent him away. This is my responsibility."

"Where are we going?"

"Out of the combat zone, I hope."

"They'll search every centimeter of these caves. You won't be able to hide."

"If they search every centimeter, they'll be here for a thousand years. These hills are honeycombed."

Nothingness lay ahead. Captivity. Questions. Torture. Death? Yet at this moment, he and she were alone. Before the crash, she would have judged that fair odds; she could have taken him. Now, she found herself an unknown quantity. She could not stand or walk. She wondered if she could even crawl.

What would Michael do?

She wound her fingers in his hair and yanked. With her full strength, the action might have broken his neck; at least it should have thrown him off-balance. But her fingers were weak, her arm muscles atrophied. He didn't even break stride.

"I'm glad you didn't succeed at *that* little maneuver," he said, and, as if she were a load of feathers, he slung her over his shoulders, her wrists clutched in one hand, her ankles in the other. "This won't be as comfortable, but it

won't allow you any more dumb ideas." His pace quick-
ened. "I can't imagine why you'd welcome a pack of trig-
ger-happy Patrollers. They'd be as likely to shoot you as
ask your name."

"I don't care much for the alternative," she said.

"Farther on—when they're past the first flush of attack,
when they're more likely to be cautious—you can wave a
white flag then."

Hanging over his shoulder, blood rushing to her head,
she puzzled over his words. "White flag?"

"I know just the spot: a cul-de-sac off the main tunnel.
We'll be there soon."

"What are you talking about?"

Around them, the rock rumbled dully, and Talley
stepped up his pace. His feet jarred against the ground,
sending shocks through both their bodies until, breaking
stride, he turned a corner and halted. "Here," he said, and
he lowered her gently to the ground. "I have a light. Better
avert your eyes."

A faceted lantern no larger than a finger ring revealed
that they were in a cubbyhole, a mere bubble in the rock,
its domed ceiling barely clearing Talley's head as he
crouched over her.

"I should have brought the blanket . . ." he murmured.
"Well—here." He stripped off his black shirt and wrapped
it around her, tucking the tail beneath her thighs. The
garment was warm from his flesh, and she clutched it
closed with both hands, conserving that warmth. In the
lantern light, his naked chest was pale and hairless and
prickled with gooseflesh.

"Keep the light, and this." He pulled a white scarf from
his hip pocket. "You'll be all right," he said. "Your fellow
Patrollers will follow my trail; they should be willing to
listen to reason by the time they get here. You can flash
your lieutenant's bars at them."

She clutched the scarf. "But what about the information,
the torture . . ."

"In my medical opinion, you were too weak to survive
extended torture; I was, therefore, given extra time to
prepare you for interrogation. Unfortunately . . . you were
rescued during the attack. I barely escaped with my own
life."

She tried to read his expression. His eyes were large and
almost colorless in the lamplight, seemed deep-sunk in his

head. His jaw was set hard. "I don't understand," Dia
said. "If you can evade the Patrol now, you can take me
with you; I don't weigh more than a bundle of sticks. Why
the lies to your friends? Why let me go? Or is this some
crazy trick on me?"

Kneeling before her, he took her face between his hands
and pressed his mouth to hers. His long fingers were a cage,
steel bars covered with flesh, but his lips were gentle, moving softly on hers. There was something magnetic in the
kiss; she felt it drawing her to him, her iron to his lode-
stone, a rush of adrenalin spreading heat from the pit of
her stomach upward to her throat, her lips, flushing her
cheeks beneath his hands. After a moment, she could not
help responding, no matter that he was the enemy, her
jailer; no matter that tremors from the Patrol attack now
shook them almost continuously. She lifted both of her
hands to his.

Talley broke away. "Don't forget me, Dia."

Then he was gone, swallowed whole by the darkness.

She waited, cupping the light in her palms as if it were
a small bird. Without a clock, she felt that hours were passing . . . days . . . millenia . . . she counted to a hundred . . .
a thousand . . . and she shivered in her two shirts, *his* shirts,
as the age-old chill of the depths crept through her thin,
wasted flesh and settled in her marrow. Her jaw ached
from clamping down on chattering teeth, and her fingers
were icy stiff, crooked around an ember that shed no heat
with its light.

And then she heard voices in the tunnel, saw the glow of
torches flashing against the walls, recognized the familiar
blue uniforms. Calling out her name and rank, she waved
the white scarf wildly, and Patrollers rushed to greet her.

A captain detailed three men to carry Dia into the sunlight while he and the rest continued to plumb the caverns.
Hours later, the entire force climbed wearily to the surface,
staggered into flyers waiting at the ledge on the hillside.
They had no prisoners, no booty but a couple of lanterns
and the pallet that Dia knew so well.

Talley and Strux and the man she called Unknown had
gotten away.

PART TWO
HERO

We landed near a medium-sized city, and as ranking officer I was the first to step onto the soil of Amphora. Surveying the area for a likely place to set our standard, I sighted a large boulder not far from the ship. With my beamer I burned the Patrol emblem into its surface to claim the planet as our new base. My staff officers ranged themselves behind me as I worked, giving silent respect to the symbol of our bond and our heritage.

Soon, a delegation of colonists came out of the city to greet us and ask our business. We told them some of the truth; if they guessed the rest, they didn't betray it. Twenty ships of the Patrol, I suppose, showed them how little their objections would mean.

—from the *Memoirs of Brigadier General
Marcus Bohannon, Commander,
36th Tactical Strike Force,
Stellar Federation Patrol*

ONE

Dia's sister moved around the room adjusting fruit bowls and trays of nuts.

"If you want anything, just lift an eyebrow; Poppa and I will both be watching."

Ensconced in a plush recliner, Dia smiled indulgently. "I'm all right, Syd. Really, I can walk across the room all by myself."

"I don't want you to get too tired."

"I worked out in the gym again today—a little more moving won't make any difference."

Sydney looked her up and down. "You do look better. Still wretched, but better."

Dia smoothed the slick fabric of her gown across one thigh, felt the cleanly defined kneecap. "I look like a diet that got out of hand." She leaned back, chose a piece of fruit from the nearest bowl, and bit off a small chunk. "Why don't you sit down and relax, Syd? I've never seen you this nervous before a party."

"Me? No. . . . Isn't it getting late?" She scrutinized the jeweled chronometer on her right thumb as if its face held the key to the future. At that moment, the annunciator chimed, and the front door opened to admit a group that included Oliver Solares and his former wife Vanessa Catlin —Dia's parents.

Sydney greeted the arrivals cheerfully, linking one arm with her father and one with her mother, and Dia had to smile at that pose—physically, Sydney was a perfect blend of the two of them: she was midway in height between them, midway in coloring, midway in build, midway in features. Perhaps that was why she got along so well with both of them, far better than they could with each other. They had not spoken to one another, except very formally,

64

in years, and Dia knew it was a great concession for them to appear at the same party. They even visited their small grandchildren, Sydney's boy and girl, separately, calling ahead to be sure of no inadvertent overlap.

There was only time for Dia to smile that once, to let it stand for a greeting to her parents, before the floodgates opened and Sydney's apartment turned into a disorganized crush. Relatives and friends crowded in, eating, drinking, laughing, and questioning Dia about her captivity. In spite of her protests, she was not allowed to move from her place in the center of the company. Wine, cake, and fruit were all delivered to her, passed from hand to hand when Sydney could not elbow through the press. At last Dia rose and, hands on hips, asked loudly, "Syd, will you go to the bathroom and piss for me?"

Grinning, the guests made a path for her.

In the bathroom, Dia leaned against the mirror. She *was* tired, though she wouldn't admit it to anyone. A long afternoon in the gymnasium had strained her depleted muscles to their limit, and she ached all over. She stepped on the scale: eight more kilos before she reached her normal weight. Her cheeks were still hollow, her elbows, knees, and hips sharp. Wretched, as Sydney had said, but not so wretched as a month ago.

The gown was green and black. Once a favorite of Sydney's own wardrobe, it had long been too tight for a figure that grew more ample every year; altered to fit Dia, its high throat and long, drooping sleeves camouflaged her thinness. She would have preferred Patrol dress uniform, but none of hers fit properly, and she balked at spending credit on clothing soon to be too snug.

Green and black. She fingered one sleeve. Michael had always liked her in green; he said it brought color to her cheeks by contrast. Frowning into the mirror, she flicked at her hair with one of Sydney's combs. Belying her illness, the tresses swung dark and glossy to her shoulders—a wig made of locks shorn when she entered the Academy. She had been a no-nonsense cadet; long hair, she reasoned, would only get in her way.

Michael asked her, one night when they had been together some weeks, to let it grow again. She had said no then, but now she thought she would do it, in memoriam.

"Nothing like a little healthy morbidity," she muttered to her reflection.

The commotion of the party died abruptly, and Dia wondered for a moment if everyone had rushed out into the corridor to view some catastrophe. Opening the bathroom door a crack, she peeked out at a sea of backs. There was a stiffness in the crowd, an air of tension that made Dia think that some high echelon officer had just arrived, probably a friend of one of her parents, come to ogle the returned prisoner of war. Beside the bathroom entrance, several guests, gazed earnestly toward the facilities. Regretfully, Dia vacated her sanctuary.

The new arrival was Brigadier Velicher himself, Commander-in-Chief of the Patrol.

He was a tall, ruddy-faced man, of an age with Dia's father, broad-shouldered, with just the first traces of a pot belly showing at his waist. As the throng parted to let Dia pass, he turned toward her, the famous public smile curving his lips, leaving his cheeks and eyes untouched. Dia thought the smile must be part of the heritage handed from Brigadier to Brigadier along with the insignia and the office furniture; official pictures showed them all wearing it.

"Good evening, Lieutenant Catlin," he said. "I see that you are making an excellent recovery." Three weeks ago he had observed her report to the Council, seated unobtrusively in the far corner of the Assembly Hall, sending an occasional note to the Chief Councillor, a request for clarification or elaboration.

"Good evening, Sir," Dia replied. "I hope to return to active duty as soon as possible."

"No one expects you to do so until you are entirely able, Lieutenant. At that time, however, you will be wearing these." He opened one broad-fingered hand to expose a pair of gleaming silver second lieutenant's bars. "Congratulations, Lieutenant."

The party guests began to applaud as Dia lifted the insignia from the Brigadier's hand and held them gingerly between two fingers. Under normal circumstances, she could not have achieved this rank for at least another year. Velicher took her free hand, shook it firmly, and Dia's stammered gratitude was drowned out by the upsurge of excited crowd chatter.

The Brigadier lifted one finger and achieved instant silence. "I thought you might also want this, as a souvenir of your imprisonment." At his nod, the short, balding captain at his elbow passed a cloth-wrapped package to Dia:

the bronze memorial plaque that had hung in the Citadel Square while she was missing.

She gripped its beveled edges. Ornate script, barely legible: *Killed in action*. Her name. The date. She thought of Michael's plaque, so similar, lost among rows and rows of comrades, like a single scale on the flank of a vast golden fish.

"Not many people get to see their own death notice," she said, and she swallowed the temptation to suggest the Brigadier keep it for use at some later date.

"And now," said Brigadier Velicher, "I wish someone would offer me a drink."

Sydney hurried forward, and Dia's parents followed, drawing the Commander-in-Chief of the Patrol aside into a small circle of older officers. Now Dia understood why *they* were at the party; if the Brigadier chose to honor the hero with his presence, could the hero's own parents do less? Dia slumped into her chair, left conspicuously vacant during her absence, and friends and relatives closed in, a human shield against the Brigadier's nearness. Velicher was not known for an easy-going nature, nor for any over-closeness to subordinates. No one was willing to suggest that his attendance at the party was a terrifying event, but hardly a soul in Dia's group could refrain from looking over a shoulder frequently and reporting that "He" was still there. From the Big Brass corner, an occasional wave of mild laughter jostled the room.

Dia slipped the plaque under her chair and tucked the silver bars into her waistband. She wondered—had Michael lived, would he have been promoted to lieutenant colonel, the youngest lieutenant colonel of the decade? She closed her eyes for a moment. *Tomorrow*, she told herself, *tomorrow I will clean the apartment of all his memories.*

When she opened her eyes, someone asked for the dozenth time about the card-playing creature Strux. Dia shrugged. "I think he was pretty intelligent. He beat me." A surge of laughter greeted this response, but Dia no longer felt she could join it. Exhaustion was beginning to foam about her like water rising in a bathtub. She short-circuited the next inquirer by suggesting a bit sharply that he direct his questions to someone who had already heard the tale and now knew as much about the rebels as did Dia herself. The group as a whole accepted her broad hint and turned to other topics, leaving Dia to lean back in her chair and stare idly at the ceiling.

The Brigadier left early, shaking the hands of the elder officers, nodding at the younger, insisting that Dia not rise from her seat to bid him farewell. Once he was gone, the party became louder, and the intoxicating beverages began disappearing with greater speed. Dia drank only a little, and when she found no extra energy forthcoming from the glass, she decided to go home, too.

"Poppa will walk with you," Sydney said, glancing toward the corner where her father lounged. Her mother had gone, protesting early appointments, but Oliver Solares stayed, his eye on Dia.

"I can make it myself, Syd; it's only a couple hundred meters."

"You should see yourself, little sister. You're out on your feet."

Dia grinned tiredly. "I wasn't ready for the strain of promotion. Did you tell *anyone* that he was coming?"

"Poppa and Mother knew."

"The ex-prisoner of war and the Brigadier himself—two social coups in one evening. You're doing pretty well for a reserve officer, Syd."

"Another party like this one could convince me to go back on active service. Somehow, tonight, I felt that sitting in some lonely garrison would be a lot easier on the nerves than having the Brigadier in for cocktails."

"Tomorrow you'll say you had a wonderful time."

"That's tomorrow. Tonight I'm tempted to rush everybody out and go to bed."

"But you won't."

"No, I might as well bask in borrowed glory while I can. I certainly don't have any exploits of my own to fall back on."

"Well, that's what you get for flying a desk."

Sydney shrugged. "With my coordination, I didn't have much choice. You know, when I was down at Sandy Ridge, we had a bomb scare. Everybody evacuated the building, and the ordnance people came in to search. They found it, too. But it was a dud. Just like my career."

Dia slipped an arm around her sister's shoulders. "You did your job, Syd. Nobody could ask any more. And now . . . I thought you liked teaching."

"I like it, but there's no glory in it. You and Paul will

have to keep up the family traditions; I couldn't seem to manage it. You two got all the talent."

"Well . . . I guess we did get all the reflexes. But I think you got your share of the brains." She smiled. "If I'm wrong, then the Council made a hell of a mistake entrusting children to your care." She gripped her sister's arm. "Listen, Syd—bask while you can. It can't last. Personally, I've had enough. I just want to get back to ordinary Patrol life, and to hell with family tradition. Let other people be heroes for a while."

Silently, their father had stolen up behind Dia. He laid a hand on her shoulder. "I see you edging toward the door."

Dia squeezed his hand. "Sydney tells me you're my bodyguard."

"No, just your mobile crutch." He linked his arm in hers. "Or would you prefer to be carried?"

A picture of Talley bending down to lift her in his arms flashed through her mind. She could almost feel his touch, cool hands, all else warm. "I can walk," she said.

"Then let us adjourn to the corridor. Good night, Sydney."

Oliver Solares was tall, gray-haired and gray-eyed; his step was firm and his grip solid, and he walked too fast for his youngest daughter. "I'll know you're completely well," he said, "when you can keep up with me again."

"I could have, earlier today, but my stamina has all faded away."

"Are you sure you don't want to move back in with me?"

"No, Poppa. I'm all right. I don't want to be waited on."

"Well, you're the best judge of your condition . . . but I hate to see you living alone right now."

"I'd rather be alone. I need breathing space."

"You didn't enjoy the party."

She shrugged. "It wasn't a matter of enjoying, Poppa— the party was an ordeal I had to go through. One last night of telling the story. Now everyone knows, and they'll stop bothering me. I hope so, anyway. It's not as if I did something heroic that I could enjoy bragging about, after all. I didn't do a damned thing but lie on my back and sleep."

"You didn't break."

"I didn't have a chance to break."

He hugged her. "Daughter, I don't care about the details. You're back safe, you've got your silver bars, and I love you."

She leaned against his chest. "I wish Paul could have been here, to see me promoted."

"I called him before the party."

She gazed up at him sidelong, one eyebrow raised. "You knew, of course."

"Of course. We senior officers have our sources."

"You couldn't . . . pull a few strings to get him here?"

Oliver Solares pursed his lips. "Well . . . he came in for your requiem, and his commanding officer didn't think a party in honor of your survival was quite so important. His tour's up in a few months anyway, and then you two can have a real reunion. That party wasn't anyplace to greet your brother."

"I'll have to write to him." A few more steps brought them to her door. "Would you like to come in, Poppa?"

He caught her hands between his own. "You don't really want me to come in, Dia; you're tired."

"Yes, I am."

Softly, he kissed her forehead. "Don't push yourself too hard. And don't let anyone else push you."

"I wish someone would push me a little. Everyone keeps telling me to take it easy—sometimes I feel like they want me to be an invalid for the rest of my life." Drawing one hand from his grasp, she laid her palm against the door, and it slid open silently, exposing darkness in the interior of her apartment. "Good night, Poppa. I'll talk to you in a few days."

He stood at the threshold for a moment as if he were about to speak again, but then he merely waved and smiled and strode away in the direction of his own quarters.

Dia moved surely in the dark, stripping her clothes off as she walked, dropping the dress on the chair opposite her bed, tossing the hairpiece unerringly to its stand on the dresser. The bed was rumpled, the pillow still marked by her head. She lay down on her back, arms flung out across the mattress, her mind's eye seeing every detail of the rooms she had shared for so many months with Michael. His bureau, still full of his underwear and socks; his closet where the uniforms still hung; the wall where his trophies clustered—all just as it had been before they left on that fateful flight. Michael's brother, on special duty in the south, had not yet been able to return to the citadel to claim his effects. Dia had come home to dusty staleness and to the relics of a dead man. She wept then, alone in their bed, and she could not bring herself to get rid of them.

Now she lay awake, dry-eyed, and she said to herself, *Tomorrow. Tomorrow I will start living all over again.*

Dozing in the darkness, she dreamed herself back in the cave, back with Strux and Talley and the damp limestone rubble sparkling in the lantern light, sparkling alternately silver and gold, like gleaming Patrol insignia.

TWO

Morning brought sunlight into her bedroom—the apartment was in an upper tower of the Citadel, its windows commanding a view of the other spires and of the Square. Michael's apartment it was, assigned in deference to his rank and his fame, a choice corner location.

Michael's apartment—though Dia's name was on file for it, too—and it reeked of him.

After a quick breakfast, she began to pack his clothes. Swiftly, she folded the shirts, the jackets, the uniform pieces into his luggage. Upon these cushions went the medals, the trophies, the tokens of the days before they met; none of it belonged to her. She called for a storage pickup, signed it all into Michael's brother's custody, to be laid away till his return. The rest, the few meager remnants of their life together—a few gilt medallions for gymnastics and marksmanship, a picture of the two of them, the matched pistols they had purchased for competition—she put away in the deepest drawer of her dresser. Someday, she thought, she would be able to look at them, even handle them without trembling, but not now, not yet. Entirely hers for the first time, the apartment seemed bare in spite of the bed and the couch and the easy-chairs. He was gone, even the dust of dead skin and the stray hairs from his body were gone. Had he ever existed at all, except as a plaque in the Square?

The annunciator chimed a mail delivery; wearily, Dia scanned the items:

—Official notice of her promotion and pay increase; she tossed it into the top drawer of her dresser, where all her other paperwork lay in haphazard order.

—An invitation to the Brigadier's Masque, one week hence, costume mandatory. She wondered who had ar-

72

ranged that, her mother or her father. Or Sydney's husband, perhaps, now on temporary duty in the West and due to become a Staff Officer at his next promotion—Dia hardly knew him, he was away so much, but Sydney had great influence with him. Such invitations were never refused, not by anyone who had the remotest desire to rise in the Patrol. As far as she knew, they were hardly ever offered to low-ranking officers. Dia sighed and dropped it on the bed. She was still the hero; her world was conspiring to keep her from putting that behind her. At a Masque, though, she might at least hope to hide her identity behind a false face. Until midnight.

—A packet from Pelham's Woods garrison.

Dearest Dia—a thousand congratulations from the hinterlands and your lonesome sibling. They tell me I'll get leave in a couple of centuries. Meanwhile, I send my love and the enclosed—I've saved them for you ever since my last promotion, and I'm happy to forward them so much sooner than expected. I'll have to jump to keep ahead of you.

Take care, Paul

The enclosed: a pair of second lieutenant's bars. She laid them beside the set that the Brigadier had presented to her.

And then, once more, the chime, and a crisp, official summons fell into the drop tube: she was due at the Brigadier's office at 1500 hours. More of the hero business, no doubt. Michael, she thought, would have been happy to know she was seeing so much of the Brigadier. Familiarity, he would have said—*had* said, after introducing her to one of his high-ranking friends—breeds promotion. She had thirty-five minutes in which to shower and dress and run.

She chose Paul's bars for her uniform. Brigadier Velicher would never know the difference. Both slacks and tunic were pitifully loose, but Dia cinched the belt tight, knowing that any uniform at all was preferable to appearing in the Brigadier's office in casual clothing.

She took a roundabout route—elevator to ground level, scooter along the service ways, elevator into the Central Tower. There were other courses that led outside through the Square or the Gardens, that wended along upper-story balconies or catwalks, that cut through recreation rooms where uniforms were seldom seen, but the elevator-scooter route made up in speed for its lack of directness. Dia arrived with two minutes to spare.

At the anteroom desk was the captain who had accompanied the Brigadier to the party. Before him was his nameplate, white letters on a blue background: Morgan Ramirez, easier to read than the tag above his breast pocket. He raised his head as she entered and indicated a nearby chair with a wave of one finger. There was no one else in the room.

Dia folded her hands and watched the captain's bald spot as it bobbed over his work. Her chronometer showed precisely the hour when he flicked the intercom on and announced her. She could not hear the reply but edged forward in her seat, assuming he would speak or motion her to rise. He did both, but not until he had settled back in his chair and given her a long, appraising look. His expression was quite neutral as he did so, only the eyes moving in his face. She thought he must be evaluating her youth, and the gleaming bars on her shoulders.

He pointed toward the door that bore no name, only the emblem of the Patrol in bold relief. "Go in, Lieutenant."

She stepped into the Brigadier's office.

As a very junior officer, she had never been there before, but she had seen the broad, bare desk, the heavily padded chair, and the panelled walls in official broadcasts. It was a sparsely furnished room, the walls devoid of ornamentation save for the Patrol emblem and a plaque bearing a gold-plated pistol inscribed as a marksmanship trophy; the lighting was indirect, fixtures hidden behind translucent ceiling panels—buried in the heart of the Citadel, the room had no windows. Two low couches faced the desk, and Dia halted beside one of them to deliver her salute.

"Lieutenant Catlin reporting, Sir."

The Brigadier sat easy in his chair, arms folded, head bent so that his eyes peered up at her from behind a fence of bushy brows. "Sit down, Lieutenant."

She obeyed and found herself below his eye level. The viewpoint made both him and the desk loom large.

"I trust last night's party did not tire you unduly," he said.

"No, Sir."

"Your most recent medical report indicates that you will be able to return to duty soon."

"I'm feeling well, Sir; I just have to pick up a little more weight."

He leaned forward, forearms flat on the desktop, fingers loosely interlaced. "I haven't had an opportunity to extend my condolences, Lieutenant. I knew Major Drew; he was a fine officer."

Stiffly, she replied, "Yes, Sir, he was."

"And he should have known better than to stretch regulations by flying a mission with his lover. No matter how safe that mission appeared."

She sat very straight, as she had during classes at the Academy when she was reprimanded. She had always accepted the blame for her own errors, never tried to make excuses. "It was my idea, Sir."

"He could have squelched the notion. *He* had the connections that made it possible."

"Yes, Sir. But I did talk him into it, Sir."

"He *wanted* to be talked into it. It was a stupid and unprofessional thing to do, and it mars his otherwise exemplary record . . . but a record means very little after a person is dead. What concerns me is you, Lieutenant. I would have expected you to lose your head at Major Drew's death; I would have expected you to botch the crash landing and get yourself killed as well. Instead, you survived and brought back valuable information on the rebels. Either it was a fluke, or you are an extraordinary person, Lieutenant Catlin." He regarded her with slitted eyes, as if focusing on some detail of her uniform. "Which is it?"

Involuntarily, she looked down at herself, searching for the object of his fascination. There was nothing but the unadorned blue uniform, hanging loosely on her thin frame. She didn't feel very extraordinary. "I'll opt for the fluke, Sir."

"I'm not interested in false modesty, Lieutenant." He pushed his chair back and rose; slowly he moved around the desk toward her, the fingertips of one hand trailing over the gleaming surface as if reluctant to break contact with that token of his office. He left it behind at last and halted a few centimeters from Dia's knees. Towering above her, he said, "I want to know what sort of third lieutenant was good enough for Mike Drew."

Dia hesitated, looking up at him. "We had a lot in common, Sir."

"I know. I know all about that—the gymnastics, the marksmanship. I know you're a good pilot, too, as he was. You come from a good family, with a long history of service to the Patrol on both sides. And you were at the top of your class at the Academy. You're bright and you're capable, but there have been other bright, capable third lieutenants. Even better-looking ones." He gripped her shoulder with one hard hand, the fingers curling into the fabric of her uniform and into the flesh beneath. "He saw something special in you, Lieutenant, something worth training, worth keeping near him. Was it more or less, I wonder, than *I* see?" He grasped both her shoulders and lifted her to her feet. Her eyes were level with his chin, and he could look down on her hair, so close that his breath fluttered a few strands.

Not the Brigadier himself! she thought, and then the proof was upon her mouth, his hands at the back of her head, at the small of her waist, his body tight against hers. She stood passive in the circle of his arms, feeling the heavy beat of his heart against her chest. She had known Michael no better on the night of their first kiss, but there had been a rapport between them. Brigadier Velicher was merely a man.

Gently, she disengaged herself. "Please, Sir, I'm still in mourning for Michael," she whispered, sliding sideways out of his embrace.

He let her slip away, except for her hand, which he gripped firmly. "You can't grieve forever, Dia. I won't let you."

"I'm flattered, Sir, believe me, that you're taking such an interest in me."

"I want only the best. I want you."

"Give me some time to think, Sir."

"Of course. Go on . . . go back to your quarters and think. And remember—a good officer makes decisions quickly." He let loose her hand and smiled at her crisp farewell salute.

She sought a long route home, a sunlit route through glass-encased tunnels cantilevered over wide gardens. She was not thinking at all, merely remembering the Brigadier's face, the relentless eyes, the cheeks tanned and toughened and creased, the lips hard and thin. What made him especially suited to be Brigadier? That he outlasted, outmaneuvered, outbrazened all opponents; that he caused the

Council to love and fear him enough to name him their superior. His word was law on Amphora. He could cause the deaths of thousands with a nod. And here was Second Lieutenant Dia Catlin . . . wondering if she dared say No.

She walked past her apartment door. She didn't want to be alone right now. She gave her name at Sydney's and was immediately admitted.

Sydney came out of the bedroom clad in a light robe. "Up so early, little sister?"

Dia smiled wryly. "Don't tell me you were still asleep! The party must have gone on a long time after I left."

"It was just getting started when you gave up."

"Didn't you have work this morning?"

"The day after your party? Uh-uh; I knew I'd need the vacation. My students are on a field trip with one of the other teachers. At a dairy farm. Soaking up a little colonial life."

"Your own two must not be back then either, if you're on a *real* vacation."

"Right," said Sydney. "Three more days with Hilary's parents. And he'll be back in two. Oh, I have my life planned *very* well. Have you had lunch?"

"I could eat something." Her sister dialed a pair of sandwiches, and while they waited for delivery, Dia said, "I came for a serious talk, Syd. I really can't discuss this with anyone else. I've had a proposition."

Sydney's eyebrows lifted. "I guess you don't look as wretched as I thought." She squinted at Dia for a moment, frowning. "But I can see that something's bothering you. What's the problem?"

"I don't know what to do about it."

"Since when have you had trouble making up your mind? Especially about sex."

"Since a little while ago."

"Oho." She reached out to stroke her sister's hair. "Listen—I know it's been a long time for you. You can't let Michael's memory keep you from living."

"It isn't that. I told him I was still in mourning, but it's not true. Syd . . . it's the Brigadier."

Sydney leaned back against the kitchen counter, silent until the thump of the sandwiches in the delivery chute caught her attention. "I thought I saw a gleam in his eye last night," she said, handing Dia her lunch. "So . . . what's the problem?"

"The problem is that he doesn't excite me."

Sydney shrugged. "Mother thinks he's attractive."

"Well, that's fine for Mother. Maybe she'd like to switch places with me."

Sydney stabbed a finger toward Dia's face. "Don't be stupid, little sister—this is the chance of a lifetime. Be good to him, and you can parlay one night into a year of steady attention. You could be there when high-level decisions are made; you could practically be a member of the Staff. And after he's tired of you . . . I've heard that he doesn't forget his ex-lovers when promotion time comes around."

Dia picked at the wrapper of her sandwich. "Do I really feel up to spending a year of nights with the Brigadier . . . for the sake of my career?"

Sydney shrugged. "He owns your body, one way or another. He can order you to go out and die for the Patrol. Sleeping with him seems such a trivial thing in comparison." Slowly, her lips curved into a grin. "And I've heard from reliable sources that it's a highly satisfying experience."

Dia made no reply.

Sydney nibbled her sandwich, gazing at her sister through lowered lashes. "Is there someone else?"

She shook her head. "No. No one."

"Then I don't see any real difficulty."

"It would be easy for you, wouldn't it?"

"If he'd made me that kind of offer a few years ago, I might still be on active service today. Take the advice of an old and jaded reserve officer—say yes. I'm sure Mother and Poppa would agree."

Dia stared past her sister, eyes unfocused. Shadows moved across her mind as she said, "Would Michael also agree?"

"Well, I don't think he'd want to share you, even with the Brigadier. . . ."

Dia caught her arm. "If I were his sister or his daughter . . . Michael would agree. Anything to make rank, he used to say. Anything." She blinked away the clinging cobwebs. "All right, I know all the opinions; now I've got to go home and think." She turned toward the door.

"You haven't eaten your lunch."

"I'm not hungry."

Sydney's voice floated out into the corridor after her. "You'll be skinny forever, you idiot! What will the Brigadier think when he finds your bones stick out?" And then the door slid shut.

Maybe I won't interest him. Maybe he'll turn me out after one night. In her quarters, she sat in Michael's favorite chair, and she tried to think as Michael would. There had been other men in her life before him, casual relationships based on friendship and the desire of the moment, nothing lasting. Then, Michael, and a warmth and tenderness she had never known before, and such passion that she ached just to remember it. Now, in the quiet of their room, she realized that she couldn't expect another Michael to appear magically, that she would have to take a Velicher or keep waiting.

I am lonely, she told herself. *I'll be less lonely with someone sleeping beside me.*

The Brigadier . . . ?

After Major Michael Drew, there was nowhere to go but up.

Reclining in the chair, she dozed, and in her dream, a tall man stood close behind her, his arms encircling her body, his lips and breath warm upon her ear. Her head rocked back on his shoulder, and as his hand moved upward to touch her cheek, she saw that the fine hair on his arm was pale as moonlight.

Upon waking, she went to the closet, where a single piece of masculine attire remained, inconspicuous in the far corner: a gray tunic, its sleeves cut off raggedly. Lightly, her fingers touched the fabric. Closing her eyes, she could envision the cave, the dim glow of the lantern, the sleek shining fur of Strux; she could recall the pressure of Talley's lips on her own. *No, I will not forget you, my enemy —not as long as I walk, not as long as I breathe.*

Then she stripped off her uniform and donned a sweatshirt and shorts. The gymnasium where she and Michael had always exercised was nearby, and there she could lose herself in physical activity for a few hours and not have to think at all.

THREE

He called that night, woke her from the dreamless slumber of exhaustion. At first she thought the chime of the viewscreen was only a random ringing in her ears such as she had experienced occasionally since the crash. After a time, she reached for the light switch and the small monitor on the headboard of the bed.

"I apologize for waking you," he said, though his tone was not at all contrite. "I hadn't thought you would retire so early."

She glanced at the wall chronometer: midnight plus half an hour. "Normally, I wouldn't . . . but I'm not really well yet, Sir. I tire easily."

"Ah. In the gym."

"Yes, Sir. I used to be able to work out for hours without getting really tired."

"I see."

"I intend to return to that level of activity, Sir."

"Commendable, Lieutenant. Commendable." Though the screen was a physical barrier between them, she could feel his eyes scrutinizing the very pores of her face. "I was going to invite you to my private quarters for a chat this evening, but I perceive that you *are* tired, and I would not care to tax you beyond your strength. I presume I will see you at the Masque?"

"Yes, sir."

"Wear green. It becomes you."

"I hadn't planned on it, Sir. I have a costume that will do well enough, but it isn't green."

"I'll send over a credit voucher in the morning—buy something green. I'll be expecting an answer." He smiled. "I hope we can reach some sort of accommodation."

She hesitated, staring back into his eyes. He was an attractive man, she decided, for his age. Was it primarily his age, she wondered, that she held against him? She had thought Michael a trifle mature as a match for a new Academy graduate, and he was only thirty-three. The Brigadier was old enough to be *his* father.

"I'll have your answer," she said, and she tried to smile, but a yawn interfered. "Sorry, Sir, I'm very tired."

"Go back to sleep, my dear." The screen went dark.

Dia rolled over and buried her head in the pillows. Her blue sea-nymph costume was undoubtedly too large for her present figure. If the Brigadier wanted to buy her a new costume, she would certainly not reject the offer; credit was nothing to the Commander-in-Chief of the Patrol.

In a way, she was glad that he was offering something tangible in exchange for her body.

Later that night, her dreams were drenched in green.

In the morning, while waiting for the voucher to arrive, Dia sketched the new costume on a scrap of paper. She would be a stylized bird, hair hidden by waving plumes, feather jewelry at her throat and wrists, green satin close upon her body. The highlight of the ensemble would be the long tail streaming behind, brushing ticklishly against anyone who came near. The cost of all those feathers would be phenomenal . . . but the voucher that arrived with the first mail delivery had a blank credit space.

Her tailor was more than willing to undertake the project. Frequented almost exclusively by junior officers, he rarely had an opportunity to make something so elaborate. He even added a few touches of his own to the sketch—brilliants to accent certain feathers, and a face mask that was a delicate curving beak molded in silver filigree. It would all be ready in three days.

Not a very self-effacing regalia, she thought. Would anyone be able to guess that she was only a second lieutenant?

Exercise consumed her time until the Masque—exercise and food. She had let her protein intake slump for a few days, and the doctor had lectured her on the inadvisability of letting her weight level off so soon. He could not, however, conceal his satisfaction with her progress, with the firm muscle slowly building up around her bones.

"You'll be a star gymnast again, don't worry," he told her.

"I don't doubt it," she replied.

And then, suddenly, it was the night of the Masque, and Sydney arrived to help her into her costume.

"Well, it's gaudy enough," said Sydney, stringing feather bracelets around her sister's forearms.

"Too gaudy for my own tastes," agreed Dia, "but perfect for an entry into the rarefied world of senior officers. I wonder what he'll be wearing."

"The grapevine says black and silver."

"The grapevine?"

"Mother. She called his tailor."

"Will she be there?"

Sydney shrugged. "She hasn't made her mind up yet."

"Weighing all the factors, I suppose. As usual." Dia laughed. "How the hell does the Council ever get anything accomplished with Mother around?" She turned slowly, eyeing her reflection in the mirror. The feathers bobbed gently with her movement.

"He'll like it, Dia, don't worry."

"I don't think he'll be able to tell who it is."

"Oh, I think he'll know."

Dia cocked her head, birdlike, toward her sister. "You are undoubtedly correct, Sydney. My tailor has a big mouth, after all, not to mention my sister and my parents. Chirp." She pretended to nibble at Sydney's shoulder. "Consider yourself kissed, elder sister. It's time to fly!"

She took a scooter, sitting awkwardly, the long, fluttery tail draped over her shoulders like a cape. As she drove, occasional green fragments floated away, leaving a trail through the labyrinthine corridors of the Citadel. Passersby stared at her—everyone knew where she must be bound, and she couldn't decide which interested them more, her flamboyant outfit or her status. Her hands clutched the steering grips harder than necessary, sweat from her palms lubricating the contoured plastic; she could not remember ever being so nervous before, not even the first time she soloed an aircraft.

At the entrance to the Grand Ballroom, she presented her embossed invitation to the doorman, whom she recognized as Captain Ramirez. He wore no costume, only a skimpy domino and his dress uniform. He stared at her for a long moment, as if trying to make out the face beneath her mask, then passed her in without a word. She moved only a pace or two beyond the threshold before glancing back; he was still staring, and their eyes met briefly. She could not name what she saw in his look—it might be curiosity, appraisal, disdain. Her name was on the invitation; he knew who she was and how poorly her rank fit the occasion. She wondered if he also knew the reason for her presence. He broke the contact first, turning smoothly to greet the next guest.

She went on.

The room was much as she remembered it from the night of graduation. Down one side was a row of tables proffering food and drink of every description and temperature. In the center was the translucent dance floor beneath which pastel colors ebbed and flowed in a river of rainbow light. Brocade draperies hid the walls, and diamond points sprinkled the ceiling like so many stars.

Dia crossed to the closest refreshment table and selected a glass of cold red punch; it would suffice to keep her hands occupied for some minutes. She retired to a vantage near one of the heavy curtains and scanned the room unhurriedly. Gaudy though Sydney judged it, her costume was far from the most elaborate present. Plumes, satins, jewels, gleaming metal were all in evidence; frothy fabrics waved in the draft of the ventilators; trains and cloaks flared; naked and partly naked limbs flashed behind screens of lace or metallic mesh or glittering dust. Perhaps a hundred Masquers moved in the room: Councillors, Staff members, some lower-echelon officers about to rise in rank, no doubt a few special guests like herself. Sydney's husband should have been there, except that he was two thousand kilometers away on special assignment; Sydney, of course, a reserve officer of only middling rank, was not invited.

Identifying anyone among the particolored throng was virtually impossible. She would have known only a few of them personally anyway—one or two of Michael's friends, perhaps, and her mother. A few of her mother's friends might be here, but Dia hardly knew any of them; she had only rarely been with her mother since her parents parted. As for her father—though she knew his social circle fairly well, he didn't move among people likely to be invited to a Brigadier's Masque. She thought she glimpsed her mother once, but she wasn't sure; nor did she have any desire to pursue the identification.

The Brigadier, however, was conspicuous. He was unmistakable in height, in build, in opulence of dress. Black and silver he was indeed, and the horned headdress made him tower over everyone else. His cloak was heavy, voluminous, floor-sweeping, and upon its back was worked the Patrol emblem in silver thread. He moved about the room with fluid grace, and an entourage moved with him, like scavengers following a master hunter. His striding seemed random, first one way, then another, and he stopped every few paces to speak to someone, to laugh, to raise a toast with the glass from which he never sipped. Occasionally he sent one of his retinue to whisper to Captain Ramirez. Dia perceived a pattern quickly—every hint of green attracted him, and after inspection he passed on, having ascertained that the bearer was not the person he sought.

He took his time, and eventually he reached the curtain where Dia stood. "Good evening," he said, a black and silver demon with hazel eyes glittering moistly behind a velvet mask.

"Good evening, Sir," she said, inclining her head.

Though it was muffled by the beak, he did not fail to recognize her voice. His whole posture changed, the tilt of his head, the twist of his shoulders. He lifted his glass. "A toast to your answer," he said softly. "May it be yes." A massive ring on his gloved right hand flashed, a jade egg twined in brambles of gold. *I should be flattered,* she thought; *he loves beautiful things.*

She lifted her own glass, still a quarter full of blood-red punch, and she met his gaze. What other answer could there be for a proper Patroller? "Yes," she said. Their glasses clinked, and for the first time since she had been watching him, he drained his. Then he made a peremptory gesture that caused his entourage to melt away, and he offered her his arm.

"Shall we dance?"

He was a fine dancer, and they swept across the floor unhindered, other couples giving way to the Brigadier and his partner. Dia laughed at the stares they must have thought were surreptitious; obviously they were wondering who she was, what her rank and her fame were, what attractions lay beneath the feathers and gems and satin

cloth. She was sure now that she saw her mother at the
edge of the dance floor, standing with hands at her back,
in a semblance of parade rest, rocking to and fro, her long
gown gently whisking the floor. Beneath a narrow domino,
her mouth was a narrower smile. Her hair was green for
the evening—perhaps in solidarity with her daughter—and
Dia wondered what sort of advantage she would make of
her child's liaison.

Unmasking came at midnight, and everyone had to kiss
his partner. Velicher swept his cloak about Dia and bent,
vampirelike, to claim her. Horns still firmly fixed atop his
head, he seemed unhumanly tall, and she felt tiny beside
him, and fragile as a flower. He held her gently, as if fear-
ing to bruise her.

"Are you tired?" he whispered in her ear.

She shook her head, and the plumes of her headdress
bobbed at the periphery of her vision, echoing the negative gesture.

"Then one more dance . . . and we'll leave."

"As you wish, Sir," she replied.

"You must call me Arlen," he murmured, "when we're
alone together."

"Arlen."

"Yes."

The dance was a leisurely one, and their unhurried movements brought them gradually to the door, where Captain
Ramirez bowed them out. The black and silver demon,
however, could not leave unobtrusively; the dancing throng
skewed doorward for a look at the Brigadier's partner, and
a sussurating babble arose as soon as the pair had passed
through the doorway. The Brigadier covered Dia's hand
with his own and strode away from the Masque without a
backward glance. His own quarters were only a short walk
from the Grand Ballroom, just below his office. No one
dared to follow them. No one was near to see them enter.

"A very becoming costume, my dear," he said, helping
her remove the headdress and wristlets and the long, fluttering tail.

"I couldn't have been much greener." She smiled at him.
"I'm surprised you took so long to find me."

"Oh, I knew you as soon as you walked in." He stroked
the sleek feathers on her shoulders. "But there wasn't any
need to rush." He slipped the horned cowl off and laid it
gently on a low table. Then he doffed his cloak and gloves,

to become merely a gray-haired man of sixty in an elegant black and silver suit.

"Your costume was very effective," Dia said, her eyes on the tapered, slightly curved horns.

"Unhuman," he said. "Appropriate, don't you think, for the Brigadier—sitting up in my office giving orders like some elder god."

She shifted her gaze to his face. "You *are* an elder god."

He smiled, and though it was not the public smile now, it was still only a cool curve of the lips. "You know . . . you're the only second lieutenant who ever looked me in the eye." He shook his head and sat down on the low couch that occupied one side of the living room. "Every year I plod past that line of graduates, clipping on bars and shaking hands and returning salutes, and they all stare straight ahead. They're usually captains before they can look at my face."

"Gaze upon the countenance of the god and tremble," she said.

He caught her arm and pulled her down beside him. "I don't see you trembling."

"That was earlier today. I got over it."

His hands slid easily along her satin-covered thighs. "How does the rest of this costume come off?"

"Simply enough," she said, guiding his fingers to the closures at the back. "Wouldn't we be more comfortable in the bedroom?"

"I was just about to suggest that."

Sydney's reliable sources turned out to be right . . . or perhaps the Brigadier was only trying to show that a man of sixty could be as good a lover as Michael Drew. Dia fell asleep against his side, and she slept soundly till his bedside chronometer chimed morning. She dreamed of other things, of past and never things, but when she woke they receded to that wellspring of the subconscious from which they had bloomed. Arlen Velicher kissed her a firm good morning.

"There's a small but comfortable apartment adjoining this one. I think you'll like it."

Dia stretched, bending her body into a taut bow and then curling into the curve of his arm. "I'm sure it's a fine place, Arlen . . . but I'd rather stay in my own apartment."

He nuzzled her hair. "I want you near me."

"I'd be no farther away than the viewscreen; I could be here in ten minutes, any time you call."

"Come now," he said, stroking her back. "It's just sentiment that's keeping you there. I'm not going to let you grieve—I told you that already."

She closed her eyes. To move out of Michael's apartment . . . *It's just a pair of rooms.*

"You can refurnish it however you like," he said. "Put a rug on the ceiling, a chandelier on the floor—whatever you please."

The old order passeth. She looked up at him. "All right."

"I'll have your things sent over immediately."

"No, I'll pack them myself." She rose from the bed and retrieved her costume from the chair where it had been tossed.

"You'll look odd walking the corridors in that," he said.

"I don't think your clothes will fit me, so I'll just have to look odd." She began to slip the satin tights up one leg.

"If you check the left side of the closet you'll find something a bit more suitable."

She dropped the costume and ambled over to the closet. Inside, in an otherwise empty compartment, was a uniform. Silver second lieutenant's bars marked the shoulders.

"Your tailor guaranteed a perfect fit. I don't want to see you in a baggy uniform again." While she dressed, he added, "You'll get a decent clothing allowance now; my lover can't look like a pauperized lower-echelon officer, even if that's what she is. Get yourself a couple of dress uniforms—you'll be wearing them often."

She pulled the sleeves straight and gave herself one inspection glance in the closet mirror. She looked trim and competent and military, none of which seemed appropriate to her new social position. "I won't be long," she said over her shoulder.

Naked and barefoot, he padded up behind her, encircled her with his arms. "You make that uniform look uncommonly beautiful." He kissed her neck just above the collar. "Come with me before you leave, and we'll imprint your hand on your two new doors."

The adjoining quarters were furnished with the standard Patrol-issue appurtenances. If ever another person had lived there, he or she had left no personal mark. *She,* Dia thought. *He didn't just dream up this arrangement for me.* Still, it was thoughtful of him to eliminate all hint of the previous occupant. The cupboard was bare of even the snack foods that most people kept there.

One door communicated to Velicher's quarters, one to the corridor. "They answer to me as well, of course," he said after programming the locks, "but I'll always ring before coming in. I believe in privacy."

"All right."

He draped an arm across her shoulders. "I don't want to interfere with your life, Dia. Go ahead with your gymnastics and your target competition. I might even join you at the target range. I'm not bad with a pistol myself."

She smiled slightly. "I saw the trophy."

He squeezed her. "I'm glad we'll be able to do things together."

She gazed at the door to his apartment, as if seeing the invisible handprint she had left upon it. The door—symbol of her new status. *Does he really believe that he hasn't interfered with my life?* Evenly, she said, "And what about my Patrol duties?"

"You'll be an aide attached to my Staff." He kissed her temple. "My own personal aide."

"Isn't that . . . what Captain Ramirez is?"

"There's enough work for two of you. More than two— he has a couple of aides of his own. Don't be afraid to ask him for help. You'll need him, at least at first. He's been with me for ten years, and he knows how to handle everything that comes to my office."

"I was supposed to be posted to one of the northern garrisons when my medical leave ended."

"That would be a bit inconvenient, wouldn't it? He gave her rump a pat. "Now get on to your packing; I'll expect you to dine with me this evening."

In her own quarters, she slumped on the bed for a moment before beginning her task. She felt neither happy nor sad, only as if she had been given an assignment by a strict instructor. The room that Michael had chosen would no longer belong to her; someone else's clothing would fill the drawers and closet, someone else's memorabilia would litter the walls and horizontal surfaces. Someone else would look out the window every morning. *If I were going north, it would be the same. Just the same.*

She packed swiftly, even the mementoes of former times, and she closed the lid of the last case upon them with a firm hand. After a quick sandwich she went out to look for a scooter. Her journey to the new residence drew little attention among the many Patrollers striding purposefully down the Citadel corridors, riding the elevators, entering and leaving offices and dwellings. Several times, she felt as if everyone must know her identity, and no one cared. She happened not to pass anyone she knew on the trip, and so she did not speak at all before arriving, unpacking, and punching Sydney's quarters on the new viewscreen.

"I've been trying to get you all morning," her sister said.

"I was only home a little while."

"And you're not there now," Sydney said, squinting past Dia's shoulder, "unless you've been redecorating since last night."

"I've moved out. These are my new quarters. Next door to the Brigadier."

"Aha! So it worked out well. Mother thought so when she saw you two leave the Masque together. She went after all."

"I saw her."

"This means you won't be leaving for the North."

"No, I'm permanent party in the Citadel now—the Brigadier's own aide. You may speak to me, after groveling."

Sydney grinned. "Can I come over and look at the new premises?"

"I suppose so, since you're a member of the immediate family."

"I meant right now, not in the abstract. I have some empty time."

Dia glanced at her chronometer. "Why don't you come over and look and then you can keep me company at the gym."

"You didn't get enough exercise last night?"

Dia had to return her sister's grin. "Not the right kind."

"Which gym are you thinking of?"

"The same one I always use."

"Isn't there one closer to you?"

She shrugged. "Maybe, but I don't have a time slot there."

"All right. I guess I don't mind being background noise while you punish your body."

Sydney was more subdued when she surveyed the new apartment, only making occasional humming noises as she inspected the impersonal furnishings that Dia had already begun to camouflage with memorabilia. "There isn't anything special about it, is there?" she said at last. "Somehow, I expected it to be . . . I don't know. Gold-plated?"

Dia pointed at the door to Velicher's apartment. "That's the only special thing. Come on—I want to get a couple of hours in before dinner with my new friend."

Sydney sat quietly while Dia did some tumbling. Three other young people were in the gym, but beyond smiles and waves of greeting they did not bother Dia. She knew them, as she knew all the gymnasts in the upper ranks of competition, but their very rivalry prevented them from becoming more than casual acquaintances. Occasionally the others would halt their own exercise to watch her for a moment, and at those times she felt embarrassed, for she knew that her form and speed were down considerably; that it would be many months before she could impress them.

"Your legs don't give you any trouble?" Sydney inquired during a rest period.

Dia shook her head. "He did a good job when he put me back together; just the muscles are weak, and that's up to me to fix." She stretched her arms. "It's hard to believe, now, that I could once see the bones just under the skin. The Patrol doctors said that he could have killed me with accelerated healing. But he knew *exactly* what he was doing. I was lucky, they said, to have such a good doctor." If she closed her eyes she could see him, telltale lights dancing across his pale cheeks as he bent over her. Sighing, she wished he could see her now, healthy and whole and active. She wished that somehow she could show him a truer picture of herself than he had already seen. *My compassionate enemy.*

"I wonder who he was," said Sydney. "You'd think a doctor would be on record."

Dia leaned back on her elbows, legs stretched out before her. "I must have looked at two hundred pictures," she said, "and none of them was him. I think . . . he must have been an Outsider really, and all that talk of his family was just to gain my sympathy. An off-worlder, with no birth certificate, no school registration, no flyer's license. If he was dropped secretly, if he's been living with the rebels, there might not be any records at all."

Sydney made a stiff, open-handed gesture of exasperation. "How could he have been dropped secretly? The warning net is supposed to prevent exactly that."

"Good question." She shrugged. "Let's not fool ourselves,

Syd—we don't have all the technology in the universe. Other planets must be more sophisticated than ours in some ways. If we can trace his sidekick's species, we'll know which one is teaming up with the rebels."

"Do you think we're ready for interplanetary war?"

Dia's eyebrows lifted. "Ask your husband; he'd know better than I would."

"You're going to know, little sister," Sydney murmured. "You're going to know whatever you want from now on."

Dia looked down at the floor between her feet. "I suppose that's true."

"You'll only have to keep your eyes and ears open."

"And my mouth shut," she said, transferring her gaze to her sister's face.

Sydney nodded. "By all means, your mouth shut. Especially as far as your sibling is concerned, so that she will never have to testify that you spilled military secrets to her." She stuck out her hand, and they shook solemnly and then grinned at each other, feeling like a pair of school children making a pact against their parents.

Dia returned to her new quarters to find the Brigadier seated in her living room, a sheaf of papers fanned out across his lap.

"I was wondering where you were," he said. "Leave a note on the screen next time, in case I have to call you."

"I was at the gym."

He eyed her sweat-stained shirt and shorts. "So I see. Come over here; I want to show you something."

The papers were flimsy computer printouts, a file on one particular individual. A small picture topped the stack—a chubby blond boy of twelve or thirteen gazing solemnly at the camera, as if his image were being captured for prison records rather than primary school.

"How old is the shot?" she asked.

"Eighteen years."

She picked up the likeness with two fingers, raised it close to her eyes. "It could be him."

"Gordon Tallentyre Magramor. Parents killed five years ago in a raid on a suspected rebel stronghold."

Dia nodded. "That's Talley." So his story was true after all.

"All right." He retrieved the picture. "You'd better shower and change for dinner now. Wear your uniform. Some of the Staff will be eating with us."

The Brigadier's dining room table unfolded to seat eight, and six colonels soon arrived to surround it. They greeted Dia with firm handshakes—obviously, they had been warned that their commander's new consort was an officer of low rank, and they were determined to pretend they didn't care. The meal was all business—rebel movements, supply lines, garrison augmentations; Velicher steered it swiftly from one topic to another, and by dessert he was speaking of Gordon Tallentyre Magramor.

"This is your assignment, Roppolo, and I expect you to study the file later, but briefly, Magramor is from Greentree Province. After a year at the University of Biscay he boarded a trade ship purportedly bound for Daphne, in the Archon System, and there our records end—twelve years ago. We know that Daphne has no intelligent native life, but he could easily have gone elsewhere from there; his father was a well-known jewelry maker, and the interplanetary trade in his work could easily have financed quite a bit of traveling. How did he come back undetected, why, from where, and with whom . . . ? I think he may be the key to some new strategy of the rebels, he and that creature of his, that Strux, and I want them found."

"What about sending an investigating team to Daphne?" asked Roppolo. He was a short, tense-looking man with fingernails trimmed—or bitten—to the quick.

Velicher shook his head. "A waste of time, I suspect. The trail is a dozen years cold, if it does lead there at all."

"Then I'll check out his relatives, childhood friends, teachers, everyone who ever came in contact with him."

"I have great faith in you, Colonel." He turned toward Dia and said, "Tell us, my dear, what is your evaluation of Magramor?"

Dia had said nothing during the meal, and now, as six pairs of eyes swiveled in her direction, she froze in the act of forking a piece of cake into her open mouth. Carefully, she set the untouched bite back on her plate. "He's a bitter man," she said slowly. "He has a lot of hatred for the Patrol bottled up inside him."

"Understandable," said Velicher. "We killed his parents."

"That's part of it, but it goes deeper. He loves Amphora, or at least what Amphora once was. He wants to bring that back. I don't really understand how he could have left for so many years, feeling the way he does."

Velicher leaned back, a glass of pale amber liqueur in his hand. "At the time his parents were killed, we couldn't be sure if they were rebels or merely innocent bystanders." He twirled his drink meditatively. "They were friends of Ostberg, the big landowner up there in Greentree. Close friends. We've suspected *he* was a rebel for a long time now, but we've never had any proof. He always has an alibi, with plenty of witnesses to back him up. And he's too rich and too powerful locally to arrest on any trumped-up ,charge. But I *know* he's a rebel, it's in his manner, his damned arrogance. He's too sure of himself. And if the son of his friends is a rebel . . ." He shook his head sharply. "No, it's still too tenuous to be *proof*, just guilt by association. That's what the Council would say, what the damned colonials would say. If I arrest him without real, solid evidence, it could make the whole province blow up in our faces. But this is what I think." He stabbed the air with a forefinger. "Magramor's parents were rebels, and their interplanetary jewelry trade was a cover for negotiations with sympathetic Outsiders. I think they sent their son as liaison. Presumably he attended medical school somewhere along the way." He paused for a tiny sip of liqueur. "He's important. Possibly he is the new rebel leader . . . replacing his father. Or possibly Ostberg has been the leader all along, with the Magramors his adjutants. That's pure conjecture, of course." He glanced at Roppolo. "What do you think?"

Roppolo moved his chair away from the table, but not far enough, for as he rose, his knee struck the undersurface, making all the glassware rattle. "If you don't mind, Sir, I think I'd better get to work on this right away."

"Certainly," Velicher replied. "You can all return to your jobs. Dinner is over." He nodded as they trooped out, and when they were gone, he put his feet up on the table and teetered his chair back on two legs. Without haste, he finished his drink.

"I've wanted Ostberg for a long time," he said, "but he's been too clever. He doesn't go to any parties that might be undercover rebel gatherings. He doesn't make calls that sound suspicious—I've had them monitored for years. If he talks to his friends in code . . . well, he must, and we just haven't cracked it yet. Now, I think we have a chance to get him; to get them all, to crush this damned rebellion once and for all. Roppolo's a good man. We'll be seeing your Doctor Talley one of these days, I'm sure."

She shook her head doubtfully. "He's a small bug in a big forest. And he must know we're after him."

"We'll find him," Velicher said, in a tone that brooked no disagreement. "We'll find him and we'll break him. He's soft." He gazed at her sidelong. "He let a pretty girl loose against the best interests of his cause."

"I wasn't very pretty when he saw me."

"He knew who you were. He could have seen pictures. You were in the news during the last gymnastic competitions. There's nothing like a hard physical workout to make a woman look her best."

"I thought he . . . pitied me."

"Oh?" Velicher chuckled. "Well, call it that if you like. Pity's a soft enough emotion. But not what a man should feel toward a woman." He stretched an arm toward her. "Come here, woman." Obediently, she approached him, and the arm encircled her hips. "Now I'm thinking that we should put all this serious discussion aside and go test the bed in your new quarters."

She looked down at the top of his gray head. "Yes," she said. "We probably should."

FOUR

She regained self-confidence in the gym, as she redis-
covered her old grace and precision. At the target range,
too, the old steady accuracy came back as the pistol stopped
feeling heavy to her arm; soon she was matching her previous records. Velicher joined her at the range occasionally.
At first he declined to take up a pistol, and Dia wondered
whether modesty or uncertainty spurred that reluctance.
Finally, on a day when she was doing particularly well,
he claimed a weapon, as if to show that the commander-
in-chief was just as good as any junior officer. Dia felt a
sudden twinge of misgiving and wondered if she should
miss a bull's-eye or two just to demonstrate inferiority . . .
and then she could almost hear Michael shouting at her
that she damned well better not be that sort of fool. She
stood aside while Velicher took his aim; the targets chimed
regularly as he placed his shots. That arm was too steady,
that eye too sharp for any self-doubt. His score was as
good as Dia's, better than most, and the other Patrollers
who stood around watching broke into applause when he
finally lowered the pistol. *They're as proud as he is,* she
told herself, reading the disdain on his face as a mask for
pleasure.

She walked beside him as he left the range. "You should
return to competition," she said. "Cover your office wall
with trophies."

He shook his head. "I haven't time for such nonsense."

He was a man possessed by time, working as if there
were never enough hours in the day and allotting time for
exercise and diversion as if they were prescribed by a doctor. For his age, he was in excellent health, with just a
slight thickening about the waist due to an overfondness
for a certain amber liqueur. A decanter of the pungent

drink reposed in the bottom left-hand drawer of his desk, and one of Dia's duties as aide was to make sure it was kept full.

She had other duties as well, though at first they seemed unimportant, just excuses to keep her close so that he could fondle her as she passed, grab a quick kiss, or even just look at her and smile. He seemed as infatuated as a new husband, and she found herself sorry, sometimes, that she did not share his feelings. At other times she viewed his behavior more cynically, as that of the proud new owner of a handsome pet or a stylish vehicle or a rare work of art. He liked to show her off, and she wore her dress uniform as often as her regular one, in addition to a new and expensive costume for each of the monthly Brigadier's Masques. He consulted on those costumes now, and they showed more of her flesh than she preferred, but she never refused to wear them. If she had to be a showthing, she reasoned, she would be a good one.

As his aide, she ordered his meals and supplies, punched information requests into the Citadel computer, and massaged his shoulders twice a day. She was also nominally in charge of protocol, arranging for inspections of garrisons, meetings with subordinates, and conferences with Councillors. For these duties she had a desk and communications console of her own tucked into a corner of the anteroom, opposite Captain Ramirez. Protocol had been his purview, among other things, before her arrival, and facing him there, she felt uncomfortable stealing part of his job—especially when she knew almost nothing about it.

"I don't mind the extra help," he said on her fourth day in the office. "The Brigadier always gives me enough work for three or four people. And I always manage to get it done. Sometimes in spite of those two youngsters next door that are supposed to be my assistants." He was looking over her shoulder at a list of Staff officers to be invited to accompany Velicher on a factory tour in a nearby industrial center. "You're a pragmatic person, aren't you, Lieutenant Catlin?"

"I hope so, Captain."

"Can I speak bluntly?"

"Yes, of course."

"I don't mean any insult; you must understand that."

"Go ahead."

His back was very straight. He was one of those people,

like her mother, who could not shed the physical formality drilled into them at the Academy. It made them look like they were always delivering some official pronouncement. He said, "I've been here a long time, Lieutenant, and I expect to be here a long time yet. I've seen the women come and go. They were all beautiful women. Some of them high-ranking, as young women go. They've gotten younger with the years, as the Brigadier has become less concerned about his image. You may repeat any of this to him, if you like; I have no secrets from him."

Dia smiled up at him. "So far I haven't heard anything treasonable."

"As I said, they have come and they have gone, but *I* am still here. And I will always be here."

That's putting me in my place, she thought. "I don't doubt it," she said. "The Brigadier speaks very highly of you."

"He speaks well of you, too, but of course that's to be expected."

"I can see that you have your own opinion."

"I have no opinion at all. You're young and inexperienced; I don't expect you to pick up the job in a few days or weeks. I do expect you to cooperate with me completely. We mustn't waste our time competing with each other. The Brigadier's business must run smoothly. That is the most important thing."

She spread her hands in a gesture of sincerity. "I'm willing to cooperate, Captain Ramirez. I just want to be useful to the Patrol."

He nodded. "Then that puts us on the same team, Lieutenant Catlin."

"I never thought otherwise."

He walked away from her slowly, gazing at his own desk, his hands clasped behind his back. "Some have, you know. Even after I had the same discussion with them that I've had with you. They thought this desk would be theirs someday." He touched it, and he was short enough that he could lay his palm flat on it without stooping. He turned to her then, smiling. "But you won't be like that, will you?" The smile was very like the Brigadier's own, the lips curved but the eyes cold. The two men made a matched set, she realized, in spite of their physical differences, and Dia felt she could well understand how this one had outlasted all the women. He was small and balding and made of steel.

"I won't be like that," she said. "After all, I'm a pilot. I'm not really interested in a long-term desk job."

"You'll do what the Brigadier says."

"Of course."

He gestured toward her with a forefinger. "You'd better start making those calls."

She bent over the viewscreen, tapped out the first code. Opposite her, he sat down at his desk and tapped, too, and she could not help wondering if he was monitoring her. She went through the list, tracking Staff members down, conveying the Brigadier's orders, arranging transportation, logging excuses, making substitutions. Then she organized the itinerary, planned meals and accommodations, and relayed the information to the proper departments. It took most of her day; she guessed it would have taken Ramirez about three hours. She apologized to him for her slowness.

He shrugged. "With practice, you'll be able to find people faster. Novick, for example, always checks in with his aide at 1200 hours. If you had called then, you would have found him easily. Salter runs in the third-level-west gymnasium every morning between nine and ten hundred. Most of the others have their own patterns."

She frowned a little. "You could have told me."

"I had other things to do."

She sighed softly. To *her* mind, he was just having a little fun with her, flaunting a bit of his superiority. She decided not to complain. She hoped he would settle down to a working relationship with her fairly soon. She wondered if any of the other women had complained about his manner. Perhaps they had, and that had only served to intensify it. He was a jealous man, obviously, jealous of his position, his power. As the Brigadier's adjutant, he could filter everything the Brigadier heard, every order he gave; he could keep people out or let them in as he chose; he could make them look good or bad. She wondered if, for all of his Academy correctness, Captain Ramirez ever chose to exercise that power for his own ends.

He opened a drawer of his desk and pulled out a sheet of paper, thrusting it toward Dia. "Take this," he said. "Compose a polite negative reply."

It was a heavy, formal-looking document, signed with multiple flourishes and embossed with the seal of one of the western provinces. She did not recognize the signature, but the word "governor" was printed below it. She weighed the paper in her hand before reading it, surprised that anyone would waste money on such an item when most correspondence, even with the Brigadier's office, was done by screen or flimsy. The contents were brief, and when she had read them, she understood that the document was one of those things that must be executed with proper ceremony—a request, on behalf of a colonial boy, for an appointment to the Academy. Good physical condition, excellent school record, top honors in the provincial student competitions, fine character, many local officials vouching for him, the governor himself recommending the appointment.

"He seems like a good prospect. What's wrong with him?"

"I don't know. Use your imagination. School record not good enough. No openings available. Anything. I'll read it when you're finished."

Dia felt puzzled as she read the document again. "I don't understand."

"No openings used to be good, but some of them try again the following year if you give them that one. I don't know; you have to use your own judgment. These things are a waste of my time."

"There *are* openings. There are always openings. None of the classes are ever filled." She shook her head. "I just don't understand."

He pursed his lips for a moment, looking up at her. "Don't be a fool, Lieutenant."

She waved the document. "You know this boy? He's some kind of congenital cripple or something? Or is it the governor—you don't trust his judgment?"

"You really don't know, do you?" He leaned forward on his elbows, interlacing his fingers. "We don't let them in."

"Who?"

"The colonials."

"We don't let them *in?*"

"Never. Not to the Academy, not to any level of the Patrol."

"Why not?"

"They're not good enough. They're not bred to it, after all."

"But . . . what if they *are* good enough?"

"They can't be."

"Surely, every once in a while, one of them is. We don't have a monopoly on excellence."

"Official policy," said Ramirez.

"But I know that colonials have served in the Patrol." She frowned. "Haven't they?" She thought back to stories she had heard while at the Academy. "Wasn't Frederick Henderson a colonial?"

"No."

"I'm sure I heard that."

"Oh, you may have heard it, but it was a lie. After he was dead for some time, the Brigadier's office gave that information out, subtly, gradually, as if it had been common knowledge all along. And not just for Henderson. But there weren't any colonials among your classmates, were there?"

She shook her head.

"Nor among your instructors."

"Not that I knew of."

"Nor among the Patrollers you've met more recently."

"I don't ask where people come from, Captain."

"Believe me. Now write that letter. It won't be the last you'll write while you have that desk. We get a few every year. The governors never say no; they just pass them on up to this office, and we take care of them. Go on. They taught you how to write a letter in school, didn't they?"

She sat down. "Somehow it doesn't seem fair," she said, "for the ones who really want to join us. The ones who want to do something more to protect their planet than work in a factory."

He regarded her with narrowed eyes. "Would you trust a colonial to stand at your back in a fight, Lieutenant?"

"Well, of course, if he was a member of the Patrol."

"I wouldn't. Once a colonial, always a colonial. There's a streak of rebel in every one of them."

"Do you really think so?"

He shook his head slowly. "I have to keep remembering that you're young. That you're younger than any of the others. You need a little more experience of the world, Lieutenant."

She labored over the letter for almost an hour, then presented it to Ramirez. He read it in a moment.

"Applied too late, all openings filled at this time." He

glanced up at her without tilting his head, so that the whites of his eyes showed beneath the irises. "I told you there was some question about the efficacy of that one. He'll be back next year. You'll have to think of something better then."

"Maybe I won't be here then," said Dia. "You'll think of something, though, if I'm not."

The corners of his mouth turned down. "Very well. Transmit it. And then throw that fancy piece of paper away—I don't have any place to put it." He looked at her letter once more before handing it back. "It's well-written, though. Concise. Straightforward. But courteous. A nice balance. Too bad it took you such a long time."

"I kept imagining myself in this boy's place."

"It was presumptuous of him even to think that he could join the Patrol."

"He must have a lot of self-confidence. This is going to shake it. It's going to tell him he isn't as good as he thought he was."

"Don't you think that's a good thing for a young person to find out?"

She looked down at her letter. "I try to think of what it would have been like for me not to be admitted to the Academy. It would have shamed my parents terribly."

"*His* parents will probably be relieved. They probably think he's crazy for even applying."

"But I wouldn't have been kept out of the Patrol entirely, even if I hadn't gotten into the Academy. I'd have started at the bottom and tried to work my way up through the noncommissioned ranks. There wouldn't have been any other choice. I couldn't have gone off to be a farmer or a factory worker. I *couldn't*."

"Of course not."

"I mean, all my life I knew I'd be a Patroller." She looked at his face. "There was never any doubt."

"Not with *your* parents."

She waved her letter. "What if he feels the same? What if he's spent his whole life preparing to be a Patroller, never doubting that it was possible, always . . . taking it for granted."

Ramirez shrugged. "Or he could be a spy."

"He's only fifteen years old."

"You think there's an age limit on spies? Let me put this to you, Lieutenant—what if the governor's letter contains nothing but false information? I'm not saying the governor himself is in league with them. No, he could just be a dupe. But what if this wonder child is really a facade? Oh, maybe he's smart enough to get by at the Academy. But his reason for applying is to worm his way into our confidence and give his rebel friends the kind of information that only a Patrol officer could give. They couldn't get it out of you, so why not try another way? Then what would we have? The enemy right here, at our backs. No, Lieutenant, that doesn't sound good to me at all. I say keep them all out, a thousand fine and loyal young people, if it will keep *one* traitor out. So transmit your letter, and don't bother feeling sorry for this child."

She went to her screen, rested her fingers lightly upon the keys but did not press any. "We should tell them what official policy is."

"Do you really think so, Lieutenant?"

"No. No, they'd hate us more than ever. Knowing we had cut them out. But it's not a good policy. We could have used those fine and loyal young people, and their families and their friends. They would have been part of us, and we of them, and the rebels wouldn't be able to point to us and say that Outsiders had stolen their world."

"They'd say it anyway. They're malcontents. There are always malcontents. They still teach Federation history at the Academy, don't they?"

She nodded.

"Maybe you should go back and reread some of that material. You'd find that no government has ever been able to please everyone." He grunted. "The rebels are just damned fools."

"Yes," she said. "That's exactly what I told them."

That night she asked Velicher if Ramirez was making daily reports on her.

"What a strange thing to ask," he said, curling the short tendrils of her hair about his fingers.

"He seems like the type who would make reports on everything. Why not on me?" She shifted the weight of her head on his shoulder. "I don't think I mind. I mean, I think I expected it, after he and I had been talking for a while. He doesn't want anyone to forget that he's doing his job."

"Was he unpleasant to you?"

"He didn't bother me, if that's what you mean."

"He's a valuable man. I don't know what I'd do without him."

"And he knows it."

"Yes."

"And he does report on me."

"Yes."

"I hope I haven't done anything terrible yet. I can't tell with him. I think he's trying to keep me off-balance."

"He thinks you're a little young."

"Well . . . I am."

"I don't think so."

She looked at him, eye to eye, so close that she could count his lashes. "Arlen, I *am* trying to do my best. But it's not like flying, all this desk work. It's going to take me a while to get used to it."

"You'll do well," he whispered. "After all, look at your father, your mother—they're desk workers."

"I must be a throwback to some earlier generation."

"I'll tell Ramirez not to overload you. He and his aides have been doing it all efficiently enough till now; they're not on vacation just because you're here."

"No, don't tell him that, please. I can handle what he gives me."

He kissed her nose. "Too proud, hmm?"

"Something like that."

"All right, then. But don't be too proud if you ever start *not* being able to handle it."

Later, before drifting off to sleep, she could not help thinking how strange it was that she should be spending her time at a desk job. All her life she had aimed at combat flying. There had never been a time when she hadn't dreamed of soaring through the sky, of striking hidden targets and screaming away while antiaircraft beams darted through the sky in search of her. Now she was so far from combat that she might as well be on another planet. Be realistic, Michael might have told her; even a combat pilot isn't in combat all the time.

She thought of the colonial boy; what, she wondered, had he dreamed of?

FIVE

She floats in the vast silence of sky. She scarcely notices the craft at first, blue against blue, a mere speck in the distance. It grows, seeming motionless against the background of nothingness. It grows, and after a time she realizes that it is heading directly toward her. Lazily, she strokes with one arm to ease from its path; the other arm is too tired even for that effort. The aircraft looms, but she has moved just enough to let it skim past her, so close that she can see the cockpit clearly, and the pilot's pale face within; he barely glances at her before sweeping on past. She tries to smile at him, a small stiff smile, as if her face were painted with plastic. She watches the tail of the retreating craft, and suddenly she wants to reach out for it, to clutch it and be swept along. She swims, and the air resists her like gelatin. The craft dwindles, dwindles, and she calls after it Wait, but in the vast blue silence no sound can be heard. Not the smallest sound, not the whisper of a human voice, not even the beat of a human heart.

She woke to silence, too, and for a moment she drifted in dark confusion, not knowing where she was or when or why. The bed was hard beneath her, though, solid to her questing hands and, beyond her own body, empty. The silence was the absence of his breathing. Then she realized she was holding her own breath.

She snapped the bedside light on. The other half of the bed was cool. He had been gone some time. She lay still another moment. It was his bedroom, not hers, and he had no reason to leave. She had never awakened before and found him gone.

A thousand thoughts skittered through her brain. That something had happened to him, that she would find him on the bathroom floor, dead, in spite of his apparent good health. That she would find him slumped just out of reach of the viewscreen keys, that he had been unwilling to wake her in his need but unable to reach other help. It was nonsense, she knew, anxiety spawned by the dream. He had probably wakened hungry and was in the kitchen having a late-night snack. Yet if that were so, she would surely hear something, the creak of a chair, the clink of cup against saucer. Instead, there was only the silence. The whisper of sheet against sheet as she threw back the covers seemed thunderous to her straining ears. Naked, she padded to the bathroom, flicked on the light. White tile reflected the soft glow from the ceiling. The room was empty. So was the rest of the apartment. So were her own quarters.

She threw on a shirt and shorts, all desire for sleep gone. She made herself a cup of cocoa. There was no note left for her, not on his pillow, not on the viewscreen or the door between their quarters—none of the logical places. That seemed to mean he wouldn't be gone long. She had a second cup of cocoa, then looked at her chronometer. 0425. She hadn't checked it before, didn't know how much time had passed since she had awakened, but it seemed like several hours. *It can't be that long.*

Where was he?

She went out through her own quarters, up the flight of stairs to his office. The anteroom door was ajar, the light on, someone at Ramirez's desk. She recognized one of the captain's aides, his elbows on the desk, his chin resting on clenched hands. He was reading a flimsy.

He looked up as she entered. "Lieutenant," he said.

"Working late, aren't you?" she remarked lightly.

He stifled a yawn with both hands. "Don't remind me."

"Where's Captain Ramirez?"

"Where he should be at this hour. Asleep."

"And you're here."

"Somebody's got to be on duty when the Brigadier's here. My turn."

She nodded toward the inner room. "He's inside?"

"He was. He said he'd be back."

"Did he say when?"

"Uh-uh. That was half an hour ago."

"Did he say where he was going?"

"No, but there's only one place he could be, isn't there?"

"Where?"

He grinned. "I thought you'd be one to know, Lieutenant Catlin."

She returned a smile, but a small one. "I'm new at this."

"Central Tower target range. He says it helps him think."

"Thanks." She turned on her heel and went out into the corridor. The range wasn't far, but she took a scooter anyway. The Citadel was quiet at that time of night, most Patrollers sleeping, though the corridors were as brightly lit as during the day. The few people she passed seemed oblivious of her, intent only on the work that kept them on this shift—communications, routine maintenance, pro forma sentry duty. There was a young sergeant at the entrance to the range, probably his first important assignment, surely the first that could bring him into contact with upper echelon officers, for this was a range reserved for them. He came to stiff attention at her approach, and he eyed her nervously, obviously trying to gauge her age as a clue to her rank. She looked too young for the range, she knew, and he would probably suggest that she go elsewhere. She forestalled him.

"If Brigadier Velicher is inside, will you ask him if he would mind Lieutenant Catlin joining him?"

He saluted stiffly and, taking the comm unit from its hook inside the doorway, repeated her message. A moment later, he nodded her in.

The target range was quiet—no shuffling feet, no muffled voices, just the steady chime of targets struck, the notes higher or lower depending on the distance of each strike from a bull's-eye. As far as she could see, Velicher was alone in his wedge-shaped segment of the range, and all the other areas of the semicircular room were empty. Dia passed the pistol rack and walked along the observation crescent till she stood behind him, and she watched for a time as he placed shot after shot on the distant moving targets. Eventually he lowered the pistol and looked over his shoulder at her.

"Would you like a turn?"

She shook her head. "I'm not at my best in the middle of the night. You obviously don't have that problem."

"Sometimes I can't sleep," he said. "Sometimes there are things left over from the day that need doing. And sometimes I don't know what to do about them. So I come down here. It helps me think. Channels my energies, you might say."

"Don't you find yourself tired the following day?"

"No." He turned toward her. "Is there something you want?"

"No. I just woke up and wondered what happened to you."

"Did I wake you when I left? I'm sorry. I thought I was being quiet."

"No. A nightmare woke me. I get them sometimes. Ever since the crash."

With his free hand he reached across the rail that separated them and touched her shoulder. "I'm sorry I wasn't there when you woke up."

She shook her head, smiling. "That wasn't a bid for sympathy. I can handle a little nightmare. I just woke up and you weren't there and I got a little worried. I thought maybe I'd kicked you out of bed in my sleep."

"No, no, nothing like that, my dear. It's just work. It doesn't leave me alone, some nights." He smiled back at her. "You're the first to come looking for me, though." He waved to encompass the room. "Ever been here before?"

"No. The company's a little too high-powered for me, during the daytime, anyway."

"You and I could show them a thing or two."

"I'm sure you do that quite adequately all by yourself."

"I never come here during the daytime. Just at night, when it's quiet, when there isn't anyone else to distract me. Target shooting isn't an end in itself to me any more. Oh, the other day I had to show them; it was childish of me. But here, alone, just me and the gun and the targets—somehow things fall into place then, when they wouldn't after half a night at my desk. Somehow things come clear here. And I feel better afterward." He shrugged lightly. "The elder god becomes more human every day, you see. He worries. He sweats like everyone else. It's not easy, this god business." He let go of her hand. "Go back to bed, Dia. People your age need their sleep."

"And what about you?"

"I'll be here for a while yet. You'd better sleep in your own quarters for the rest of the night—that way I won't disturb you when I come in."

"All right."

By the time she reached the doorway, he had resumed firing. The chime of the targets accompanied her out into the corridor.

He didn't do that often, she discovered—much to the relief of Ramirez's assistants, who hated night duty. Most nights he slept soundly, having put the work of the day aside at the bedroom threshold. But some nights a detail or two would nag at him, would not wait for daylight, and he was a man for whom details were of supreme importance. Then he would slip out of bed, trying not to wake Dia. But she was a light sleeper, alert to outside stimuli when the nightmares stayed away. She would feel the bed shift, hear the soft tread of bare feet and the snick of the door opening. But knowing where he was going and that he didn't need—or want—her there, she had no trouble going back to sleep.

He woke her when he rose in the morning, too. And he rose early, so that he could be at his office earlier than any business could arrive, earlier than anyone but Ramirez. He dressed swiftly, he grabbed coffee and toast and was gone. He never required that of Dia, though; if she had spent the night in his bedroom, she could lie under the covers, savoring the last minutes of leisure as she watched him move about impatiently. She could get up after he was gone and have an unhurried shower while waiting for her own more sumptuous breakfast to arrive. If food service was slow, she had time to browse through his library, opening volumes at random, more as a means of reading his personality than for any real interest in their contents. He was not an easily accessible man. After weeks of working, eating, and sleeping with him, Dia felt she hardly knew him. She knew some things that pleased him and some that annoyed him, but the inner person, Arlen Velicher, was still as much a mystery as the demon of the Masque. Had he ever opened up, she wondered, to any of his lovers?

One morning, while waiting for breakfast, she found a book that was locked.

It was an old volume that had somehow slipped behind a row of newer ones. Well-worn, the lettering faded on its cover, the binding cracked, it was sealed in a transparent jacket, locked with a thumb-plate that she guessed would open only to Velicher's touch.

Memoirs of Brigadier General Marcus Bohannon, Commander, 36th Tactical Strike Force, Stellar Federation Patrol.

Bohannon was a name familiar to any Amphoran. He was the first Brigadier, who led his fleet to this planet at the Federation's dissolution. An official biography was required reading in the Academy. Dia recalled that the Brigadier's own words had often been quoted in that text, and she wondered if this were the source. Curious, she ordered a copy for herself from the Citadel library.

Instead of a confirmation of her request, the screen flashed a brief message:

NO SUCH BOOK HAS BEEN PUBLISHED ON AMPHORA.

Puzzled, she punched the order again, and this time a librarian appeared to assure her rather crisply that the library did indeed house all Amphoran publications, both paper and film, as well as those brought in by interstellar traders, but that no memoirs of Brigadier Bohannon were in its collection. Dia had no chance to display the book before the librarian signed off.

She weighed the volume in her hand. It was an ordinary-looking book, clothbound, stamped in gilt. The jacket and lock were rubbed and crackled with much handling—they had been protecting the book for a long time.

From whom? The jacket she could understand, for an old book, a valuable book, perhaps inscribed to Velicher from some high official of bygone days, perhaps inscribed by Bohannon himself, though not to Velicher, who had not yet been born when Bohannon died. But the lock and the book's absence from the library meant there was some reason for hiding the contents from casual eyes. What, she wondered, could the first Brigadier have possibly said that must still be kept secret after eighty years?

She could have asked Velicher about it. But she thought she knew whom the lock was meant to keep out. A number of people had access to these rooms, some when the Brigadier was here, some when he was not. Of the latter, who would be likely to browse through the library—cleaners, painters, plumbers . . . or the various attractive women who had shared his bed through the years? The lock, she thought, was for them. For her.

She set the volume on the shelf, pushed it back where it had come from. Something was strange here—she felt it. The book was part of the heritage of the Patrol; rightly, it ought to belong to all the men and woman who wore the Patrol emblem. Why, then, was it denied to them? Could this be the only copy, reserved for the Brigadier alone?

She could have asked Ramirez, but she knew he would report it.

Frowning, she turned her back on the bookcase. Work was waiting for her at the Brigadier's office. Ramirez was already there, and under his tutelage, she spent her day arranging a working dinner for twenty-two. The Brigadier's quarters were too small for such a gathering, and Ramirez left the choice of another site entirely up to her. She requisitioned a conference room, had extra chairs and serving equipment moved in. And all the time, she could not help thinking of the book.

Late in the afternoon, she contrived to spend a few minutes in her father's office. As a full colonel, Oliver Solares was privy to many high-echelon concerns, and his favorite daughter trusted him to give her straight answers.

He smiled as she perched on the corner of his cluttered desk and leaned over to plant a kiss on the crown of his head. "Is this a social visit?" he inquired. "Or do you want something special from stores?"

She smoothed his fine gray hair, combing it gently with her fingertips. "As a matter of fact, I do want something, Poppa—a copy of the memoirs of Brigadier Bohannon."

He looked up at her in puzzlement. "I didn't know there *were* any memoirs."

"I thought you might have a personal copy."

He shook his head, causing gray elflocks to spring up under her fingers. "Why don't you try the library?"

"I did. They're not on file."

"Are you sure they exist?"

"Brigadier Velicher has a copy."

"Maybe it was just a private edition for Staff-level officers, a sort of upper-echelon morale boost; the trials and tribulations of the early days as told by the first Brigadier himself; that sort of thing."

Dia pursed her lips, and after long hesitation, she said, "Do you think Mother might have a copy?"

He shrugged. "I wasn't part of her life when she made her star." He stroked his daughter's knee. "Why don't you ask to borrow Velicher's copy?"

"I'd rather not." She frowned. "It's locked."

His eyebrows lifted. "Oho."

"What can it mean, Poppa? Any information in that book is eighty years out of date! It can't be secret any more."

"Maybe it isn't the book at all but something inside it—Velicher's own notes. Or love letters." He smiled. "Though I can't imagine Arlen Velicher *hiding* any love letters."

"I've been thinking about this all day, Poppa. I don't understand why it isn't in the library. He was our leader. Don't we have a right to know what he said about himself?"

"Maybe he was self-critical in his old age. Maybe . . . he wrote about shameful things."

"It's history, Poppa. And if Brigadier Bohannon was just human, don't we have a right to know that, too?" She leaned toward him, her hand planted palm down on the paper-littered surface in front of him. "I want to know what that lock means. I want to read it, Poppa. And if it turns out that the text is nothing at all, that the lock is really protecting something other than the book itself, then that, truly, is none of my business." She slid off the desk. "I'm going to try Mother."

As she moved toward the door, her father called after her: "If she has a copy . . . I'd like to read it, too."

Dia flashed a grin over her shoulder and stepped into the corridor.

Vanessa Catlin was a woman of considerable prestige, and almost all of it due to her membership on the Council. The Council was the legislative body of the Citadel and of Amphora; it drafted laws for the Brigadier's signature, provided him with information and advice, and was kept well-briefed on his activities. Only upper echelon officers could serve on it, elected by the Patrol at large every six years. Most Councillors served term after term, their seats becoming vacant only when they died, and competition for those few vacancies was fierce. Rank counted strongly in a candidate's favor, though, and when Vanessa achieved her star, her chances for election had improved dramatically. She was now midway through her second term of office.

Vanessa required more formality from her family than did her ex-husband, and Dia had to make an appointment to see her that evening, during the period when she would normally be working out at the gymnasium. As a member of the Council, Vanessa qualified for a suite of rooms anywhere she pleased, and she had chosen the spire of the North Tower, highest of them all. A pair of elevators led to her aerie. Dia entered the one which opened when she spoke her name.

Vanessa's apartment was lush with furred divans and

thick carpeting, with brocade draperies and ornamental hangings, with sparkling crystal and polished metal. Vanessa was a collector who traveled annually, inspecting the far corners of the world in her official capacity, and selecting luxuries in her private one. She even owned a few off-planet *objets d'art*—a sculpture in polished bronzewood, a painting of exotic landscape and multiple moons, a cluster of dried windblossoms. Other Councillors invested their salaries in seaside vacation homes or lavish gifts for their children; Vanessa preferred to see hers, touch it, admire it every day of her life.

She came forward, a small woman with blue-white hair and dark eyes, her plump figure swathed in feather-light purple silks. She halted some distance from her daughter and said, "How have you been, Dia? I haven't seen you in quite a while."

"I've been fine, Mother."

"And Arlen? You and he are getting along well?"

"Quite well, thank you."

"Come and sit down, my dear." She seated herself on a couch, putting her feet up on the cushions so that only a very little room was left at the far end; Dia chose to sit on an armchair rather than at her mother's feet. "Since you never visit me for the joy of my conversation," said Vanessa, "I presume you have some request."

"Yes, Mother. I want you to loan me a book."

"A novel request." She smiled icily at her own pun. "Has the library ceased its customary function?"

"This book isn't in the library."

"No? Then how could you expect me to have a copy of it?"

"You might."

"I'm sure I don't have any books that aren't in the library."

"The title is *Memoirs of Brigadier General Marcus Bohannon.*"

Her mother's eyes slitted for a moment. "Wherever did you hear of such a book?"

"Will you loan me your copy?"

Vanessa stared at her daughter silently, stared too long, and Dia knew that she was searching for a careful answer, not an honest one. At last she said, "The *Memoirs* exist in manuscript in sealed archives accessible only to the Bohannon family. I am not a member of that inner circle."

"Neither is Brigadier Velicher," said Dia.

"So?"

"He has a copy."

"I presume you have seen this copy."

"Yes."

"Obviously you have not been able to read it, or you would not be here asking me for mine."

"He keeps it locked."

"As he should! To keep out the inquisitive noses of junior officers." Vanessa swung her feet off the couch and stood up abruptly. "Listen to me, Dia—I speak to you as a fellow officer: the *Memoirs* are restricted information. I can tell you nothing about them and I cannot loan you a copy until you have a top-level clearance. Forget them."

"You have a copy, then?"

"I have read them."

"I'll have to wait twenty years for that kind of clearance."

"You'll just have to hold your curiosity in check until then."

Dia shook her head. "I can't imagine information that could still be restricted after almost a century."

"If every second lieutenant could imagine it, perhaps it wouldn't be worth restricting."

Dia gazed at her mother, trying to penetrate that wall which always hung between them. What she had ever done to deserve it, she didn't know. Perhaps, she thought, Vanessa just had too much pride of self for any feeling to be left over for her children. Even Sydney, who could carry on a conversation with her that could fool outsiders, often said she felt more like a dinner guest to Vanessa than a daughter. Now there was knowledge behind that wall, and no way that Dia could break through to it. More than ever, she wanted to know; every barrier she struck in her search made the goal that much more important.

She rose from her chair. "All right, Mother. If you don't want to help me, I won't press you any further. I'll find some other way."

Vanessa's voice was higher-pitched than usual, falsely pleasant in tone. "You're not going to ask Arlen to let you read his copy, are you?"

Dia shrugged. "I was thinking about it."

"Don't."

"No? Will he throw me out of bed?"

"He might."

"Well, I don't think I care. I want to know what Brigadier Bohannon said. I want to know why only highest level officers are allowed to read the opinions of a man dead for over sixty years."

"Think of your career, Dia. Why risk it over a *book?*"

"I *am* thinking of my career. And you are thinking of yours. Good night, Mother." She stepped into the elevator, but Vanessa held the doors apart with her arms.

"Don't be absurd, Dia. There's nothing in the book worth reading. The restricted classification is a formality."

Dia smiled sweetly. "Then Arlen won't have any objection to my reading it."

"You'll disgrace me, Dia!"

"Mother, you're going to force me to take the emergency stairs."

Vanessa jerked her arms away as if the doors had suddenly become red-hot. As they closed, she muttered, "Why are both of my daughters idiots?"

Dia stopped at the gymnasium, changed into the light clothing she kept in her locker there, and went through an abbreviated version of her usual workout. Her body swung through its routine automatically while her brain grappled with the problem of the book. Her father's ignorance, her mother's uneasiness, the lock and the very position of the book behind other volumes stirred her curiosity. Instinctively, she grasped some fragment of the import of the *Memoirs,* the very words of the first Brigadier, striking at the heart of the establishment of the Patrol on Amphora. What secret guilts were in those pages, what dirty desires not consonant with the lofty aims of the Patrol she knew? *We should know. We should all know.*

She decided to ask the Brigadier, when he was in a good mood. Perhaps while they were in bed tonight.

She showered, donned her uniform, and walked briskly back to her quarters. They were empty, the door joining them with Velicher's apartment shut. She knocked gently, speaking her name, and the panel slid aside.

He was seated at the table, eating a sandwich. "Have you had dinner?"

"No."

"You'd better order something right away—the kitchen is running slow."

Nodding, she punched up a light meal.

"I trust your mother is well."

He was aware of the visit, of course; she had left a note on his apartment screen. "She looks all right."

"You had a pleasant chat."

"Pleasant enough, all things considered. She doesn't change much over the years."

"And how is your father?"

She looked over her shoulder at him, wondering if he had had her followed. Or, more likely, if Ramirez had ordered it. But she saw her father frequently; there was nothing unusual about that. "He's fine."

"They weren't very helpful, were they?"

He knows. "Sir?"

He smiled. "Come here, my dear." He beckoned as a parent would call a child, and when she was close he pulled her down on his lap. "You haven't the gift of deviousness, Lieutenant Catlin. Finding you out was easy—the book pushed too far back on the shelf, with clean places on the jacket where someone with small fingers handled it. Visits to both of your parents in a single day. Especially to your mother. Did you really think I wouldn't wonder about *that?* I only had to call the library to confirm your interest in the *Memoirs.* They remember things like requests for nonexistent books."

"Yes, I'm interested," she said. His arms were easy about her, no tension in them, no anger. She smiled down at him, at his face level with her breasts and very near them. "Mother has decided that you'll dump me because of that."

"If you don't mind my saying so, your mother is a frigid bitch and probably jealous of you as well."

Dia shrugged. "I can't argue with that."

"I knew you'd find the book, eventually. If you hadn't in a few more weeks, I'd have moved it to a more conspicuous spot. I wanted to see what you'd do about it."

"You mean . . . it was some sort of a *test?*"

"You might say that."

"And did I pass or fail?"

"You could have failed by breaking the lock," he said. "You could still fail."

"How?"

"The *Memoirs* contain a great deal of personal material concerning Brigadier Bohannon—his life, his loves, his hates, his dreams. A man's dreams are his private property, and we upper-level officers are, in a sense, trespassing on his privacy by sharing them. But we think we're justified in prying because we've inherited his responsibilities to the Patrol. When and if you're ready for those responsibilities, you can share his dreams, too. Till then, it's best that you forget they exist."

I don't agree, Brigadier Velicher. We are all his heirs. But his face was very serious, so aloud she said, "I think I understand, Sir."

His arms tightened, and he pressed his face against her. "Your methods were legitimate. I can't fault you for asking your parents for help. But no one is going to break his oath as an officer by revealing restricted information, not even to his own kin."

"Of course not," said Dia. She rested a hand on the back of his neck, her fingers moving softly, to underline her words.

"And this is *not* important enough to lose a commission over." He stood up, lifting her in his arms as if she were a child. "I hope you're not *too* hungry for dinner," he said, and he carried her toward the big bed in his sleeping quarters.

She would not mention the *Memoirs* again, would not make any further attempt to determine their contents, to question other relatives or some of Michael's high-ranking friends. He would be watching for that, she knew. No, she would pass the test. He would be pleased and proud. His selection of her would be justified, and Michael's judgment would be confirmed. Dia Catlin would be a proper Patroller.

Not important enough—the words rang in her mind, but as she gazed over his shoulder, toward the shelf where the locked book lay, she knew that he lied. Something terribly important was hidden in those pages. She guessed that an alarm would ring if the lock were broken. *What a joke,* she thought, *if the pages are blank and the real copy of the Memoirs is stored where no one but Velicher can reach it.* But she looked up into his eyes and knew it was not so. For a man like him, the test would only be valid if the prize were real.

Where would I be if I'd opened it, read it?
Dead?

PART THREE
COLLABORATOR

The task we set ourselves was not an easy one. Some other world would have been better suited to our ends—a world where high-technology industries were well-established. Such worlds were numerous near the heart of the former Federation, and thus they were banned to us. Amphora was secluded, a safe haven, but its society was primarily agrarian, without great centers of industry and the great cities that grow up around them. We would have to build proper facilities, train thousands of workers, mine ores in quantity. We found our first manpower in the city beside the emblem stone. When a sufficient number of workers had left for the newly opened mines and factories, we requisitioned the city and moved all twenty crews into quarters more comfortable than aboard ship.

—from the *Memoirs of Brigadier General Marcus Bohannon, Commander, 36th Tactical Strike Force, Stellar Federation Patrol*

ONE

She was dropping free of the parallel bars when she noticed that Sydney had entered the gym. Dia strode across the springy mats toward her sister.

"I didn't want to interrupt you," said Sydney.

"I'm finished for today. What's up?"

"I was moving furniture, and I found this under a chair." From the capacious bag slung over her shoulder, Sydney drew the memorial plaque with Dia's name inscribed on it. "Did you intend to leave it there?"

Dia smiled wryly. "Not consciously." She turned it over in her hands, leaving damp, salty fingerprints on the polished surface. "I haven't given it a thought since the night of the party."

"Too busy?"

"Yes." She sank to the floor, cross-legged, setting the plaque beside her thigh. "The Brigadier keeps me running. I must have met every officer above light colonel by now, and arranged to feed most of them at least once. I never paid so much attention to food before in my life."

"How are you doing?" asked Sydney, seating herself beside Dia. "The two of you, I mean."

"Well enough. He doesn't seem to be bored yet."

"You're not having any problems, are you?"

Dia glanced up from the plaque. "You must have a reason for prying so hard, big sister."

Sydney shrugged. "Mother seemed to think things were turning sour. I don't know where she got her information."

"Mother worries too easily. Tell her everything is fine. He can't stay away from my body."

"You *are* looking good."

"It's about time." Dia stretched out on the floor. "I'll be getting back to flying this week."

"Oh?"

"The doctor says I'm normal. There isn't any reason to stay away from it. I can use the change, I'll tell you. Desk work is beginning to get to me."

Sydney frowned. "I'm surprised the Brigadier would allow you to be exposed to that kind of danger. That is . . . if things are really all right."

"I won't be flying any missions, just soloing in a trainer to keep up my hours. He certainly doesn't want to expose me to any danger—I've become indispensable. Or so he says." She glanced sidelong at her sister. "I imagine they all became indispensable, for a while."

Sydney looked down at her hands. "You're not . . . happy, are you? You're not even pleased."

"Does that matter?"

"I thought . . . you'd adjust to it after a while."

"I think I've adjusted."

"I know you better than that, little sister." She raised her eyes slowly. "I know the way you talk. I know your tone of voice."

"I'm an open book to you," said Dia.

"Open enough. And don't you think *he* knows how you feel? He didn't get where he is without knowing how to read people."

"I don't think he cares how I feel about him, as long as I put on a good show. Appearances matter to him. He displays me like a trophy. It doesn't matter if I'm really brass as long as I *look* like gold. The flying fits in there, you see —I'm supposed to be this fantastic pilot, so how would it look if I lost my flight rating?"

Softly, her sister said, "And you'll need your flight rating . . . afterward."

Dia nodded. "I've thought about that." She rolled to her side and leaned on one elbow. "I expect I'll get another promotion . . . as you say, *afterward*."

"They usually do."

"Enough of this premature postmortem on my love life." In a single smooth motion, Dia bounced to her feet. "How about some handball?"

Sydney made no effort to rise. "I'm rusty, little sister. We reserve officers should be allowed to rest on our laurels." She stretched out both legs and leaned back on her arms. "I've had my exercise for today—a leisurely morning of cleaning my apartment."

"Nonsense. That's terrible exercise. You need to sweat a little. What will your husband say if he comes home to a flabby wife?"

"He's come home to her numerous times, and being a trifle flabby himself, he keeps his mouth wisely shut."

"I'll go easy on you."

Sydney shook her head. "You'd better wait for Paul—he's more your sort of competition."

"But I'm not going to see Paul for months."

"I'd say two weeks was a closer estimate."

Dia grabbed her sister's arm, hauled her to her feet, and shook her. "Are you joking? No, you're not. Paul's really coming home! When did you hear?"

"Mother told me. She swung it for her birthday."

"Her birthday?" Dia's elation faded. "Don't tell me she wants to be surrounded by her children on her birthday?"

"That seems to be it."

"I can't even remember the date."

"Don't worry, you'll get an invitation."

"How large a crowd does she plan to have?"

"Intimate, she said. That can't mean more than thirty or so."

"I suppose I'll have to go." She expelled a short, tight breath. "I wouldn't want Mother's *prestige* to suffer because the Brigadier's lover didn't show up at her own mother's birthday celebration." She turned away angrily. "What am I, a two-headed baby, to be paraded around like this? Damn her!"

Sydney touched her shoulder gently. "Don't be so hard on her, Dia. After all, she's bringing Paul home for it."

"Easy enough for a Councillor to do!"

"She couldn't do it for your welcome-home party."

"Couldn't? Or wouldn't?" She took her sister's hand, squeezed it tight. "Syd, you know she wouldn't go out of her way to do anything for *me*."

Sydney sighed. "Well, you were Poppa's favorite, and I guess when she stopped liking him . . . look, you don't make it easy for her to be friendly to you! You always took Poppa's side in every argument!"

"Poppa was always right."

Sydney shook her head. "You should have had *his* last name instead of hers. You and Paul have always been strictly *his* children."

"And what about you? You're certainly not strictly hers."

"I'd pity any child who was." Then she smiled. "I'm the go-between, forever caught in the middle. Not usually a very comfortable spot. You're not going to make it worse for me, are you?"

Dia flapped her hands in a gesture of resignation. "All right, I suppose I'll have to take the good with the bad. If Paul can survive it, I can, too, and smile all the while."

Sydney linked her arm with her sister's. "Now how about a mid-afternoon snack?"

"You're going to substitute food for exercise? What kind of trade-off is that?"

"I didn't come here for exercise. And you wouldn't be hurt by a few more calories. Come on."

"Only if you don't eat. I don't want to be responsible for adding to your flab."

"I'll have a glass of water. Or something. But let's get out of this gym and sit down in some decent chairs."

As they walked toward the door, Dia could not help thinking, *Good old Vanessa.* The only way she could ever get what she wanted from her children was by buying it. *How will it feel, dear brother, to be the purchase price of a two-headed baby?*

TWO

She set the plaque on the wall above her bed. Memories flooded her as she stared at her image in the mirror-bright surface. She could almost imagine herself deep underground, with the cavern chill closing around her body, and she shivered. Once more she could see Michael's bloody skull, the familiar horror that became real in her dreams. Consciously, she blotted that image out with remembrance buried in an unmarked grave with Michael. Some of her of her own battered, bandaged face. *I am all right,* she told herself, searching the bronze reflection for scars—there were none, as Talley promised. But she did not feel all right. She did not feel the same woman who took the co-pilot's seat that sunny, cloudless morning. Some of her was was lost in caverns filled with darkness. What had come home to the Citadel? A creature of shadow, filled with aching emptiness. *Well,* she thought, *it's not his fault. He was a good doctor. He did his best.* She wondered where he was this moment, what labyrinths he traversed. He was the target of the most intensive search ever mounted by the Patrol on Amphora. She wondered if he would ever be found. Staring at her own scarless face, she hoped not. Even though she had done her best to aid that search, she hoped not. She owed him that hope, at least.

Velicher's voice behind her: "Isn't that a trifle macabre?" He stood in the doorway. "Putting that plaque up there like a tombstone . . . surely you don't think of your bed as a grave?"

She stepped off the mattress. "I don't want to forget that Dia Catlin died in that crash." She touched her chest with one hand and said, "This is an entirely different person."

He took her in his arms. "This person pleases me greatly."

124

Lying beside him in the darkness, dozing, she could not prevent her thoughts from straying back to that other life, to the security and sense of well-being that had always come to her in Michael's embrace. Velicher satisfied her body, but inside she was still hungry. They participated in an activity together, but it meant nothing to her. She knew that if they were separated she would never miss him. To her, their relationship was just one more tour of duty.

She could almost hear Michael saying it: *You entered this relationship knowing that you would never have picked him yourself.*

Who would I have picked? She couldn't think of any Patroller she cared to live with, though there were some who had been receptive to the notion in the past. Now, of course, everyone treated the Brigadier's lover with exaggerated courtesy, with cool and polite distance. She wondered what it would be like . . . afterward. Were his former lovers much in demand, perhaps as status symbols, or did they remain unapproachable, alone? She would have to ask Sydney about that—Sydney, who seemed to know a great deal about the subject.

Being alone had its appeal—sometimes Dia yearned for it, yearned for the empty bed to match her empty heart, for the lonely nights when she could be solitary with her memories. *Unhealthy desires,* she warned herself. Memories impinged upon her too often already. Only in the gymnasium was her mind ever at peace, as she reveled in the purely physical act of exercise, reveled in youth and vigor for their own sake.

She stirred restlessly, and in his sleep, Velicher threw an arm over her breasts. *Is my career really this important?* She rolled over, letting his hand slide to her back. *Do I really care about my career, without Michael?*

She could almost hear him saying, *You must care. There is nothing else for a Patroller except a career.* He had despised Sydney when she retired to the reserve. *Not your family,* he had said, when Dia protested that someone had to teach the young. *Your family is made for greater things. You are made for greater things. You must care.*

He groomed me, she thought, *and look what it got him.*

She slept at last, and she woke to Velicher's kiss on her ear.

"Good morning." He was fully dressed. "I've ordered eggs for your breakfast. Over easy, with toast."

She blinked away sleep and stretched without rising. "Thank you."

"And I thought I would give this to you now." He drew a small blue velvet bundle from his breast pocket and unrolled it to reveal a silver pendant—the head of a horned demon, its unhuman features delineated in burnished metal and black oxide; between its curving horns, like the disc of a sun god, lay a glinting black opal. "Now you know what I based my Masque costume on."

She took it from his hand, and the silver chain slipped through her fingers to swing against her upraised arm. "Yes," she said, tilting it to watch the multicolored play of light within the stone. "What a beautiful piece." She turned it over, and on the plain, flat back she saw a stylized letter *M*. "What's this?"

"The maker's mark," said Velicher. "It's one of a kind."

She closed her fingers on it. "I like it very much."

"So do I. I want to see you wear it. Often."

When he had gone, she draped it over one corner of the plaque. "With this the demon made his final payment on my soul," she murmured.

She had numerous opportunities to wear the pendant in the ensuing weeks—a formal dinner given by a newly promoted general, a Staff gathering over cocktails, a live concert where the Brigadier's stall was prominent in the audience, and, of course, her mother's birthday celebration. Velicher, who had received an invitation jointly with Dia, agreed to escort her but declined to stay past the first hour; he greeted Vanessa Catlin affably enough, wished her well, and took his leave. Privately, he told Dia, "We're not close, your mother the Councillor and I." Publically, he protested that the crush of work prevented him from remaining. He left Dia to mingle on her own with family and her mother's friends.

Other Councillors were there, committee heads, the most senior members, even the Chairman himself. Everyone seemed to be on first-name terms with everyone else, and everyone wanted to speak a word or two to the Brigadier's new love; she found herself bombarded by conversation on all sides. She smiled dutifully. She was not required to say much, merely to exist.

Gradually, she worked her way across the room. She had not found Paul yet, had not seen the top of his dark head among the sea of celebrants. Through an occasional rift in the crowd, she discerned a youngish group chatting on a low divan in one corner—she headed in that direction, hoping he might be among them. He was not, but the door to the bedroom was ajar, and the buzz of voices flowing from it indicated another cluster within; he was sitting on the scarlet-draped bed, listening to four elderly Councillors rehash the day's dull official proceedings. When he saw her slip into the room, he reached out and pulled her onto his lap for a hug and a kiss. The Councillors did not seem to notice. Paul swung her around so that her back was to them.

"I remember the days when neither of us would have been invited to a party like this," he said, grinning. "*I* didn't do anything, so it must be all your fault."

"Must be," she replied, clasping her hands behind his head and leaning back to look at his face. When he smiled, she saw their father's features in his, the same gray eyes crinkling at the corners, the same faint dimples showing in the cheeks. He looked very handsome in his fine-fitting dress uniform. She could easily understand why her mother didn't mind showing him off, especially with the bright first lieutenant's insignia on his broad shoulders. They were both young, Paul and Dia, for their ranks.

"The gossip has run rampant, you know. Up at the garrison, the guys have begun to salute me every time I walk into the rec room."

She smiled. "It'll die down soon, I'm sure. People will get tired of it. How are things in the wild north country?"

"We had a touch of excitement a few weeks back. Rebels blew up one of the assembly lines at the big factory in Northriver. About forty of us went in to track them, but they might as well have vanished into thin air. We couldn't find a trace."

"Maybe the assembly line workers did it themselves."

He shrugged. "Maybe. You never know who might be a rebel. But there wasn't any evidence against any of them, or at least nobody would talk, and we couldn't very well arrest the whole bunch—they had to rebuild the line."

"Any casualties?"

"No, it happened while the line was down, nobody there. That *does* make it sound like the workers were involved, doesn't it? They wouldn't want to take any chances on killing themselves."

"I think the rebels, whether they're workers at the factory or not, are more interested in killing Patrollers than their fellow colonials."

"So I've always thought. But they sure didn't try to get us when we went looking for them. I never felt like such a failure before in my life. Not a single clue. You'd think *someone* would know *something*, someone would turn *somebody* in, for a personal grudge if nothing else. We didn't even get any false leads. I don't know. The first action we've seen in months, and nobody fires a shot. And it was nothing, really, just a petty annoyance. One factory." He laughed drily. "If that's the best they can do, I don't know why the Brigadier is worried. Things were a lot livelier back when I was first commissioned. Except for this little business, my garrison has been so quiet we might as well be on vacation. We spend most of our time playing pool. I've become very good at it. Nobody offers any trophies for it yet, but I've picked up a lot of money on side bets."

"Yet another sport?" She shook her head, then kissed his eyebrow. "How can I possibly keep up with you?"

"You have too much competition in your soul, little sister."

"I come by it naturally, big brother."

He squinted at the bedroom door, where the crush of bodies in the living room was only too visible. "There isn't any other way out of this place, is there?" Since childhood, and his parents' separation, he had seen even less of his mother than Dia had, and he had rarely visited her plush Councillor's apartment.

"Not unless you can climb down the outside wall."

He dumped her off his lap and went to the window, opened it, and leaned out.

"No stairs," Dia said, moving to his side.

He glanced toward the bed. "I have an idea." Leaning over the bedside viewscreen, he punched a familiar number; his father's face was resolved on the monitor. They had a brief exchange which Dia could not make out because the elderly Councillors' conversation had grown loud and heated. Paul switched the screen off and turned back to her. "Watch this," he said, and he raised the window as far as it would go and straddled the sill.

Dia caught his arm. "I know you're probably a bit intoxicated," she said, "but don't you think you'd be happier away from that window? I know *I* would be if you were."

He laughed. "I'm not intoxicated at all. Poppa's going to pick us up. You don't really want to stay here, do you?"

About five minutes later, a small aircar drifted up to hover a few centimeters from the window. Inside, illuminated by the faint green telltales of the dash, sat Oliver Solares. He waved at his children and raised the transparent hatch.

Paul, one foot already on the rim of the car, reached for Dia's hand. "Don't tell me you're afraid of heights?" he said.

She smiled, squeezing his fingers and then letting go. "Just waiting for you to get your carcass out of my way." She watched him step into the vehicle, and then she gathered her long skirt in one hand, lifted it above her knees, and followed him.

"Hello, my dears," said their father. In the green light they saw him smile, and then the car swooped downward to snug into its cradle in the pleasure craft hangar a dozen stories below. "A novel way to leave a party," he remarked as they climbed out.

"I don't think anyone even noticed," said Paul. He linked arms with his father on one side and his sister on the other. "How have you been, Poppa? I wanted to call you earlier, but Mother kept me busy."

Oliver Solares shrugged. "What did you expect? She didn't bring you here to see *me*." He gripped his son's arm with both hands. "I'm glad to see you, Paul. I've been well, and so has your sister over there. In fact, she's been better than I have, and pretty soon she'll outrank me, too."

"Poppa!"

"Well, you do have a certain advantage, my dear—there's never been a female Brigadier to lust after my body. Or a male one, for that matter." They had arrived at his rooms by this time, and he slid the door open and gestured them in. The soft lights revealed well-cushioned chairs, a thick rug, and a low table bearing an aluminized chill-bottle of wine and four glasses. Oliver poured three of them full. "I thought you might bring Sydney along," he said, indicating the fourth.

"I told her we were coming here after Mother's party was over," said Paul. "But I'm sure she couldn't guess it would be over so soon. For us, anyway." He lifted his glass. "To you, Poppa—who made us human in spite of Mother. We love you."

Dia met his toast.

"Modesty forbids my agreeing with you," said Oliver. "I trust your mother was her usual self on her fifty-third birthday."

Dia shrugged, put her feet up on the table. "She doesn't change."

"All top brass, I suppose."

"What else?"

"She used to have other friends. I still have them. Well, that's your mother—always a climber. We broke up because she realized I'd never make a star. Not enough ambition." He nodded toward Dia. "There's some of your mother in you, like it or not."

"Me? Not much, I hope."

Oliver leaned far forward, lifted the pendant away from her throat. "He gave this to you, didn't he?"

"Yes."

"Beautiful. Expensive. Of course, he can afford anything he wants." It slipped from his fingers. "Don't tell me you love him, daughter—I won't believe that."

"I wouldn't lie to you, Poppa. I don't love him. I never did."

He eased back in his chair. "Well, you didn't ask my advice, and I'm glad of that. I don't know what I would have said."

"Being the Brigadier's lover is good for her career," said Paul.

Oliver nodded slowly. "That's certainly true. That's exactly what your mother would say."

"Well, Mother isn't wrong about everything."

"No, and Dia will make her star, too, if she keeps on this way."

"It's obvious," said Paul, "that you don't approve."

His father swirled the wine in his glass, gazing meditatively into the pale pink fluid. "I think my daughter would be . . . more content . . . on a regular tour of duty. I know she'd rather fly an aircraft than a desk."

"Poppa, there's no point in discussing this," said Dia. "I made a decision, and I'm standing by it."

He reached for her hand. "I've watched you these past months. I know you, Dia, better than Paul does, better than Sydney. And I can tell you're not happy."

"I haven't been happy since Michael died." Paul took her free hand, and as if a circuit had been completed, she felt a flow of warmth from her father and her brother. She smiled at each of them. "But this moment, with both of you here beside me—it's the best moment in a long, long time." She shook her head. "Enough, Poppa, enough. Can't we talk about Paul's career instead of mine? After all, he's the visitor. My life is old news."

Without releasing her hand, Paul said, "Poppa already knows about the only break in the monotony up north. I wish I had something more exciting to add to the story."

"There's nothing wrong with a lack of excitement," said Oliver.

"Well, it does mean fewer commendations and slower promotion. I don't care much for *that* situation."

"It also means no one is getting killed. There's something to be said for that, too."

Paul leaned to one side in his chair, one elbow cocked on its low back. "I think we ought to be more aggressive in how we handle the rebellion. Even if it does require some killing. The rebels seem weaker now than they've been in decades. We could really trounce them and end it once and for all."

"You think so?" said his father.

"It's gone on far too long. I don't think there'll be a better time than now to strike and strike hard."

"That's been thought before and it's been done before, and they always come back."

"Then it's never been done properly."

Oliver finished his wine and poured himself a second glass. "I don't know," he said. "Guerrilla warfare is very difficult to deal with. There aren't any decisive battles, just endless skirmishing. The guerrillas always have the advantage of the terrain. And of knowing who to shoot at."

"I've read history, too, Poppa."

"If I were at the top . . . I'd have given up long ago."

"Given up?" said Dia. "And done what? Left Amphora? For where?"

He shook his head. "I'm sure it's just as well that I'm not at the top. I haven't the faintest idea how I would resolve the situation."

"It would be a lot easier if the colonials would help us clean up the rebels," said Paul. "They give their tacit approval to the rebellion by sitting back while we do all the work."

Oliver drained his glass and set it on the table. "Well,

they figure we're the police, it's our job to take care of civil disorder. And some of them certainly are in sympathy with the rebels."

"I wonder how many."

His father shrugged. "I suspect we'll never know. Even if we do somehow stamp out the rebellion, a lot of those sympathizers are bound to deny ever being involved. And we'll probably have no proof to convict them, so we'll have to leave them alone. And maybe they'll turn into the core of a new rebellion, somewhere down the line."

Paul shook his head. "That's too pessimistic for me."

"After so many years of conflict, I don't think pessimism is unjustified."

"I hope you're wrong, Poppa, because we *are* going to move on the rebels soon."

"What makes you think that?"

"Our garrison commander's brother is a light colonel; the commander likes me, and I keep my ears open. Something big seems to be coming up."

Dia said, "Should you be telling us this?"

He smiled at her. "I don't see why I can't tell *you*. Haven't you heard something about it already?"

"No. Not that I know of. But maybe I wouldn't recognize it. I don't really know the difference between ordinary business and special matters yet, in the office." She smiled back at him. "And even if I did, I wouldn't be discussing it with my brother, whose ears are open."

"Touché," he said, and he stood up, stretching as if he had been sitting in a cramped position for hours. "All right, enough of this serious stuff. Why don't we run down to the nearest rec room, liberate a pool table, and I'll teach you two the fundamentals?"

"Sounds great," said Dia.

Oliver reached for the control console behind his chair. "Upon receiving your last letter, in which you detailed at tiresome length the extent of your interest in this new pastime, I had a table installed here." He touched a stud, and a panel of the far wall slid aside to reveal an upended pool table. "Such are the perquisites of a chief of Materiel. Help me move the furniture, please."

Oliver had obviously had some practice in the game, and between two sets of conflicting advice, Dia managed a creditable performance. Halfway through the second round, Sydney arrived and was promptly handed a cue. Fumble-fingered, she was soon left behind and retired from play, content to offer snide remarks from the sidelines.

After the third game, she said, "Mother wasn't too happy that you left without saying goodbye."

Paul racked the balls casually. "We couldn't get near her." Over his shoulder, he grinned conspiratorially at Dia. "I didn't want to break any ribs elbowing my way through the mob."

"One of the guests said he saw you climb out the window. Of course, he was pretty far gone by that time—he couldn't be sure if you had come back in or not."

"I sprouted wings," Paul replied. "But they're very filmy, and tuck neatly into my pants. I suppose, to forestall a lecture on protocol, I'll have to send flowers in the morning."

"I already arranged for a gift in your name."

He bent over the table, cue in hand. "I swear, Sydney, if you weren't around to smooth her feathers, Mother wouldn't be speaking to either Dia or me. Which is not such a terrible notion." He broke the clustered balls and proceeded to mop up the table.

"You might need her someday, brother. Best to keep on good terms. Though sometimes you make it damned difficult."

"I'll make my star without her," he said.

Sydney shrugged. "Poppa couldn't."

Oliver Solares laid a hand on his eldest daughter's shoulder. "I didn't want it," he said.

She looked up at him. "You say that now, Poppa, but I remember how you talked when you were passed over."

"I was wrong then. I'm better off where I am. I'm not decisive enough to be on the Staff, I'm not political enough to be on the Council, and I'm not adventurous enough to be in the field. I wouldn't be happy as a top-level officer."

"I would," said Paul.

"That's what you think now." He turned to Dia. "What about you, my dear? Will you be happy with a star?"

She smiled. "Isn't it a little early to ask me that?"

"No," said her father. "I don't think so. I think that now is exactly the right time."

"You'll make it," said Paul. He planted the cue on the floor and leaned against it. "I've watched you, little sister, all through school, all through the Academy. And with Mike. He knew, just like I did. You've got it, whatever it is

—the call to glory. I don't know if it means happiness. Maybe just . . . satisfaction. But my prediction is that you'll outrank us all someday. You'll make this family famous."

"Well, thanks for the vote of confidence."

"I'm serious, Dia. I think you've got a good chance of becoming the first woman Brigadier."

Dia felt a chill climb up her spine. "I don't know why you should say that, and I don't think I want to be the first woman Brigadier. That's more Mother's speed."

"Mother! She'll never get any farther than she is now."

"It would be more than enough for me, Paul. Much more. I'm not even sure I won't retire next year."

"Re*tire?*" The cue stick clattered against the table as Paul swung around to face her. "What are you talking about?"

Dia shrugged. "I haven't felt . . . useful lately. Captain Ramirez can do everything I do, faster and better."

Paul said, "Surely not everything."

Sydney shot him a sharp look and moved to her sister's side. "One retirement in this venerable family is enough, don't you think?"

"You can't be serious, Dia," said Paul. "You can't throw away everything to take a teaching job. Apologies to Syd, but it just won't look right. Especially at your age."

"I wasn't thinking of teaching." She looked down at the table, unable to meet the eyes that were focused on her. "I didn't mean retiring to the reserve. I meant resigning my commission. Leaving the Patrol."

"No," said Paul. "You can't do that."

"I've been giving it serious thought."

"It would disgrace us all!"

Softly, she said, "I suppose it would."

"And Mike—what the hell do you think he'd say?"

She nodded. "I know what he'd say. I know."

"You're young, my dear," said her father, "and every day seems endless. But time will pass, and so will grief. Believe me. Things will brighten, I promise you; just give them time. Your relationship with the Brigadier won't last forever, not if he runs true to form. Afterward, you can probably get any assignment you want." He collected the cue sticks and stacked them under the table. "If you want action, there are plenty of garrisons more active than Paul's. Or I could find you something in Materiel—plenty of flying there." He punched a button and the table retracted into its recess. "But if you leave the Patrol . . . what would you do? Work in a factory? Run farm equipment? Or are you just thinking of being a hermit?"

She shook her head. "I don't know what I want to do. I don't seem to be very good at making decisions either, Poppa. I'm obviously not Brigadier material."

Paul picked up his glass, freshened its contents and took a deep drink. "You *used* to know what you wanted," he said.

"That was a long time ago."

He sighed. "All right; I shouldn't try to give you advice. You've got to do what feels best to you." He drank again, draining the glass. "I only hope that whatever you choose is right in the long run. But it'll be rough, little sister, outside the Patrol. I can't imagine it myself."

"I don't know if I can either." She lifted her eyes at last to look into his, and she saw sadness there, and concern. "I'm not rushing into anything, Paul."

"I hope not. It's not like you." He tried to smile, but the result was meager. "I want the best for you, little sister, I can't help it. But whatever you do—I'm on your side. We all are. You know that."

"I know," she said, reaching for his hand and pulling him close for a hug. "I know, and I love you, all of you." They crowded together then, all touching her, in silent communion.

"I feel like it's *my* birthday, with all of you here," Oliver Solares said at last, and he smiled at his children. "But now the hour is late, and your father has a full schedule tomorrow."

They kissed him in turn, then kissed each other and promised to gather at Sydney's apartment the following night, to make the most of Paul's brief leave. Dia was the last to depart, held back by her father's light touch on her arm.

"I didn't want to ask you in front of the others . . . what ever happened about that book?"

Dia shook her head. "There's no such book, Poppa. It doesn't exist. Unless you have a star."

"Then I'll never read it."

"Maybe I won't either."

"Remember what I said, Dia. Don't do anything hasty. Don't do anything you'll regret."

She looked down at the pendant lying against her pale

skin, and she touched it with the tips of her fingers, as if testing its reality. "It's too late for that advice, Poppa. Far too late." She kissed him once again. "Good night. Try not to worry about me. I'll work it all out."

He held her close for a moment. "Take it easy, daughter. I love you."

She found the Brigadier in her bed, but he was asleep and she managed to slip in without rousing him. She lay listening to his quiet breathing, feeling his body heat across the centimeters that separated them. If he were Michael, she would have wakened him. But he was Arlen Velicher, and she lay still and pondered the chain of events that had brought them together in this room. Once more, her mind turned to the crash and the cave and Strux and Dr. Talley Magramor.

Does he ever think of me?

THREE

The trainer was a two-person craft, but Dia took it into the sky above the Citadel alone. From the air, Patrol headquarters was a prickly nest of multicolored spires set in the midst of garden greenery. Beyond the shrubs and flower beds, carefully planted in a complex maze pattern by the second Brigadier, lay grain and bean fields serviced by a few farmers and much automated machinery. The nearest colonial town was forty kilometers distant, a hamlet on the surface route to Anderson University City, where non-Patrol children from all over the province attended advanced classes. Offspring of Patrollers, of course, attended the Citadel schools. Dia knew now that the two groups never mixed at any educational level. She had been taught to look down on the colonial universities, no matter how excellent their reputations; she had never known anyone who had seriously contemplated attending one—there was too much family pressure, peer pressure, Patrol pressure to stay in the Citadel. Now she was sure that such attendance wouldn't be allowed. Separate, colonials and Patrollers— forever separate. She wondered how much that encouraged their mutual distrust.

Dia circled the hamlet. She had enough stored power to fly twice as far as Anderson, but the Brigadier's orders kept her within a more circumscribed area. And other officers were waiting to use the same craft to keep up their own hours in the air. After ninety minutes, Dia reluctantly turned toward her home base.

She loved flying, had loved it since her first day aloft. She had even been on the senior aerobatics team at the Academy. Now the other team members all had regular flying assignments and were logging hundreds of hours in the air, much of it over dangerous territory, while she had

to be content with a scant few sessions of uneventful flying
in the safest airspace on the planet. She was restless for
something a little more interesting.

I wonder if I could skim past Mother's window?

The trainer was a giant compared to the aircar with
which her father had rescued her and Paul from the party.
That had been a tricky stunt, but rounding the tower at
close range in a larger craft would be far more difficult.
She pulled the trainer into a tight curve and headed for
her mother's sanctum.

If there was anyone in the apartment, no one rushed to
the window as the gale shrieked by. The edge of one back-
swept stabilizer seemed almost to brush the smooth wall.
And then she was soaring away, her paraboloid turn complete; she leveled, then circled, losing speed and altitude
until she could slip quietly into the hangar on the south
wall of the Citadel.

By the time she reached Velicher's office to take up the
official duties of the day, he had received word of her
escapade. He called her into the inner room and had her
close the door. He was at his desk, both arms laid flat on
the smooth surface. "I understand that you buzzed the
North Tower a little while ago."

"Just a bit of close maneuvering," Dia replied. She
smiled slightly, trying to appear casual about the accom-
plishment when she was really feeling more pleased with
herself than in a long time. The old skill was still there.
She was still someone special, not just the Brigadier's lover
who spent her days in make-work.

"You just . . . happened to choose the tower that your
mother lives in, I suppose."

Dia shrugged. "I figured if I was going to bother anyone,
it might as well be her."

She stood facing him, with the desk between them. She
was not prepared for him to reach out suddenly, grab her
arm and drag her down across that broad surface till they
were nose to nose. His fingers tightened till she had to bite
back a cry of pain.

"I don't want any of that fool-ass stuff near the Citadel,
Lieutenant Catlin," he said in a low, hard voice. "If you
must play games, take them to the colonial towns—not my
towers!" He relaxed his grip abruptly, almost thrusting her
away, and she scrambled to her feet and stood, shamefaced
and rigid before his anger.

He turned his back to her, appeared to contemplate the marksmanship trophy on the wall behind the desk for long minutes. At last he said, "But it *was* a neat bit of maneuvering. You impressed the hell out of the hangar crew." Slowly, he pulled his chair around. "Sometimes I forget . . . that you're so young." Frowning, he opened the bottom drawer of his desk and poured himself a snifter of amber liqueur. "You'll think twice before you're tempted to do something like this again, won't you? I'd hate to suspend your flying privileges."

"I won't do it again, Sir," she said very quietly.

He offered her a glass, and when she shook her head, he drained his own. "I'll chalk it up to the strain of the other night's party. After all, I don't much care for your mother, either." He dumped the empty glass in the drawer. "Did I hurt you?"

She could still feel the pressure of his fingers, but pride kept her from admitting it. "No, Sir. And if you had, I would have deserved it."

"Very well, Lieutenant; the subject is now closed. Punch up Colonel Roppolo; I want a Staff meeting this afternoon at 1400, and a full report on the status of the search for Magramor."

Dia went to her viewscreen, and though she felt Ramirez's eyes upon her, she refused to look up at him. Ramirez knew, of course; he knew everything the Brigadier said and did. But she didn't want to give him the satisfaction of seeing her embarrassed by a reprimand. She tracked Roppolo down in a sauna—he had taken an early lunch hour and was obviously dismayed at having to cut it short and rush around gathering information. By the time Dia finished her job, her hands were shaking. She no longer felt cocky about shearing so neatly past her mother's window, but was beginning to visualize the consequences of failure. She was a good pilot, but what if she hadn't been good enough? What if that side fin had touched the tower instead of barely missing? At that speed the damage would have been incredible—the tower demolished, masonry raining down on the Citadel, bodies plummeting a dozen stories to the ground . . . and her craft and herself mixed together in jagged fragments, falling and falling and falling. She had seen the stunt as a test of her own skill, as a sort of competition with her father, as a taunt to her mother, as an assertion of her individuality, but now she could not help wondering if the whole incident had not really been spurred by some sick, submerged desire to join Michael in oblivion. Her stomach churned. *Not that kind of retirement!*

She jumped up, trying to shake off the mood of horror with physical activity. In the inner office she slid the couches aside and opened the storage well in the floor to draw up the panel that extended Velicher's desk into a long table. She unfolded eight chairs and set them at comfortable distances apart. She ordered a list of refreshments to be delivered at 1400, and then she stood at the far end of the table and waited for the Brigadier to tell her what to do next.

He was leafing through some printouts. "Get me a light lunch," he said without looking up. "And yourself, too."

She hardly ate, but he didn't notice.

Several of the Staff arrived early. Roppolo, however, rushed in apologetically well after the appointed hour.

"Good news," he said. "Magramor was captured four days ago in Eugenia Province. He's being held at the provincial garrison pending instructions."

Velicher straightened abruptly, his hands flat on the top of his desk. "Four days ago?" His voice was low but edged. "Why has it taken four days to bring this news to my attention?"

Roppolo grinned nervously. "My department has been badly overworked. I asked for more personnel last spring, but I was assigned a very low priority."

Velicher cut him short with a gesture. "I don't want to hear alibis, Colonel. We've lost too much time already—have him flown here immediately."

"Here, Sir? He can be questioned where he is, if you don't want to waste time."

"Here, Colonel. His friends might be able to rescue him from Eugenia garrison, but they're not going to get him out of the Citadel."

"Yes, Sir." Having scarcely had a chance to sit down, Roppolo hurried away.

Dia sat through the rest of the meeting without paying any attention to the topics discussed. Her mind was racing. *Talley captured.* She wanted to know everything about it. Where was he captured, how, with whom—Strux, or the secretive Unknown, or some other rebels. Or was he found alone? Had he been injured in a fight or taken peacefully?

Who had betrayed him—a friend, a relative, an anonymous passerby? Eugenia Province—he had traveled far from their last meeting place, from the hilly north country to the flat farmlands of the east; how many narrow escapes had he suffered along the way, and where had he been going when they took him? She wanted to run after Roppolo, to cross-examine him, squeeze every gram of information from his little body; but she suspected he knew no more than he had just related. There would be an official report, and she would manage a look at it. She calculated the length of the air trip from Eugenia: perhaps three hours if they used the fastest craft.

Talley captured. Now the Patrol had dug its talons into his flesh, and it would twist them 'till all his secrets were revealed. Dia shuddered at the mental image of the Patrol as some vast bird of prey. *My own talons,* she told herself. *I am a fledgling of this nest.*

FOUR

She was in the Brigadier's apartment that evening, trying to disguise her restlessness by reading one of his books on the military history of the Federation. He was relaxing with a liqueur and recorded music when the viewscreen signaled an incoming call: Roppolo announcing that Magramor was in the Citadel.

"Have you talked to him?" asked Velicher.

"I asked what his role in the rebel movement was. He insists that he's just a doctor."

"Well, I'm sure your people will work on him with their usual efficiency. Let me know when you get some results—and use your own judgment about waking me."

"Yes, Sir." The screen darkened, and music swelled to fill the room once more.

Velicher glanced at Dia. "I suppose you'd be interested in the details of the capture. . . ?"

The book lay unheeded, the pages slowly fluttering shut, in her lap. "Yes. Yes, I would." She tried to sound cool, detached. Velicher was already leaning over the viewscreen. "To be honest, Arlen, I thought we wouldn't find him."

"You underestimated Roppolo's desire for promotion, my dear." He punched his private code; the machine began to print the report in luminous letters on its dark surface.

The trail had been tortuous, replete with false leads and dead ends. Yet from the tangle of conflicting stories, from the lies and half-truths, from the inadvertent admissions of old and young, neighbors and relatives, teachers and schoolmates, Roppolo's people had drawn a thread of reality and followed it relentlessly. With bribes and with less pleasant forms of persuasion, they tracked Talley Magramor through the people he passed on his way from Greentree to Eugenia, leaping the gap of those off-planet

years as if it were a mere crack in the sidewalk. He had
returned to familiar scenes and moved onward swiftly.

A lonely farmhouse, a small gathering of friends on a
cool evening, a Patrol squad descending unheralded. In the
fight that followed, three rebels were killed, and one Patroller. When the house was taken at last, two people were
found alive inside—a wounded boy and the man who
tended him. The boy died within hours. The man could not
be persuaded to speak. Routine pictures and coronal
prints were dispatched to the Citadel, but it was four days
before Roppolo himself confirmed that the prisoner was
Dr. Gordon Tallentyre Magramor.

A face flashed on the screen, and Dia found herself staring at Talley's gaunt features. He had grown a beard since
their parting, a thick blond frame for his haggard, pouchy
eyes. The corners of his mouth sagged. He looked exhausted.

"I presume there's no mistake," said Velicher. He stood
behind Dia, his hands on her shoulders.

"No mistake," she said. "He's grown the beard, but I'd
know him anywhere."

The picture faded into a welter of statistics—height,
weight, retinal index. Velicher shut the screen off.

His hand slid beneath Dia's chin and tipped her face up.
"Would you like to see him?"

She frowned. "He won't have anything pleasant to say to
me."

"I should think not, since he owes his captivity to you.
In his position, I would be quite abusive if I saw you. Perhaps he's rather creative in his abuse. Let's find out."

"You really want me to see him?"

"Yes."

"Right now?"

"Oh, tomorrow is soon enough." His hand was warm
against her cheek now, slipping upward to her temple.
"Tomorrow morning, my dear, right after breakfast."

She lay beside him that night until his breathing indicated sleep; then she returned to her own quarters, her own
bed. She shut his sleeping body away with a firmly closed
door, but he remained awake in her thoughts, saying over
and over again, *Would you like to see him?* She wondered
at his motives. Surely he could not expect the rebel doctor
to confess all when suddenly confronted with his be-
trayer; Talley would be stupid indeed had he not foreseen

her telling her superiors everything about the cavern experience. Was this, then, another test of herself, of her steadfastness before a storm of revilement, of her indifference to the enemy who saved her life, of her Patrol-bred implacability toward even the most personal pleas for sympathy? Or was the Brigadier merely going to indulge in a little gloating? Not knowing what he expected of her, she vowed to present a bland and unruffled exterior, to exhibit no feeling, no curiosity, no opinion at all. To be in all ways a proper Patroller.

If I can.

She dreamed uneasily of Talley on the rack, his bones stretching grotesquely like caramel, his mouth wide and screaming as time expanded infinitely in all directions. She woke without any desire for breakfast, dressed, and knocked at the Brigadier's door.

As usual, he had risen early and was ready to commence the day's activities. "Restless night?" he inquired, kissing her lightly.

"No, I woke up hungry at 0200 and didn't want to disturb you."

"I take it you're ready to see Dr. Magramor."

"As ready as I'll ever be."

"Then let's go." A scooter was waiting at his front door; they mounted side by side and headed down the south branch of the corridor. At the nearest elevator, Velicher braked and entered smoothly, swiveling on one wheel to face front.

Talley was being held in an interior, middle-level, high-security chamber; its single door was at the back of a narrow anteroom. A first lieutenant, the paired silver bars on his shoulders gleaming bright under the intense illumination of a desk light, sat in the anteroom, playing cards with himself. He wore a sidearm in a closed holster so shiny he must have oiled it daily. At the Brigadier's first step through the doorway, he looked up and then sprang to his feet.

"At ease, Lieutenant Schain," said Velicher. "Has Colonel Roppolo been in yet this morning?"

"No, Sir, he hasn't. He's due in half an hour, Sir."

"Call him, then, and have him verify my identity. I want to see the prisoner."

"No need to call, Sir. I know you by sight, Sir."

"Do you? When was the last time you saw me?"

"On a broadcast three weeks ago, Sir."

"You've never met me?"

"Seven years ago, Sir, at graduation ceremonies."

"Seven years is a long time. I could be a clever impostor. I could be a rebel spy."

"In the middle of the Citadel, Sir?"

"Call Roppolo. I don't want any chances taken with this prisoner."

"Yes, Sir." His face pink, the lieutenant punched a code on his desk screen, and Roppolo at the breakfast table was resolved on its surface. The colonel was annoyed at being disturbed, until Velicher leaned over the desk to greet him, and then he gave the guard a curt order to let the Brigadier do whatever he wished.

"All right," said Velicher, "you know me now. No one is to go in that room without my authorization or Colonel Roppolo's."

"Yes, Sir," said the lieutenant, and he palmed the door open.

Talley lay on the unpadded bench that served as chair, bed, and table for his cell. There was no window, only diffuse artificial light radiating from the junctures of cream-colored walls and ceiling. In the far corner was a coverless toilet, above it a single spigot for water. The floor was hard and gray and cold. As they entered, Talley sat up, knuckling sleep out of his eyes. He wore a green tunic and green slacks, smeared and stiffened here and there by some darker hue, and his feet were bare. He had no blanket.

"Dr. Magramor?" said Velicher.

Talley's gaze slid past the Brigadier and lit on Dia, standing straight and silent beside him. "You look very well, Lieutenant Catlin," he said.

Dia made no reply, only stared at him, her expression bland by an effort of will. The picture accompanying the report of his capture had prepared her to see him haggard and bearded; it had not prepared her for the slump of shoulders, the drooping head, the listless limbs. He held his body as though the effort were too much for him.

"Do you know who I am?" asked Velicher.

Talley's shoulders lifted in a halfhearted shrug. "I know what the uniform means. Commanding officer of the Patrol."

Velicher turned to the guard. "Bring chairs for Lieutenant Catlin and myself." When the two of them were seated opposite Talley, with the guard standing easy behind them, Velicher leaned forward and spoke earnestly. "You must know why you're here, Dr. Magramor. There's no point in pretending that you have no information to give us."

"What would a simple doctor know that could possibly be of any importance to you?" Talley said, his eyes on Dia. They told her, *I can play the same game you did.* His lips twitched in a shadowy smile. "I'm not privy to any secrets."

Velicher shook his head. "It won't do, Doctor. I advise you to tell us everything immediately. Delay will only mean discomfort for you."

"Ah . . . discomfort. Why don't you just call it pain? I've already been beaten and starved; what's next?"

"Lieutenant Catlin has already provided us a detailed account of her experiences in your camp, and a detailed description of your friend Strux. We gather that he is the emissary of a foreign power aiding the rebel cause. Tell us about Strux, Doctor. Where is he from, and how many of his kind are on Amphora?"

Talley did not bother to look at Velicher.

"You would be wise to answer," said the Brigadier, his voice low and hard. "Our methods are thorough, and you won't find a sympathetic jailer here to set you free!"

"I wouldn't think so," said Talley, and his gaze dropped to the floor.

Dia sat motionless, knees together, hands flat on her thighs. She said nothing but only watched the prisoner sink into himself. He seemed to dwindle in size, drawing his legs, up, his arms in, as if shielding his vulnerable belly from a blow. His sleeve rode up, and she saw marks upon his skin, red welts and discolored swelling.

How does it feel, Talley, to be in my place?

Velicher rose to his feet, and his chair skidded back. He grasped Talley's shirt and yanked him to his feet, and the rebel doctor let himself hang limp in the Brigadier's grip, his head lolling back.

"If you don't talk," Velicher whispered, "I will personally see that you die slowly, by centimeters, and that you suffer every second of it!" Their eyes met, and for a moment hatred was an almost tangible force in the air between them. Then Velicher threw his captive to the bench and stepped back. "All right, Lieutenant Schain, we're finished here. Tell Colonel Roppolo I'll talk to him later in the day." He stalked out of the room.

Dia had to lengthen her stride to keep up with the Brigadier's furious pace; he spurned the scooter and marched down the corridor in silence. His arms and legs worked stiffly, as if the joints were poorly oiled. At the Southeast Tower, the broadest of all the Citadel's towers, he took the elevator to an upper level and went outdoors to the catwalk that communicated to the next spire. Halfway between, high above the Citadel Square where countless bronze memorial plaques gleamed in the morning sunshine, he stopped and leaned on the rail, staring down.

Dia waited, feeling the brisk wind in her hair; beneath scattered clouds she could see the dark delta-shapes that were probably middle-level officers logging their flight hours. She wondered how many of them thought of what awaited them in enemy hands.

"Cocky bastard," Velicher muttered.

Far below, figures moved across the Square; Dia watched them pass the pillar that held Michael's plaque without pausing. Who, she thought, besides herself, ever stopped to read his name?

"They're all the same," said Velicher. "Every one of them." His clasped hands shook with vehemence. "And now they've *dared* to go offplanet with their lies, to con some other race into helping them push us off *our* world!" He turned his head and impaled Dia with his stare. His face was livid. "Take a lesson from this, Lieutenant Catlin: the universe laughs at softness. If the old Brigadier had listened to my advice, we could have wiped out the rebels before they scattered. Instead, he let the Council sway him with their calls for a truce. I've had to spend most of my career regaining the position he lost!" His mouth tightened. "But they won't escape me this time. I can feel it—after eighty years, we're finally going to destroy them." He gazed toward the horizon, toward nothing at all save the images in his own mind. His hands gripped the rail, his elbows straightening slowly as he shifted to the erect, military stance that had been bred and drilled into him.

Dia spoke in a low voice. "What about their off-planet allies? Will we be able to destroy them, too?"

"We have an ace or two up our sleeves," he said. "They haven't caught us unprepared." He glanced at her sidelong. "Keep up your flying hours."

"Is something . . . big . . . going to happen?"

He took her by the arms, holding her as if she were a

painting and he an art collector trying to decide whether to buy. "Something big. Yes. Soon. And when the crunch does come, my dear, we'll need every pilot we have for combat duty. Even you. Even the Brigadier's own aide."

So Paul was right. I should be excited. Action at last. Goodbye desk. Soon. But she felt no exhilaration. She could only think of Talley in his cell, waiting. "I understand," she said.

"We still have some time. And you grow lovelier with every passing day, my dear. I could stand out here and look at you . . ." His voice trailed off, and then he eyed the chronometer on his sleeve. "Unfortunately, the morning includes a number of important appointments, and therefore we must return to the office."

This day was like any other for the man who ruled the Patrol—and Amphora—from the Central Tower of the Citadel. There were instructions to be given, inspectors to be dispatched, reports to be reviewed. The Council had met the evening before, and the transcript was waiting on Velicher's screen; he had Dia give him a summary of it during lunch. Over coffee, he called Roppolo, expressing his dissatisfaction loudly when the Colonel could only offer negative results.

"He's had some training in resistance to pain," said Roppolo.

"I expect you to get past his resistance, Colonel."

"Of course, Sir, but we have to strike a median—too little and he won't talk, too much and he won't be able to talk, not coherently at least."

Velicher shut the screen off in disgust. "I wish we had one of those babble-gadgets they used on you. What did you call it? An Inducer. If it really worked."

"Did he have a medical kit with him when he was captured?" asked Dia.

Velicher looked up sharply. "There might be one in it." He returned to the screen, found Roppolo again, and conferred with him rapidly. "What do you mean you don't know? Well, find out, Colonel! Do I have to do your job for you?"

Dia had little faith in the Inducer as an instrument for the extraction of information; even if it worked as well as the rebels said, they had still wanted her conscious cooperation to make full sense of its results. Otherwise they wouldn't have bothered with threats and cajolery. But her store of knowledge had been skimpy; even the Inducer could not elicit what wasn't there. Talley, on the other hand, had to be a fund of data. Coherent or not, his mind could yield facts the Patrol required . . . and with the Inducer, there would be no more pain. No more pain. She could not forget the sight of him in his cell. Defeat was written all over his body, but his voice was still defiant. As hers had been, down in the caves, out on the mountain ledge. They shared a damnable stubbornness. Did the prospect of pain frighten him, she wondered, as much as it had frightened her? But there would be no more pain with the Inducer—she could buy him that much with her suggestion.

I owe him at least that, she thought, waiting in the Brigadier's office for Roppolo's reply. *At least that.* By the time the message arrived—relayed by the Colonel's adjutant —her appointed hour at the gymnasium was imminent. She wanted to go, to put everything out of her mind, but she waited, watching Velicher's face redden and his voice dip ominously low.

"Left at Eugenia?" he said to the image on the screen. "I expect more than that from the Colonel's office. Get it here immediately."

The adjutant assured him that Colonel Roppolo was seeing to the matter personally.

"I hold you responsible for it, too," said Velicher, and he broke the connection. His hands curled into fists, and one pressed against his mouth as he glared at the blank screen.

Dia let a long moment pass before she approached the desk to ask if the Brigadier needed anything else before she took her turn at the gym.

"Greater efficiency," he muttered, and he waved her out.

As she passed through the anteroom, Ramirez beckoned her to him. He spoke softly, and she knew that he had been listening in on Velicher's screen conversation. "I've never seen him like this," he said. "Be careful of what you say and do. It'll be easier for all of us."

Coldly, she said, "Are you afraid he'll hold you responsible, too?"

"I'm just trying to do my job, Lieutenant. For the good of the Patrol."

She looked down at him, at the desk that was the symbol of his power, at the cool, disdainful eyes. Had he hated every one of the Brigadier's women? "I don't forget that,

Captain. Believe me. I have a job, too—for the good of the Patrol." She turned her back on him and walked out.

At the parallel bars, she leaned her forehead against the cool metal. Her teeth, her jaws, the backs of her eyes throbbed from the strain of maintaining a bland exterior. *Why fool myself? I wasn't thinking of my debt when I identified the picture of a schoolboy.* In the detention room, she had wanted to shout, *Tell him, Talley; tell him everything!* But of course, he wouldn't listen to such a cry from his enemy.

She tried to lose herself in exercise, to blank out her brain while her body strained to its utmost, but this time there was no oblivion on the bars, the rings, the balance beam. Everywhere she thought of him. Of the welts, the bruises. Of the pain that Roppolo had administered so carefully. Everywhere she thought, *This is how I've paid him back.*

Her vision momentarily blurred, she missed her hold on one of the bars, slammed her forearms against it, and ricocheted to the mat. Immediately, half a dozen fellow gymnasts were bending over her, asking anxious questions, prodding, poking. She shook her head and threw them off, rolling to her feet. Bruises, nothing more. Someone brought cold packs, and she retired to a corner to nurse her arms with them. She sat there for a long time, huddled over, wishing that she could numb all of her, not just the flesh. In the corner, no one could see her tears.

For the good of the Patrol.

FIVE

After showering she barely reached the Brigadier's quarters in time for dinner. She found Roppolo there, eating fruit salad with his commanding officer.

"Here is our expert," said Velicher, waving his fork toward Dia.

"Expert in what, Sir?" Dia responded, seating herself at his left and selecting a melon slice from the platter in the center of the table. She was cool now, in command of herself once more, ignoring the throb of bruised arms. The cold packs had prevented them from swelling, and the growing discoloration was hidden by her uniform.

"Aside from Magramor himself, and any rebel spies in our midst, you are the only person in the Citadel who has seen the Inducer in use."

" 'Experienced' would be a better term, Sir," she replied. "I never *saw* it being used."

"I threatened Magramor with the Inducer," said Roppolo. "He told me that we'd be more likely to kill him than to dig out any information."

"But you must remember something about it," said Velicher. "Which button made you fall asleep, at least."

"I could guess, Sir, but . . ." she shrugged. "It has a lot of buttons. Surely we have technicians who could figure it out."

Roppolo shook his head. "Our best technicians have examined it. They said it might take a year to analyze properly."

"We don't have a year," said Velicher. "And the other way, testing all the controls on a volunteer—well, I can't ask one of my Patrollers to volunteer for something like that. Not if there's a possibility of death."

"He could be lying," said Roppolo. "But we can't take that chance."

"Close your eyes, Lieutenant. Think back. Where did Dr. Magramor touch your head when he put you to sleep?"

"It was Strux, Sir, who did that. At my temples." She fingered either side of her head. "There was a red light in the center, directly above my nose." Roppolo leaned forward across his half-eaten dinner, measuring tape in hand, to determine the exact placement of the remembered controls.

"Show him which buttons you're going to press," Velicher said. "See what his reaction is. But don't do anything until you've talked to me again."

Roppolo wolfed his meal and hurried away.

"You don't think he *wants* to die, do you?" the Brigadier said to Dia over dessert.

"No, I don't think he's that crazy."

"I wonder. Some of them are damnably fanatical." He frowned down at his plate. "Now that we have it, I hate to try the thing. We know our own methods, but this . . . this alien gadget is so uncertain. What if he's counting on us to kill him with it?"

"Then he wouldn't have warned us that might happen," Dia said.

"These rebels—they're perverse bastards, every one of them. The sooner we get rid of them all, the better."

He stayed wakeful late that night, reading, listening to music, watching Dia read. Until Roppolo called to report the arrival of the Inducer and its presentation to Magramor —who merely smiled when the two critical buttons were indicated. With a curt nod, Velicher gave the go-ahead for its use. "Call me as soon as something happens," he said. Notification came some fifteen minutes later; manipulation of the controls had caused Magramor to fall into a deep sleep, and he could not be wakened by shaking, nor by vigorous slaps.

"Press the buttons again," said Velicher.

Roppolo grinned in self-satisfaction. "I tried that right away, Sir, and it woke him up. I've put him back to sleep now."

"Record everything he says tonight, no matter how garbled. Try asking him questions while he's in this state. I don't expect you to leave him, Colonel."

Roppolo's grin faded. "I'll do my best, Sir. Good night."

Velicher turned to Dia. "Let's go to bed."

He noticed the bruises on her arms but did not question her explanation—that she had miscalculated while trying a new maneuver on the parallel bars. She slept at last, long after his breathing became deep and even, and she woke first in the morning, stealing silently out of bed to order breakfast. He rose just as it arrived.

"I suppose he hasn't called?"

Dia shook her head.

Velicher toyed with his food. "Call him."

"Do you really want to disturb him? He might be busy."

Velicher nodded slowly. "You're right. I'll wait. Half an hour."

At precisely 0800, the viewscreen chimed: Ropollo's adjutant.

"Where's your commanding officer, Lieutenant?" Velicher said sharply.

"Asleep, sir. He was up all night, in compliance with your orders. I have his report."

"He wasn't supposed to leave while the prisoner was asleep."

"The prisoner is awake, Sir. Colonel Roppolo wakened him at 0730."

Velicher's voice was tight. "Why did he do that, Lieutenant?"

"He judged that the experimental intelligence-gathering technique was a failure, Sir. The prisoner did not say a single word all night."

Velicher's fist pounded the screen, striking the adjutant's image square in the face, and the man flinched as from an actual blow. "Resume our previous techniques, Lieutenant. And tell the colonel to call me when he wakes up."

Dia passed him a fresh cup of coffee. "Talking must be controlled by other buttons."

"Or the whole thing was a lie. I wouldn't doubt it—the damned rebels trying to force you to talk by saying you'd already betrayed virtually everything. Well, we've wasted a night, and he's had a good sleep on top of that, but it's the last sleep he'll have until he talks!" He gulped the coffee, then stalked into the bedroom to dress.

Dia dumped the dishes down the chute, then leaned against the wall to steady herself. The time she had bought was gone, one pitiful night's sleep. Well, he had surely slept better than she had. Now his body would be the battlefield once more in the war between his will and the Brigadier's.

Damn you, why should I care what happens to you? It's your own damned fault for being on the wrong side!

An image of Strux rose in her mind—Strux saying, "I am on the winning side, Lieutenant."

Whatever happened, whoever came out the victor, Talley Magramor had already lost.

She was combing her hair when Velicher returned, fully dressed and looking twice as formidable in uniform as in robe and slippers. He stepped up behind her, encircling her with his arms. "I meant to tell you, my dear, that I was pleased with your behavior in the detention room. He was obviously making a bid for your sympathy, staring at you like that and using the same excuse you gave him when you were his prisoner."

"I noticed," Dia said coolly.

He kissed her ear. "You should have seen the look of disdain on your face. You fairly withered him—the woman whose life he saved betraying him. He didn't know the Patrol, my dear; he didn't know us at all. Maybe if more of them knew what we were like, they'd give up this insane resistance."

"I think they must suspect," she said. "Remember, he said I was stubborn, just like all Patrollers."

"Stubborn? They don't know the half of it! Come on, let's go to the office and start the day before I call the detention room and get another useless report."

"I'm ready." As they climbed the short stairway to his office, Dia behind him, she watched his straight back. *So you used me, Brigadier Velicher—used me to wreak some petty vengeance; not on Talley, not on a man you'd never met before, but on a symbol of the whole rebel movement. You said he was the key, but for the time we were in that room, especially for the moment you held him in your hands, he was everything.*

Inside the office, she stood beside the desk as he eased into his chair, her face a careful mask of neutrality. *Is this what he reads for disdain?* she wondered, and she forced a faint smile to her lips. Glancing up at her, he smiled back. Then he began to punch messages on his desk screen.

For Dia, the day crept by, in spite of the errands that required her to scooter around the Citadel, in spite of a Staff conference that included a colonel recently arrived from the southern continent. Velicher, too, seemed uneasy and was physically more active than usual, taking his lunch break for target practice. Only Ramirez appeared unaffected by the tense atmosphere; smoothly efficient, he dealt with a thousand details of the Brigadier's office without ever leaving his desk. Late in the day, he relayed a call from Roppolo.

At her own desk, Dia heard him announce it—her ears were tuned to that name. In the silence of the anteroom, she could hear the murmur of the Brigadier's voice, accepting the call. And then there were further murmurs, too faint for her to make out the words, from Ramirez's viewscreen. That was nothing new—Ramirez was always communicating with someone. But this time he was listening, saying nothing, and Dia knew that he was eavesdropping on the Brigadier's call. She looked up at him, trying to be unobtrusive about it, and saw his gaze aimed at the screen, and his hands, which so often were punching codes on his keyboard or making notes on his desk pad, were still. A minute passed. He did not move. The murmur of human voices was gone now, replaced by a thick silence; only by the bluish highlights on Ramirez's face could Dia tell that his screen was still on. And by his rapt attention.

Her fingers strayed to the keys of her own screen. Like Ramirez's, it intercepted calls to the Brigadier—allowing either of them to handle routine matters without disturbing him. It also allowed them to monitor all of the Brigadier's calls, to violate his privacy and see what he saw, hear what he heard. Dia had never eavesdropped. If Ramirez wanted to risk his career by doing so, that was up to him. Let him be the one who knew all the gossip first. Let him have that petty pleasure.

Still, he did not move.

What are they watching?

And then she knew. Her mind made the logical leap, without words, without images. What would the Brigadier and his long-time aide, his shadow, be watching for so long?

She touched the key, and her screen brightened.

Talley's cell.

At first she could not make sense out of the scene. Talley was seated in a straight-backed chair, Roppolo in another, facing him. Behind Talley stood a first lieutenant, one hand on Talley's head. Roppolo was bending forward, almost leaning into Talley's lap. Then Talley jerked sharply, and the tableau came into sudden focus for Dia, as if a gauze curtain had been whisked away.

He was manacled to the chair by wrists and ankles. The lieutenant gripped his hair, holding his head still while his body heaved. The filthy green trousers were gone, and Roppolo bent over Talley's naked thighs, a burning splint in his hand. There were marks on the inside of the far thigh, all the way up to the groin, and as Dia watched, Roppolo made another one. Talley jerked again, his whole body thrusting sideways, and the chair teetered on two legs for a moment before the lieutenant righted it with his free hand. Talley's mouth opened wide, but the sound was off on Dia's screen and she couldn't hear his cry. Roppolo glanced away, but not out of pity, only to re-light the splint, which had gone out against Talley's skin.

She hit the Off key with her fist and sat there, her eyes trapped by the screen, though it was blank now. She could feel cold sweat starting all over her body, and she clenched her teeth against it. With some effort, she finally raised her head. Across the room, Ramirez was still watching his own screen, as if human pain were the greatest of all entertainments. Dia spread her hands flat on the surface of her desk and levered herself out of her chair. Ramirez never looked up as she left the room.

She made for the nearest stairway, not running, though she wanted to run, but walking with purposeful stride, as if on an errand too important to be interrupted. She descended the single story to her apartment and shut the door that sealed away the rest of the world. Only then did she let herself sag to the floor, pressing her hands to her face. Behind her eyes, the image of Talley and Roppolo still loomed, though she squeezed her lids shut till she saw dancing lights against the darkness.

Ramirez was still watching, which meant that Velicher, too, had his screen tuned to Talley's cell. And Roppolo was sending that image. *Ghouls*, she thought.

Her eyes began to ache, and she had to open them. She shivered, her sweat-soaked clothing clammy against her skin. According to her chronometer, there were still two hours left of office duty. She stripped, took a quick shower, and donned a fresh uniform. She felt no better then but went upstairs anyway, before someone started wondering what had happened to her.

Shortly after she returned, Talley Magramor broke.

SIX

Roppolo brought the news in person, and the transcript of the confession. Dia and Ramirez stood in the doorway of Velicher's office to hear it. Garbled though it was, wrung out of the prisoner over a period of hours, the facts were clear enough, and Colonel Roppolo summarized them aloud: "The creature Strux comes from the planet Avdotya, in system GR 2672; his race is the dominant intelligent native life form and lives in cooperation with a human colony established about two hundred years ago. They have a high technology culture and have established hegemony over their own and two neighboring stellar systems.

"Magramor met Strux at medical school on Quixote, the largest human facility convenient to Avdotya, and after their internships, he followed the creature to its home world. There he was able to enlist the sympathies of the human colonials, who influenced the native government to offer a substantial expeditionary force to the Amphoran rebels. Strux himself was dispatched to reconnoiter the scene of hostilities, to render a detailed report, and to signal the launching of the invasion."

"And?" said Velicher.

"And the Avdotyan Armada is due here sometime in the next few weeks."

Velicher pounded his desk. "I don't believe it! What did he offer them that they're so ready to spend men and materiel?"

"A colony."

"A colony?"

"The south continent, to be precise."

"What an idiot!" He lurched out of his chair and rounded the desk, turning to stare at his empty place. "Is he so stupid that he believes they're willing to cross three-hundred-odd parsecs for one measly continent? He sold his people down the drain!" He snatched the transcript from Roppolo's hands and devoured it in silence. "Bastard!" he muttered at last. He looked up sharply. "Where is Avdotya, and what do they have to send against us?"

Roppolo summoned a star map on the desk screen and indicated an insignificant yellow sun amid a thousand others; like Amphora, it lay on the fringe of the territory formerly known as the Stellar Federation. "It's a seven week trip each way, and Strux left eleven weeks ago."

"On what? No ship left Amphora eleven weeks ago, or twelve, or twenty!"

Roppolo shrugged. "They must have evaded our detectors. They have a high technology."

"How high?"

"Sir, we don't know anything about Avdotya except that system GR 2672 exists."

"You haven't been doing your job, Roppolo."

Roppolo straightened his back. "Sir, the Stellar Federation numbered more than three thousand inhabited worlds. System GR 2672 was *not* included in its jurisdiction." He hesitated. "Not according to our records, anyway."

"Our records are obviously sadly lacking."

"We do our best, Sir, but it's quite a distance. . . ."

Velicher glared at him. "Stop making excuses, Colonel. We know nothing but what Magramor tells us. What condition is he in?"

"He'll survive."

Velicher rattled the transcript. "There's a lot of information here, but not as much as we need."

"If I may say so, Sir—he seems to have given us everything he has. He's not a technically minded man, except insofar as medicine is concerned. He spoke quite a bit about medicine." He gestured toward the transcript. "You'll see that in the supplement."

"I saw it." Slowly, the Brigadier paced the width of his office. "Well, what does it matter? We have certain weapons; we can't conjure better ones out of air. We'll have to be prepared for the worst."

"Well, Sir," said Roppolo, "we have at least three weeks."

"That doesn't give us much margin." He turned to Dia. "Call a Staff meeting for tonight. No, a dinner—formal dress. For morale." He nodded to Roppolo. "I'll expect you to be there with a briefing on this material." He threw the transcript at the colonel.

"What about Magramor, Sir?"

"What about him?"

"Well . . . shall I feed him?"

"Feed him? He'll eat no Citadel food as long as I'm alive. But you can let him *sleep*." He threw himself into his chair, which tilted hard against the wall, and he put his feet up on the desk. "I'm not finished with him . . . not yet."

Dinner stretched late into the night; Roppolo delivered his briefing with the fruit cup, and the subsequent courses were awash with lengthy debate on the disposition of personnel and armaments, on strategy and supply lines for the coming conflict.

Dia listened intently from her vantage at the Brigadier's left, until the wealth of information began to blend into an amorphous mass in her mind—too many numbers, too many names, too many alternative courses of action suggested. Only by taking notes could she have retained the whole in some coherent form. The Staff members, each responsible for only a fraction of the whole operation, were recording memoranda on their portable memory units; Velicher, who already knew exactly what he wanted from all of them and steered the debate in his chosen directions, did not need to record trivia. The essential plan was to set Patrol craft in orbit about Amphora, ready to strike as soon as the Avdotyan fleet approached. His scheme involved a vast array of ships—Dia was astonished that so many could have been built with Amphora's meager facilities, even in eighty years of Patrol supervision.

No wonder he told me to keep up my flight hours.

And she realized, too, that in spite of her closeness to him, in spite of the bed they shared and the other services she rendered him, she knew next to nothing about the real decisions that governed the Patrol and the planet. He had allowed her to observe the superficialities; but the real secrets, like the *Memoirs* of the first Brigadier, like the existence of these ships—which must be scattered about the planet in the most secluded regions to remain unsuspected by the lower echelons—the real secrets were locked away from her.

Velicher stood, leaned forward, his hands flat on the table on either side of his empty dessert plate. Towering over the seated Staff, he was an imposing figure in his bemedalled dress uniform, and his voice was imperious. "They will be here in no less than three weeks. We must and will be ready in two. That is all."

There was no talking as the Staff members filed out of the room. Each person seemed lost in his own thoughts, his own plans, his own responsibilities, and out in the corridor they moved quickly and purposefully apart, as if the few moments gained by that hurry could make the difference between victory and defeat.

"My dear," said Velicher to Dia when they were finally alone. "You look lovely tonight."

She lifted an empty long-stemmed glass, twirled it between two fingers, watched the play of light on its polished surface. "Can we really be ready in two weeks?" she asked

"I don't doubt it." He slung an arm about her waist. "I've had more than enough official discussion for tonight, haven't you?"

Nodding, she leaned toward him, tilting her face upward for his kiss. Shortly, they retired to the bedroom.

In the quietest hour of the night, when the gentle rhythm of his breathing betrayed the depth of his slumber, she stole naked from the bed. She moved by touch, by memory, silently. She could not see him in the darkness, but she knew that seeing would only confirm her decision. Negotiating the dining area, still crowded with table and chairs, she found the bookcase and, by touch again, selected the single book that was locked into its cover. Then she padded to her own quarters and sealed the communicating door.

She dressed swiftly in her regular uniform. From the bottom drawer of the bureau, she drew the matched set of slim target pistols and slipped one into each deep pocket of her slacks—the two slight bulges were covered by the overlap of her tunic, and one was further camouflaged by the rectangular shape of the book in her tunic pocket. The corridor was silent as she stepped from her apartment; she went to the nearest scooter station and, once mounted, proceeded southward.

As she had expected, the familiar first lieutenant was on duty, his shift only an hour old and due to run till midmorning. He rose as she entered the anteroom, not tired or bored enough yet to be engrossed in a card game with himself.

"Lieutenant Catlin," he said.

"Do you remember me?"

"Of course. You were here with the Brigadier the day before yesterday."

"I'm to see the prisoner."

"Your authorization?"

"Brigadier's orders."

He hesitated, and his uncertainties were visible on his face. He recognized her as the Brigadier's aide, but Velicher's reprimand was still fresh in his memory. He glanced at his chronometer. "Is the Brigadier in his office?"

"No, he's in his quarters. He worked most of the night, and he's asleep now."

The guard grimaced. "I have to do this, Lieutenant." He reached toward the keyboard set in one side of his desk.

"Don't touch those keys," said Dia. One of her hands had already dipped into a pocket, and when the guard looked up, he found himself staring down the muzzle of a target pistol. "Raise your hands above your head, stand up slowly, and move away from the desk." He hesitated only a moment before obeying. "Against the wall; on your elbows." She relieved him of his sidearm. It was a light stunner—Velicher and Roppolo were taking no chances on the prisoner being killed in any jailhouse fracas. "Open the inner door."

He shook his head. "You know I can't do that."

"I don't want to hurt you, Lieutenant, but if I have to, the gun I'm holding will do a lot worse than the one I took from you. Now open the door." She stepped back, out of reach. "And no heroics. There's no career advancement in a memorial plaque."

He palmed the door. Inside the cell, Talley huddled on the bench, his legs drawn up against his stomach. He turned his head and blinked blearily at the two who entered.

"Get up, Doctor," said Dia. She motioned the guard to the far side of the room. "Lieutenant, take off your clothes and toss them gently toward the doctor."

They seemed to obey with equal reluctance. Talley was unsteady on his feet and had to sit down almost immediately. The guard unfastened his tunic with fumbling fingers.

"What's going on?" said Talley. "What is this?"

"You're coming with me," said Dia.

He peered at her, his brow furrowing. "With you? For what reason?"

"Strip and put on his uniform. We'll discuss the reasons later."

Talley laughed hollowly. "There must be some simpler way to get rid of me than by staging a fake escape attempt."

"Do as I say!" she hissed.

He shook his head. "No, no; I'm staying right here in my safe little cell."

Without taking her eyes off the guard, she reached out, wound the fingers of her free hand in his hair, and rocked his head violently from side to side. "Do as I say or I'll put you out of your misery right here and now!" She dragged him off the bench by his hair. "We're not playing games here, Doctor! Change your clothes!"

He changed, while the naked guard stood in the corner, shifting from foot to foot. Dia drew the stunner and shot the man, then turned to face Talley, who was struggling into the tunic—he apparently needed the wall to hold him up. The uniform was broad in the shoulders, but not too short in the cuff; the boots stretched to fit his feet. "You make a pretty sorry-looking officer," she said, eyeing his wilting posture. "Can you stand up straight?"

"You wouldn't stand very straight if you hadn't eaten in days."

She fished a nut bar out of one breast pocket—a protein concentrate she often ate after workouts at the gym—and thrust it into his hands. "You can chew on this after we've gotten out of here. Come on." With a hand in his armpit, she hustled him out of the cell. Reprogramming the open lock took only a moment, and then the door shut, accessible only to Dia's palm or to a locksmith. If the guard regained consciousness before his shift was over, he would not be able to set off an alarm. She strapped the stunner to her waist, and tucked the target pistol back in her pocket. She felt like a walking arsenal.

She stepped into the corridor, determined that it was empty, and pulled Talley along behind her. They mounted the scooter, and she had to prod his back sharply with her knuckles to make him sit up in some semblance of military bearing. She drove one-handed, choosing corridors that were likely to be little-traveled in the middle of the night; they passed three or four pedestrians who paid no particular attention to their speeding progress.

As they rounded the final corner, she said, "For the next

ten minutes, you are Lieutenant Murray Schain. I'll do the talking, but you've *got* to act bright-eyed and alert!"

"Are you really going to get me—"

"Shut up!" She eased the scooter into a parking stall and climbed off, gesturing peremptorily for him to follow.

The night hangar crew was clustered about a chess board, and only the chief looked up as Dia and Talley approached. "Your trainer's ready, Lieutenants," she said, escorting them to its cradle, "but I'm afraid I can only give you an hour in the air tonight. There's a major wants to make a dawn-twilight run, and we'll barely have a chance to refuel from your flight before he gets here."

Dia pulled a flight suit and helmet from the nearest rack, tossed a set to Talley. "Can't you assign him some other craft?"

The chief shrugged. "Sorry—everything else is spoken for or docked for repairs. You're lucky to get this, as late as you called."

"Well, I guess we'll have to take what we can get." She pressed the seams of her suit together and flicked a glance at Talley, who was moving slowly but not having any obvious difficulty. "Ready, Lieutenant?" she asked him.

He nodded. His back was reasonably straight, and if his eyes were a trifle unfocused, he was careful to keep his face turned away from the hangar chief.

"You take the front," said Dia, and she pinched his elbow to give him some impetus to climb into his seat. She settled in behind him, and the chief checked their safety harnesses and secured the canopy over their heads. The cradle clamps fell away, the hangar roof slid back, and the trainer rose vertically into the sky above the Citadel.

Beyond the artificial lights, the stars were bright and crisp and cold. Dia found the North Star, checked her compass, and set the autopilot for the course she had filed when reserving the craft the previous afternoon. For the first ten minutes they would follow that course.

She spoke into the intercom. "All right, Doctor—we have an hour clear and maybe another hour before the search gets frantic. They'll be looking for a landing site pretty far from where we'll really be, so we probably don't have to start worrying until the Brigadier joins in. That could be as late as 0700, if no one thinks of waking him earlier. It won't take him long to figure out what happened, but by that time we should be down in the caverns where I was picked up by the Patrol. I hope you can hide the two of us as well as you hid yourself that time."

His voice crackled in her ears like an old man's. "The cavern entrance was bombed. We can't get in that way."

"There must be another—you certainly weren't buried alive."

He was silent for a long time. Over her instrument panel, Dia could see his helmet canted to the left, resting against the lower edge of the canopy.

Sharply, she said, "Doctor, you're not asleep, are you?"

His response was faint. "Why did you do it?"

"There was a debt to be paid." And then the autopilot buzzed, signaling the end of the first leg of their journey. She switched it off and banked hard to the right, northward. "You'd better think about that other entrance, Doctor; we'll be there in a shade less than two hours."

"You'll have to turn back, Lieutenant. I'm not going to fall for this fake escape routine. I'm not going to tell you where the other entrance is."

Dia swore. "Lack of food has put your brain to sleep, Doctor. If Intelligence had been interested in the location of any cavern entrance, they would have tortured the information out of you along with the rest, not set up an elaborate fraud to trick you into revealing it." She bit her lips, tasted the bitter tang of blood. "I suppose I should have killed the guard, to demonstrate my sincerity."

"It wouldn't have proved a thing, if you'd done it under orders."

"We don't give orders to kill each other in the Patrol!"

His whisper was harsh, grating on her ears. "And you're such a good little Patroller."

Her hands tightened on the steering grips. Ahead, the North Star winked solemnly; ten minutes earlier she had seen it as a welcoming signpost, but now it seemed to send a tremulous warning. "Talley," she said, her voice rigidly controlled, "as of this night, I am no longer a member of the Patrol." Spoken aloud at last, the words chilled her. She had thrown it all away: past, present, future, all her family's hopes and her childhood dreams. There was no turning back now. If the decision had been hard to make, the words were twice as hard to say. There had been a time, not so long ago, when she would not have been able to imagine them coming from her lips. Not so long ago . . .

yet it seemed more than a lifetime. Too much had happened. Too much.

"Do you really expect me to believe that?"

"He was going to kill you. Velicher. He was going to get a great deal of satisfaction out of your death. I . . . couldn't allow it."

"What? The satisfaction?"

"No." She swallowed with difficulty, her throat suddenly tight. "I couldn't let you die."

"Why not, Lieutenant? I'm just another rebel."

"Damn you!" she shouted, and his helmet jerked as her voice blasted through his earphones. He turned slowly, as far as his harness would permit, and peered at her over the instrument panel.

"Damn you," she muttered, almost to herself, and she reached inside her flight suit to rip the insignia from her shoulders. She thrust the bright bars toward his face, then opened her palm to show them, to let them slide away, clinking, into his section of the craft. "I resign my commission. I am now a civilian. I am now a rebel." She leaned back, drained. In her line of sight were other stars besides the North, and constellations familiar since childhood. A few green and amber streaks, distorted reflections from the instruments, mingled with the cold white pinpoints of space. *If they don't want me, where will I go? There is nothing else. Nothing.*

Talley watched her face for a time, and then he said, "You've stolen a Patrol vehicle."

She met his eye. "Good. Now where's that other entrance?"

"Fifty-three kilometers north-northwest of the bombed one." He turned away, settling once more with the blank back of his helmet toward her. "It'll be dawn by the time we reach the area—I'll be able to point it out to you."

Dia projected a map on the twin screens of the cockpit. She touched her own with the tip of one finger. "Here?"

The shadow of his finger indicated a spot slightly westward. Dia altered course for the new destination.

PART FOUR
REBEL

With a sufficiently large fleet of Amphoran-built craft, we will be able to overwhelm the caretaker force that guards the mothballed fleet. Hundreds of ships wait for us there, as perfect as when they were retired, requiring only minimal servicing and refueling. Once they are in our possession, we will control the greatest armada the universe has ever known. Then the glory of the Patrol will be rekindled—it will outreach this insignificant planet and claim the stars we once policed.

Ultimately, there will be peace and stability in our empire.

—from the *Memoirs of Brigadier General Marcus Bohannon, Commander, 36th Tactical Strike Force, Stellar Federation Patrol*

ONE

Seen from a few thousand meters of altitude, the sun had already cleared the horizon, but on the ground the morning light was still gray and diffuse. Dia helped Talley scramble from the cockpit, then leaned inside to retrieve the two emergency kits from their niche beneath the front instrument panel.

"We can't very well hide a thing as big as this," she said, waving at the vehicle, which rested in the one grassy clearing in a hilly landscape of trees.

"I'll send some friends to dismantle it," said Talley. He stood on unsteady legs, both of his hands clutching her arm. "After a couple of hours, no one will know it was ever here."

"I hope we still have a couple of hours. We'd better get going."

"This way." He pointed westward, and they entered the forest. Here it was dim, and Dia brought out a pocket flash. The ground began to rise, and Talley walked with more difficulty, pausing often to breathe heavily. They had endured perhaps half a kilometer of uphill effort when he stopped and, swaying like a sapling in a breeze, pointed ahead.

To Dia's eyes, the cave mouth was a shadow, unreal until she stepped close and felt the cold air blowing from it. "This is it?"

Talley nodded. By the light of the flash, his face was too pale, his lips bloodless. He took one slow step, as if his legs were weighted with steel. Then Dia slung his arm across her shoulders and walked him inside, splashing through puddles, kicking free of clinging mud. The damp, familiar smell of the underworld surrounded them, and the flash showed the wide tunnel leading back, back, into

170

the heart of the hills. Talley's feet dragged; she was almost carrying him now, but he was not too heavy for her gymnast's muscles.

The tunnel floor was thick with mud and decaying vegetation. Farther inside, the rotten greenery gave way to more mud, and to slippery broken rock. Dia walked carefully, her eyes on the floor, on the pool of light made by the flash, and only when Talley whispered, "Stop," did she lift her eyes and realize they had entered a large room with walls laced and convoluted by rock formations.

Talley found his own footing, leaning gingerly against a limestone outcrop. He made passes over the rock with his hands, seemed to be wiping the dampness from its surface, and then suddenly the whole mass tilted upward on hidden hinges, revealing a dark hole.

"Shine the light down there," he said.

Dia obeyed and saw a flight of steps leading to the abyss. Talley descended first, one careful step at a time. Dia followed closely, directing the beam of the flash past his shoulder. Behind them, the rock returned to its former position, softly, silently, sealing them into the depths.

Walls and ceiling were close upon the stairway, and a low steel railing ran down one side, bolted to the naked stone. Talley clung to the rail with both hands, Dia with one, manipulating the flash with the other; the rail was icy to the touch, drawing warmth from their flesh till their numbed fingers could barely curve to grip it. Talley slid once on the moisture-coated steps, but Dia hooked her free arm about his waist and held him safe. The flash slipped from her fingers, clattered downward, and came to rest at the foot of the stairs, a wan marker for their destination. More slowly than ever, they negotiated the remaining distance, and Dia retrieved the light to examine their surroundings.

The stairway made a right angle with a horizontal tunnel; peering into it, Dia found that it stretched to right and left beyond the limit of the flash, and she wondered what natural processes had formed it. Talley motioned her back to the shelter of the stairway. "You don't want to get hit." He palmed a spot on the wall above the lowest step, and a small, square panel opened; inside was an instrument board—a luminous map, telltales, buttons. He stabbed a green button.

"Welcome to the subway," he said.

A section of the seemingly solid floor of the tunnel slid aside, and a cylinder perhaps three meters long and one and a half in diameter rose out of the well. The upper half of the cylinder was transparent, and a hatch opened in this part. Within was a cushioned floor.

"Climb in," said Talley.

Dia obeyed, helping Talley in after her. While she shut the hatch, he knelt over another instrument board set in one end of the cylinder. He punched a code and the vehicle commenced to glide down the tunnel, suspended in mid-air. It made a faint noise as it moved, a high-pitched note almost beyond the range of human hearing, part sound, part shiver. Dia remembered that sound, remembered it from a dream she had had during her cavern captivity, and now she knew that she had traveled the subway before, sleeping, with Strux and Talley. The flash revealed rock walls passing in a blur on all sides.

Talley swayed on his knees, leaned against the curve of the cylinder, then gradually slipped forward till his forehead rested against the clear front plate.

"Are you all right?" Dia asked, touching his shoulders. When he made no answer, she pulled him back, and he sagged against her. His eyes were closed, and he breathed hoarsely through a half-open mouth. She shook him, and his eyelids flickered.

"I won't die on you," he muttered. "Just a nap . . ." His voice faded on the last word. He was asleep.

Dia's arms closed around him. His head was pillowed on her breast, his body touching hers along its full length, his legs sprawled between her own. They had never been so close, not even when he carried her in his arms. But she didn't want to push him away this time. This time he was cold, he shivered faintly in his sleep, and she wanted to warm him with her nearness. And she wanted the subway ride to go on forever, wanted the two of them to be suspended in time and space, without past or future, without dread, without pain. She bent her head and pressed her lips against his fine, pale hair. The glow of the flash limned his scalp with white, almost as if the hair shone with some inner radiance. The light gleamed off the insignia on his shoulders, too, inside the open collar of his flight suit, and Dia moved one hand to strip them off. Outside the car, kilometers of stone whipped by. They were in his world now, for better or worse.

The vehicle slowed finally, stopped, settled to the floor of the tunnel. Nothing marked this portion of the tunnel as different from any other, but one of the telltales on the instrument panel was blinking red. Gently, Dia shook Talley awake.

"We seem to have arrived," she said, "or else this thing has broken down."

He sat up groggily. "Oh, we're here all right. Lift the hatch for me?"

With Dia's help he clambered out, found another hidden panel, and caused the cylinder to sink downward and be covered with a perfect camouflage of stone. Then he punched another button, and a section of the wall beside him swung inward, exposing an upward-angling tunnel. His arm across Dia's shoulders, one hand braced against the rocky wall, which here was almost dry, he began to climb. The incline was shallow, the roof well above their heads. After fifty or sixty paces, Dia was certain she saw a glimmer of light ahead. After a hundred paces, she knew that the light was artificial.

The cavern was vast, its ceiling vaulting thirty meters and more, the walls so distant that their detail blurred. In this open space, instead of tumbled limestone slabs, instead of fat stalagmites like half-melted trees, was a neat little underground village. One and two story buildings of dressed limestone blocks lined wide, clean-swept avenues. Tall tripod lamps stood at regular intervals along the streets, shedding a pale twilight upon them, and beneath these lamps and among these buildings walked men and women, and furry creatures that looked like Strux.

Dia's arms were gripped suddenly from behind. Looking over her shoulder, she found she was in the custody of a tall, stern-faced man. She could have broken his grip, but she chose not to. Talley had been taken similarly by a husky woman—two guards at the entry to the village, *only to be expected*, Dia told herself.

Talley gasped in pain. "Damn you, Fairborne, you know me!"

His captor let him go abruptly, then caught him as he collapsed, easing him to the floor. "We didn't expect you," she said in gruff apology. "Especially not in those clothes."

Talley pointed at Dia. "Let her go. She's with us."

Dia's guard let go but frisked her, taking the weapons. "You're hurt," Fairborne said to Talley.

He nodded. "I don't think I can make it any farther under my own power. Better get help. And we've got some evidence to hide back at Station Eight, fast. An aircraft. Top priority."

Fairborne pulled a communicator from her belt, repeated Talley's message to it, and ordered a litter. While she was talking, the nearest strollers, both human and alien, were beginning to approach. They all seemed to know who Tally was, murmuring his name to each other, some even addressing him. He closed his eyes and ignored them, and Fairborne tried to wave them away; they did not leave at her gesture, but they did fall silent, waiting in a ring around Dia, Talley, and the guards for the next act of the drama. The ring parted to let the litter through. The two men who carried it eased Talley onto it with practiced smoothness. Then they lifted their burden and marched in neat tandem toward the nearest avenue. The crowd followed, leaving the guards and Dia at the subway entrance.

Dia looked at the guards. "Am I free to go?"

Fairborne shrugged. "Dr. Magramor vouched for you. I can't stop you."

So he's a real V.I.P., Dia thought. *Like Velicher said.* A chill touched her back. She could almost hear his voice again: "We must and will be ready in two weeks." Were there really only two weeks left for these guards, this village, Talley? For ex-lieutenant Dia Catlin? Her brain was foggy with fatigue. She couldn't think. She didn't want to think. Because every time her brain started working, it came up with the same conclusion.

And this time, she knew, there would be no memorial plaque in the Citadel Square. Not for a traitor.

TWO

Dia trudged down the central avenue of the village, weariness lapping at her bones. She had been awake too long, under too much stress, and at last her body was failing her. She felt as though her flesh were dead metal that must be forced forward, one short step after another, and only by sheer willpower would her muscles undertake the task. Talley and the pursuing crowd had disappeared rapidly down this same street, leaving her nothing to follow, not even a clear memory. The guards had pointed her toward the hospital, his destination. You can't miss it, they said, not in a village this size. Largest building on the street, and the word HOSPITAL in big plastic letters clamped to the front wall. Double-wide doorway, always open. Bright lights inside, human-level lighting, much stronger than the tripod lamps.

Talley was safe now, surrounded by his friends, and Dia was safe, too, at this moment, surrounded by no one. She wanted to lie down and rest, there in the street, on the cold, hard stone. A couple of people passed her, eyed her briefly, but did not stop. She wondered if they would stop if she fell, if they would gather around her and call for a litter and carry her to the hospital, too. It seemed so much easier than trying to walk the whole way, even though the guards said it wasn't far. Nothing was far, they said, in the cavern. Nothing was far, except that the hospital seemed to be on the other side of the world.

Pride kept her going. *I can walk it. I don't need their help. Show them the stubborn Patroller*, she thought. *The stubborn ex-Patroller*. Pride, she knew, was all she had left.

Buildings crept by in dreamlike slow motion. Low, arched doorways sealed with dark panels, small square win-

dows shuttered with the same. Houses on shallow plat-
forms, ankle-high to the street, as if there were some threat
of occasional water, though there were no drains at the
curbs. *Well, where would it go?* she thought. *We're already underground.* But that was hard to believe, harder
with each passing moment. The air was dank, true, but
no danker than on a night promising rain. A faint breeze
blew from the direction of the subway entrance. The ceiling was virtually invisible—it might as well be an overcast
sky, no moon or stars showing through the clouds. As long
as she didn't look past the houses to the cavern walls, the
illusion persisted. It was aided by the growing things along
the fronts of some of the houses—pale-stemmed, fragile-
looking things, no larger than her little finger, topped with
down-turned cups. In the lamp-spawned twilight, they
looked like flowers, strange leafless flowers springing from
darker strips on the cream-colored cavern floor, but she
knew they must be fungi—nothing else could grow with so
little light.

She lost track of how long she had been walking. The
avenue seemed to stretch on and on, as if it were length-
ening ahead of her. She turned around once, to make sure
she had not passed the hospital, and was surprised to see
how little ground she had covered; the two guards at the
subway entrance were clearly visible, though she thought
they would have vanished in the distance by now. She
closed her eyes and swayed on her feet a moment. *It's
just reaction. I can't really be this tired.* She fumbled at her
belt for one of the emergency kits, pulled a nut bar from
it and gnawed at one end. *Sugar,* she thought, savoring the
sweetness of the bar. *I just need some sugar.* Whether it was
the sugar itself or just the idea of delivering nutrients into
her bloodstream, she felt a little better afterward and
turned to walk again.

HOSPITAL.

She almost passed it, so mechanical was her pace by
then. With an effort, she climbed the steps and entered the
two-story structure.

Just inside the doorway was a waiting room, suddenly
warm in contrast to the coolness of the cavern. A few people stood around it, talking softly. Dia hardly saw them.
She found a chair, a deep, cushioned chair that tilted back
as she sank into it. Her head drooped, her eyelids eased
shut, and she dozed.

Only a moment seemed to pass before a touch on her shoulder wakened her, and a furry, goggled face greeted her opening eyes. For a second, she thought it must be Strux, but then she recalled that he had to be parsecs away, en route from Avdotya with the fleet.

"Are you in good health, Lieutenant Catlin?" the creature inquired.

She smiled tiredly. "Very good health, but I need some rest."

"Come with me," it said, taking her hand in its warm paw.

She stood, and for the first time she realized how small Strux's people were; like a six-year-old child, this one barely cleared her waist. Its walk was a rapid waddle, tail twitching with every step. It led her along a short corridor to a small, windowless room where a bed and a toilet cubicle occupied almost the entire floor space.

"This is yours, Lieutenant," it said. "Should you require anything, an attendant is on duty at all times in the pharmacy across the hall."

"Thank you." She fell on the bed and was asleep immediately.

In her dreams, she found herself once more in the subway, passenger on another cylinder, but this time her route was straight down. She stood on the transparent front plate, and the tunnel rushed upward between her feet. Talley hovered beside her, weightless in the wild fall, and he jostled her as he floated, saying, "Welcome, welcome, welcome to the underworld."

She woke feeling refreshed in spite of the dream. Sitting up in bed, she discovered that she had been undressed and tucked beneath a fluffy comforter. The room contained a chair now, crowded beside the bed; her flight suit and uniform hung on the back of it, and clean civilian clothes were draped on the seat. She donned the latter—pale blue flannel shirt, black slacks, a leather jacket. Without rank insignia, her uniform tunic looked naked, and as she lifted it in her hands, the lightweight fabric felt somehow alien, as if all those years she had spent wearing it belonged to someone else. *Forgive me, Poppa.*

The weapons were gone, but the *Memoirs* of the first Brigadier remained in the tunic pocket, and the emergency kits were still clipped to the belt. Hungry and thirsty, she breakfasted on a nut bar and cold water from the cubicle's tiny sink. She ran her fingers through her hair and turned to the door.

The hall was empty, but as the furry creature had said, there was someone at the pharmacy. She sat at a desk, reading. As Dia approached, she looked up. "Good afternoon, Lieutenant Catlin. Can I help you?"

Dia glanced at her chronometer. 1345 in the Citadel's time zone. She couldn't guess what time it was here, wherever here might be. Not that it mattered. "Good afternoon. Is Doctor Magramor awake?"

"No, he'll be sleeping for some hours yet."

"All right." She pointed to the corridor behind her. "Am I allowed to go out and look around?"

The woman frowned. "It wouldn't be a good idea, not without a guide—you might get lost." She closed her book firmly. "You must be hungry. I have some cold meat back here, and a pot of coffee."

"I'll only walk around the building. I was too tired when we got here to take a good look at the place."

"Why don't you eat something first?"

Dia shrugged, sensing the imperative behind the suggestion. "All right."

By the time Dia had consumed lunch another person had arrived, a man of middling height and age—summoned, she was sure, by a hidden alarm. He nodded perfunctorily at the pharmacy attendant, who found some mumbled excuse to retreat to the back of the room, and he leaned against the doorjamb, gazing at Dia.

"Hello, Lieutenant Catlin."

"It certainly is nice that everyone here knows me," Dia said, "but it does put me at a disadvantage." She smiled into his brilliant blue eyes, trying to divine their familiarity, and then her glance skimmed down his body to his boots of fine Kyrlian leather. "Ah, Mr. Unknown. I perceive we meet again. And you are far handsomer than I ever suspected—really, the mask did not become you."

"Very astute, Lieutenant."

"I trust you haven't any plans for torturing me this time. After all, I'm on your side now."

"Are you?"

"Ask the doctor if you don't believe me."

He shook his head. "Why, Lieutenant? Why are you here?"

"You ought to know the answer to that, John. It's your fault."

"Mine?" He was suddenly defensive, his voice rising in the single word. "What are you talking about?"

"Well, if you hadn't threatened to torture me, the doctor wouldn't have set me free; I wouldn't have told the Patrol about him, he wouldn't have been hunted down, *he* wouldn't have been tortured at the Citadel, and I wouldn't have been compelled to rescue him. It's very simple, isn't it?"

"All except that last part."

"Ah, the last part . . . well, I'm sure Talley could explain it to you. He seemed to understand."

"You had quite a few weapons with you when you arrived, Lieutenant."

"I wouldn't have been able to get out of the Citadel without them." She folded her arms across her chest. "And John, drop the 'Lieutenant,' please. I'm not a Patroller anymore."

"Very well, Miss Catlin," he said. "You realize, of course, that you are a prisoner."

"I presumed I would be. Though when Talley vouched for me back at the subway entrance, the guards didn't seem interested in me anymore. I could have gone anywhere then, you know. I didn't have to come here."

"Not anywhere," he said. "You couldn't have gotten out of the cavern without authorization. And the place isn't so large that we couldn't have found you, no matter where you tried to hide."

"But I didn't try to leave. Ask Fairborne if you don't believe me. And I didn't try to hide. I came straight here. Doesn't that give you sort of an impression . . . that I want to cooperate?"

"I'm not jumping to any conclusions, Lieutenant—sorry, *Miss* Catlin."

"I think you are. I think you've decided I'm a spy."

He showed his teeth in an expression that wasn't quite a smile. "Let's just say that I trust you somewhat less than the doctor does. Therefore, for the time being, you are restricted to this building."

Dia shrugged. "You're giving the orders."

"We'll speak further when the doctor awakens."

"I'm sure we will." She left the pharmacy and walked to her room without looking back.

She closed the door. Faced with an indefinite length of empty time, she took the *Memoirs* out of her pocket; the volume might be requisitioned soon, and she wanted to read it first. She wanted to know what truths were there, what secrets; what black, unmentionable secrets. That was why she had taken it—the penultimate disobedience.

Tucked under a flap on the bottom of each emergency kit was a small knife; Dia fished one out and attacked the transparent strap that sealed the book. Tough material though it was, it yielded ultimately, though the knife was considerably dulled in the process. Dia settled back on the bed, doubling over the pillow to prop her head up.

The first sentence:

I was a career Patrol officer, like my parents and their parents before them.

Dia read on, thinking, *We have something in common, Bohannon and I. Or we used to.*

THREE

She turned the last page and closed the book. Now she knew the man Marcus Bohannon, knew his inmost hopes and fears, his dreams, his goals. But not his uncertainties. There were no uncertainties in the *Memoirs;* there was only the great design to bring back the glory of the Patrol, and Bohannon never doubted that it could be accomplished. He had been young, as officers of the old Patrol went, back when the rank of Brigadier was not the highest of them all. He had expected to become Commander-in-Chief someday. But his ambitions were short-circuited by the dissolution of the Federation, and he had chosen to become Commander-in-Chief of twenty ships rather than none at all.

He cared nothing for Amphora or the Amphorans. He merely used the planet as a munitions factory, with the people at forced labor—not for their own good, as young Patrollers had been taught, but for the fulfillment of his greater plan of conquest. He must have known that his dream could not be realized in his lifetime; he left it as a legacy to the descendants of his body and mind.

Part of his passion was the drive for vengeance; those whose decision had abolished his career would be brought low. Part of his passion was a drive for glory, for the medals and the scrolls and the public adulation that accompanied successful military exploits; if he could not win them from the Federation, he would wrest them from a conquered empire. Part of his passion was a salve for wounded pride; he would show the universe—and, more immediately, the officers of his own small fleet—that a Brigadier of the Patrol was not a man to be decommissioned and given some sop of a job behind a civilian desk.

Now Dia knew why only upper-level officers were allowed to read the volume, for there was shame in it, and pettiness, and megalomania. Yet for all his flaws, Brigadier Bohannon had set in motion a planet-sized machine that had not ceased to churn out war materiel. Slowly at first, because the people of Amphora had never previously bothered with much heavy industry, factories had been built and workers trained, till now almost a third of the adult population labored for the Patrol. After eighty years, great stockpiles of ships and equipment existed on the planet. Not nearly as much as Velicher had detailed at the Staff meeting, but enough, surely enough, to take the rest by force from the planet where they were stored away. The old Patrol HQ.

But HQ was eleven weeks away. If the Patrol would be ready in two weeks, that meant the mothball fleets under its command were already on their way to Amphora. Velicher must have sent an expedition to hijack them as soon as he heard about Strux.

Well, I'm sure the rebels will be delighted to find out that I've made it possible for their allies to take on the biggest fleet in the history of the Galaxy.

She rolled off the bed and went in search of Unknown, but all she found was locked doors and the pharmacy attendant.

"You'd better call your superior," Dia said to her. "I have some interesting news."

"He's with Doctor Magramor."

"Is Talley awake?"

"Yes, he is."

"Can I see him?"

"Not right now."

"Which door is his?"

"Third on the right."

Dia headed for it.

"You can't go in!" called the attendant.

"I can sit in front of it till it opens," Dia replied.

She listened at the panel, but it was soundproofed, so she settled on the floor to leaf through the *Memoirs* and fold down the corners of the most significant pages. She wondered if Unknown would suggest she be executed for her crimes against the revolution. The possibility worried her little—after so many weeks as the Brigadier's aide, she was too valuable to kill. The ignorant transport co-pilot had been transformed into a fount of information.

Unknown almost stepped on her when he came out. "I was just about to call you," he said, pulling the door shut behind him.

She climbed to her feet. "Good. I wanted to talk to you, too."

"The doctor seems quite sure of your sincerity. I hope he isn't wrong."

"I hope Strux wasn't wrong."

"What do you mean?"

"When he said he was on the winning side." She held the book up. "You'll find this significant reading, especially the pages I've marked."

"I haven't time for reading, Miss Catlin."

"No? Well, I'd suggest you find time, before the Patrol fleets arrive."

He frowned. "What are you talking about?"

"Brigadier Velicher sent a task force to commandeer the fleets that were in storage at the old Patrol Headquarters. They should be here in something like two weeks."

Unknown snatched the book from her hands, looked at the spine. "Bohannon—the first Brigadier. That was eighty years ago. What does this have to do with those ships?"

"It was Bohannon's idea, spelled out in that book. I heard enough at Staff meetings to make me reasonably sure that Velicher is implementing it."

He growled deep in his throat. "Something like two weeks, you say? How much like it?"

"I don't know exactly when they left Amphora, but if it was the earliest conceivable date, and if they were lucky and efficient . . . well, Velicher said two weeks, but I figure it could be as little as six days from now."

His fingers tightened on the volume. "Well, it doesn't matter. It doesn't matter at all." He shoved the book into a pocket of his jacket, and then he slid the door open. "Go on in if you want."

She stepped inside a room twice as large as her own. Behind her, the door closed. Unknown had stayed in the corridor. Before her was Talley, sitting up in bed, eating a light meal. One of the furry creatures was curled up on a bedside chair.

Talley smiled at her. "Have they fed you?"

"I had lunch. How are you feeling?"

"Strux says I'll live."

"Strux?"

"Ask him yourself." He waved at his furry companion.

Dia stared at Strux's twitching nose; she sensed that he was laughing silently, knowing quite well that she had failed to recognize him. "I thought you were with the Avdotyan fleet—not due for at least three weeks."

"What gave you that idea?" said Strux.

"Why . . . that's what Talley told the Patrol interrogators."

"Well," said Talley, "I may have lied a little under duress."

Dia was confused. She looked at Strux. "Didn't you go? Or . . ." And now she felt a light dawning. "Have you been here all along? Your entire fleet?"

Strux answered, "Indeed, we are all here, and have been for quite some time."

Dia wondered how they had escaped detection by the Patrol's system-wide sensor net. But there were more urgent matters to discuss. She said, "Then you'd better make your move now."

"Why?" asked Talley.

She spoke of the book, the Brigadier's confident two-week target date, the old HQ, the oncoming ships.

Talley was frozen for a moment when she finished, his eyes unblinking, their gaze turned inward. Then he glanced at Strux, and some message passed between them. Strux's whiskers twitched, and his fur rippled as muscles beneath the skin shifted and tensed; no longer did he merely lie upon the chair—rather, he crouched there, as if ready to spring upon an enemy.

"Here," murmured Talley. "Yes, it's here all right. We can't afford to wait any longer." Gingerly, he touched his sheeted thigh with one hand. "I suppose I won't be taking a very active role."

Hesitantly, she said, "Did they . . . do much damage?"

He shrugged. "Burns mostly. Very unpleasant smell, charring flesh. They doctored me somewhat, afterward."

"You will heal," said Strux.

"Ah yes, the marvels of medicine."

"Velicher watched," Dia said. "Part of the time, at least."

Talley nodded slowly. "I'm not surprised. I suspected he had a strong streak of sadism in him. Roppolo certainly has, and his assistant. Do they recruit that kind special for Intelligence, or are all Patrollers like that?"

"Not all." Her voice was very low.

"Most?"

She swallowed thickly. "I don't know. I don't know anything about the Patrol any more. Everything I thought I knew . . . turns out to be wrong." She looked down at the sheet, at the long ridges that were his legs beneath that whiteness. "I caught Velicher watching. So I saw, too. More than I wanted to see." Now her memory played the scene back, imagination adding the details too small for resolution on the viewscreen—the blackened, crisping rims encircling raw, oozing meat. For a moment, the old horror of Michael's death washed over her once more, and she swayed on her feet.

Talley caught at her arm and said, "I think you'd better sit down." He moved over to make room for her at the edge of the bed. "I didn't feel much of it. Implanted nerve blocks took care of that."

"Do not be deceived, Miss Catlin," said Strux. "Implanted nerve blocks are of limited efficacy; otherwise the carrier cannot function."

"Don't make me too much of a hero, Strux. I didn't suffer as much as an unprotected person would have. And I made my confession before they did any permanent damage."

Strux slipped off his chair and, putting one paw on Talley's near arm, said, "Miss Catlin's news will undoubtedly stimulate considerable discussion. If you have no need of me at present, I would like to add my opinions to the debate."

"Go on, Strux. I'll be all right."

The door opened barely wide enough for his exit.

Talley took Dia's left hand in both of his own. "I never did say thank you."

She raised her eyes to his face, letting the sight of his unblemished features banish the last tatters of nightmare from her mind. "Velicher was going to have you killed. Slowly. You represented all rebels to him. By killing you he was destroying the rebellion, symbolically. He hates you all so much."

"Because he knows he can never really defeat us."

"Maybe. Or maybe . . . because unrest here on Amphora is holding the Patrol back from greater things."

His eyes narrowed. "Greater things? You don't really think he wants to fulfill Bohannon's dream, do you? That's a hell of a job. The Federation was awfully big. I'd guess that if it was too big to be a Federation, it's too big to be an Empire."

"I don't know. Why else keep the *Memoirs* a secret? Sure, they give a negative image of the first Brigadier. He wasn't the pure, altruistic hero they told us about in school. But Patrollers could live with that truth if later Brigadiers had been different. If their ideals were truth for *our* generation. But the *Memoirs* are still secret, so maybe Bohannon's goals are still the Patrol's. Maybe Velicher himself wasn't planning on leading the conquest; maybe he figured that would be up to some future Brigadier. But now . . . suddenly he'll have all those ships. It'll be so damned tempting. What else would he do with them afterward?"

"You think . . . we're going to lose?"

She shook her head wearily. "I don't know. The Patrol is stronger than I ever dreamed. And they know so much now; about you, the Avdotyans, everything."

He pursed his lips. "They don't know that much. I had plenty of information left to give them. I was going to string them out, tantalize them with bits and pieces, and hope my friends would rescue me before anything drastic happened." He shrugged. "Maybe that wasn't a very realistic hope. But it was all I had, and a lot better than constantly reminding myself that I probably didn't have long to live." He slipped one arm around her waist and drew her closer, till their hips touched, though the sheet was bunched between them. "And suddenly, like a miracle, there was a friend." He leaned his forehead against hers. "I suppose this makes us even . . . though I have to admit your job was a lot harder than mine."

"It just took nerve."

"And now you're with us."

"Absolutely."

"Why, Dia? Why throw away your whole career just to . . . pay a debt?"

She sighed softly. "Don't you know?"

His voice was low. "Tell me."

"A career based on honor is hollow when the honor itself is hollow. When the morality behind it is a sham; when all you have is the gleaming suit of armor, but nothing inside it. That's something you knew all along, and it took me a while to learn."

"Is that all?"

She closed her eyes. "No." Her fingers traced his collar bone where it showed above the hospital gown. "I couldn't be a Patroller any more if the Patrol killed you. I couldn't face it. Your life meant more to me than any career."

His breath fluttered her hair, and he moved his hand up to smooth the few straying wisps back into place. "You know, you were right, back at the cave."

"About what?"

He tipped her face up and smiled. "You really are beautiful." Then they kissed and he pulled her back against the mounded pillows, holding her as close and tight as she held him. For a long moment they breathed each other's breath, and then he loosened his embrace with a sigh. "I'm not in any condition for this. My medical conscience tells me that if I don't let you go, I'll mess up all of Strux's work and keep myself out of action for an extra week." He interlocked his fingers with hers. "Eventually, we'll both be whole and healthy at the same time."

"If the world doesn't come to an end first," she murmured. "What will happen, Talley? Will the Avdotyan fleet attack immediately? I'm sure that's the best course. No one at the Citadel even dreams that it's here already."

"Our leaders will want to talk to you. You seem to have a wealth of information."

She raised his hand to her cheek, pressed it there with strong fingers. "You made me famous, Talley. Everyone wanted to hear about my adventures underground. Even the Brigadier. He was so impressed that he made me his aide."

"So—no longer the ignorant junior officer."

Now she had to tell him the rest. "I became his lover, too."

He caught a breath, then exhaled long and slow. His voice dropped to a whisper. "I'm not surprised." He kissed her fingers. "You're not a woman that many men could let be lonely. And the Commander-in-Chief would certainly beat out all the competition."

"I did it for my career, Talley. I didn't love him."

He smiled wryly. "He didn't seem a very lovable fellow, the one time I met him."

Dia recalled the interview in the detention cell with pain. "I think I must have begun to hate him then. He didn't seem quite human afterward. But I stayed with him. For my career."

"That doesn't seem strange . . . for a Patroller."

She gazed at him levelly. "You must know that if it hadn't been for my report, you would never have been hunted down."

"That was a chance I took when I let you go. I assumed a loyal Patrol officer would do her duty and spill everything."

"I can't regret it, Talley," she said softly. "For what I was, that was the only proper thing to do."

"I understand."

"Michael would have been proud of me." She frowned. His name still brought pain. His memory still had power to touch her. But he could not make her feel any shame. Not now. She gripped Talley's arm tightly. "I used to evaluate everything by his standards—the Patrol's standards. I was a good officer. I never questioned my superiors; I assumed they had to be right. And then. . . . Because of you, I was suddenly not an ordinary troop anymore. I was a hero, an important person; I was working in the Brigadier's office and sleeping in the Brigadier's bed. I was seeing and hearing things I shouldn't have seen or heard for another twenty years. And I didn't like it. My family was so proud of me, all they could see was *status*. But *I* could see lies, and I wasn't ready to know they were lies." She shook her head, feeling as if cobwebs were parting inside. "Small lies. Big ones. Nothing about the Patrol was quite as . . . as clean as I had been brought up to think. But the biggest lie of all was the one we'd been told by our own parents. That we were here to protect Amphora; that we were making this planet safe for the people who lived here. That we *cared* about them. I was so proud of that when I graduated from the Academy. I was so proud of it when you and I argued about it, when you said the Patrol was here for its own benefit. I *knew* you were wrong." She paused. "But you weren't wrong. The Patrol doesn't care about the people; it only cares about the real estate. Maybe if I'd risen in the ranks the ordinary way, maybe that attitude would have grown on me slowly. Maybe I wouldn't have noticed my feelings shifting. Maybe I would have wound up hating all of you . . . you colonials." She looked him in the eye, sad and serious. "They do, you know. The upper level officers. They hate you all, not just the rebels. It's . . . official policy."

"I've often suspected it."

She bent her head to his shoulder and closed her eyes. His skin smelled faintly of sweat and disinfectant. "But I couldn't. Not after meeting you. And now I don't care what Michael would think any more. He's part of the life I'm finished with. You're here, alive, and so am I, and that's all that matters."

Lightly, he stroked her neck. "You know . . . if we lose, you'll be in big trouble."

"I won't be the only one."

His lips brushed her temple. "I know a deep, dark cavern where they'll never think of looking."

"Sounds wonderful."

"I love you, Dia. Back in the cave I wanted so much to forget that we were enemies. I wanted to hold you in my arms and blot out everything else. I've thought of you so often since then."

"And I've thought of you, and wanted you . . . and wouldn't admit it to myself."

Their mouths met and clung for a long moment, but at last he pushed her away. "That's enough for now; you'd better get off this bed."

She sat in the chair that Strux had vacated, edging it closer to the bed till her hand could rest in his. He fell asleep clutching her fingers, and she must have dozed as well, for a series of sharp raps at the door jarred her like hammer blows. Talley woke, rubbed his eyes, and called out permission to enter.

A throng of men and women surged in.

"We have questions, Miss Catlin," said the man she called Unknown, "and we've decided to bring them here, where Doctor Magramor can listen, too." He nudged the two men nearest him and pointed to the wall on his left. "Take that down." In a few moments they had tripled the size of the room, exposing empty beds that could be used as seats.

Unknown sat atop a tall stool at the foot of Talley's bed. He leaned forward, his gaze keen on Dia's face, the hunter in sight of his quarry. Dia felt Talley's fingers tighten on her own, and she glanced at him and grinned, unruffled. "How may I be of service, Mr. Interrogator?" she said to Unknown.

"Miss Catlin," he replied, "we are going to pick your brains."

And for three hours the questions came, from Unknown and from all corners of the room, from young men and middle-aged women, from grizzled elders and bright-eyed youths—all the diverse types that the Patrol had always lumped under a single name: rebel. She gave freely and in detail, everything she could remember—strategy and supply lines, troop allocations and aerial tactics, and all the intelligence on rebel activity that had passed through her hands.

"Of course, he'll assume I'm telling you all of this," she said, "but he thinks he still has a margin of three weeks in which to change his plans. I'd say your best hope would be a quick, decisive blow with the Avdotyan fleet. Fifty percent of the Patrol is in the Citadel right now. Take it—tomorrow, if you can. You can handle the oncoming ships later—they'll be undermanned; without help from the ground they'll have a tough time against even a substantially smaller force."

"Why undermanned?" asked Unknown.

"I was in the Citadel when the operation must have been launched, but I didn't even hear a rumor about it then. To keep it that quiet, it had to be small, maybe less than a thousand troops, and none of them drawn from the Citadel itself. That means the returning ships will only have skeleton crews; Velicher probably intends to bring them down at the Citadel spaceport and staff them there. He recently told me to keep up my flying hours, that he'd need every officer he had for something big coming up. A couple of hundred good-sized ships would take that many."

"I would agree that we must take the Citadel," said Unknown.

"It won't be easy," Dia told him. Her throat constricted at the thought of Sydney and her father as casualties, but she felt compelled to give her honest opinion. "You'll probably have to bomb it to rubble before they'll surrender."

"There will be no bombing," he replied, and at his peremptory gesture, a youth from the rear of the crowd came forward, carrying a large sheaf of papers. Unknown spread several of them out on the floor, and each measured a meter on a side; their surfaces were covered with incomplete architectural plans. "We have sketchy cross-sections of all the Citadel buildings. You're a native—we want you to fill them in. Weapons stores, offices and quarters of high-echelon officers, strategic positions, vehicles, communications."

"What do you think you're going to do?" she gasped. "A ground force couldn't get within ten kilometers of the outer wall, and there's no way in from above until the air defenses are destroyed!"

"Let us worry about that, Miss Catlin. Get to work."

She accepted a stylus from his hands and knelt on the floor to study the first sketch. All around her, the crowd edged closer, and as she worked they snatched the pages that she set aside, passing them from hand to hand to peer at the details that filled in the diagrams. Occasionally, she had to call back a sheet to insert another item or to correct a first approximation. She knew the Citadel well, but still there were areas that she was uncertain about, and some that she was forced to leave blank. At last—it seemed like hours later—she rocked back on her heels.

"That's the best I can do, I think. Actually, you know quite a bit about the place. Velicher wasn't joking when he talked about spies."

"We've had plenty of time to collect that information," said Unknown. "Now that we've speeded the process up by a couple of orders of magnitude . . . I hope you haven't left out anything important."

"I don't think so. The antiaircraft emplacements are spaced along the outer walls here. I've marked the armories at the base of each tower. You have to remember, though, that there are also pistols stored at all the target ranges, and most people interested in competition have guns in their quarters." She glanced up at him. "If you do get inside, you'll be sniped at from all directions." When he made no reply, she continued. "The viewscreens all tie into the Central Switchboard in the South Tower *and* into the alternate switchboard in the North Tower—you'll have to take both of them to knock out communications. Staff offices and quarters are concentrated here and here, and Velicher's own are in the Central Tower." She pinpointed them with the stylus. "You'll run into strong opposition there, unless he's somewhere else. But I don't think he would be—that office is an extension of his personality, and he'd certainly direct the fight from there." She paused, frowning. "Frankly, I don't see how you could get that far. There are over fifty thousand Patrollers in the Citadel right now, and they're not going to let you walk in, even if they have to fight you hand to hand."

"Tell her," said Talley.

She had almost forgotten that the meeting was taking place in his enlarged hospital room, that he was watching and listening to everything. "Tell me what?" she asked.

Unknown said, "Doctor Magramor wants me to tell you our plans. He trusts you."

"Yes, I trust her," said Talley.

"He's read you fairly well until now, Miss Catlin—I have to admit that. But I'm not prepared to tell all to a person so recently our enemy."

"You'll tell her," said Talley, "because she's going to lead us into the Citadel."

"What?" croaked Dia.

Unknown shook his head. "No, we can't do it that way."

"We have to act now," said Talley, "before those ships get here. She has all the plans of the Citadel in her head. She knows how to move around inside, fast. And she was Velicher's aide—she knows all his habits, and every place he goes."

Unknown crossed his arms over his chest. "It can't depend on her. Not after so many years of careful planning."

"She's exactly what we need."

"Exactly what we need to raise the alarm at the wrong moment. You're out of your mind, Magramor!"

"I don't think so." Talley stretched his arm out toward Dia. "Come here."

She eyed Unknown as she took Talley's hand. "You misjudge me," she said. "I will do whatever I can to help you." Then her gaze shifted to Talley, and her fingers tightened on his. "But you can't expect me to throw my life away."

"We have a way into the Citadel," said Talley. "A way that bypasses all their safeguards. If we enter in Patrol uniform, a few of us at a time, we have a good chance to hit the armories, the comm centers, and even Velicher and his Staff before they realize something's wrong. We could use a native guide."

"How will we get in?"

"There's a tunnel."

"That's impossible. The foundations are wired for seismic disturbance—you can't do any digging without being detected."

"The sensors have been disconnected."

"How?"

Talley glanced toward the foot of the bed, where Unknown crouched, stony-faced. "I can tell her," he said, "and then we'll have made the decision."

Unknown straightened slowly. "All right, Doctor," he muttered. "We scanned her with microwave and sound while she slept—she isn't carrying any implanted transmitters. Whatever she hears now won't be passed on . . . *won't* be, because I will not leave her side from now until the operation is over. At the first suspicious action, though, I swear I'll kill her."

"You haven't changed at all," said Dia.

"Have you?"

"Yes."

He made a sound of disgust deep in his throat, and then he waved an arm at the crowd. "What are you all standing there for? You've got floor plans to memorize! Get out of here and let the doctor have some rest!"

The last few out replaced the walls that made the room a cubicle once more.

"I don't like you," said Unknown, when the three of them were alone.

"So I noticed," said Dia. Of Talley she inquired, "Are you the boss?"

"In a manner of speaking," he said. "I'm supposed to listen to his advice. Or he's supposed to listen to mine."

"Your father always took my advice," said Unknown.

"And look where he is today," replied Talley. "Events have come to a nexus, my friend, and we have to act."

"And here you are in bed!"

"I'll be with you. Just don't expect any gymnastics from me." He looked up into Dia's eyes. "You're coming, aren't you?"

"I thought we were going to hide in a cavern."

"I guess that will have to wait."

"Are you sure you're well enough to go?"

"No, but I'm going anyway. It's my father's plan, and I owe it to his memory to be there."

"You must have a pretty deep-rooted death wish."

"I think we can pull it off, if you come along."

"Not unless I know what I'm getting into."

He pulled her closer to the bed. "The tunnel was started twenty years ago, so you see this is not a hastily conceived scheme. For some time, it's been complete to within a meter of the lowest level of the Citadel—and according to your information, and some fairly reliable reports we had before, it will open into the armory at the base of the West Tower. It can be finished by tomorrow morning."

She shook her head. "I don't understand how you could have dug it without being detected."

"One small creature," he said, "burrowing a route no wider than its body—too small and silent to be picked up by instruments designed for earthquakes and heavy machinery. One small creature to start—to short out the sensors under the Citadel. After that, the tunnel was enlarged to accommodate human beings."

"What creature?" asked Dia.

"Strux. His people. Our allies."

"You mean Strux and his people have been here for twenty years? How could that be? You've only been back on Amphora a short time."

Talley smiled. "I've been back on Amphora for several years, but we decided to let the Patrol think otherwise. I returned on a trade ship; I was designated 'art objects' on the manifest. As for Strux and his people—they've been here a lot longer than twenty years. They're native to Amphora."

Dia glanced from Talley to Unknown. "There are no native intelligent life forms on Amphora," she said firmly, repeating verbatim the statement of every biology text she had ever seen.

"Amphora was colonized," said Unknown, "because the first explorers found no intelligent life."

"They were wrong," said Talley. "The natives were shy, nocturnal burrowers, and their society existed totally underground. They had domesticated animals and plants, a high-level metallurgical technology, an elaborate social organization, art, literature . . . all where no human could see them. The cavern we're in right now was originally a steelworks, with furnaces along one wall and huge vents to the surface. They moved the operation away and plugged the vents when a human settlement was established in the area, afraid the smoke would be seen. They nearly gave up large-scale metalworking, just to avoid discovery. For over a century they hid, and when they finally showed themselves, they posed as ordinary animals. Farmers would occasionally take them in as pets, never suspecting that those delightful creatures were learning human language over the shoulders of the farmer's children. Once in a while a child followed his straying pet into the woods and came home with a wild story about visiting 'the underground kingdom' . . . but he was almost never believed, and the story could never be checked. When they were quite ready, the burrowers let a few discreet humans in on their secret. My grandfather was one of them; he was taken down into the deep caverns where the burrowers have their cities. And the burrowers visited him in his home; as a child I romped with Strux as much as with my human friends. A little trade started up between species; the burrowers wanted things from the human society that they could not make for themselves. My grandfather gave them plastics in return for precious gems. The burrowers were very happy with the arrangement, but, being practical people, they realized that the status quo was only temporary. Someday, in spite of all the good intentions of their friends, the secret of their existence would leak out to the Patrol. The Patrol had been on Amphora for almost sixty years at that time, and the burrowers had been watching it from a distance for quite a while; they were sure that as soon as it discovered they were intelligent it would try to force them to work in its factories. They didn't care for that idea, and so they approached my family—which, like many families on Amphora, was not precisely in sympathy with the Patrol—to discuss getting rid of the newcomers."

Dia tried to digest all this information—an entire intelligent species plotting the downfall of a Patrol which didn't even suspect its existence. "But what about the Avdotyan fleet?"

"It doesn't exist."

"But Avdotya is real."

"Yes. I heard of it on Quixote, but the natives aren't interested in helping us. I'm sure they've never even heard of us."

"Then you invented it all under torture?"

He shook his head. "Not then. Those were carefully planned lies, Dia, designed to match the story we thought you had taken back with you. In fact, we let you go in order to be sure that some word of me, and of Strux, got back to the Patrol."

"Let me go? Ah . . ." Her voice drifted into a sigh. "It begins to make real sense now."

"We put on a show for you, Dia." He gripped her hand

tighter, as if afraid she would back away from him, though she made no move to do so. "Something of a show, anyway—enough to convince you that we had some trick up our sleeves that wasn't at all the actual trick. It was the perfect opportunity to start the Patrol working on a wrong hypothesis."

Dia nodded slowly. "They'll be looking toward the sky, but the threat will be coming from beneath their feet."

"From their own midst," said Unknown. "Remember, we'll be in uniform. We have plenty of Patrol uniforms."

"And when the task force comes back from the old headquarters planet, you'll just order them all to land, as if nothing had happened while they were gone."

"Exactly. I don't think we'll have any trouble managing them."

"Very clever," she said softly. "Very neatly thought out."

"There was just one thing that wasn't part of the plan," Talley said. "One thing that wasn't part of the show. My falling in love with you. Believe me, Dia; that was real."

She smiled. "I believe you." Then she shook her head. "But how can I possibly go along?" She turned to Unknown. "How can Talley go? Someone might recognize us. I'll bet our faces have been splashed on every viewscreen in the Citadel!"

"We'll bleach your hair blond," said Talley, "and dye mine dark. And I'll get rid of the beard and mustache."

"I'd feel better with plastic surgery."

"I could give you some facial implants, but there's no time for the bruises to heal. Dentures might help—over your own teeth, altering the set of your jaw. It won't be very comfortable, but you'll look a lot less like you."

She looked down at their clasped hands, a silent promise atop the white sheet. "I'll go on one condition: that my parents and my sister won't be harmed."

"We can't make that kind of promise," said Unknown. "A lot of people are going to be killed in this operation—we can't gurantee anyone's safety."

"Then you'll go without me."

"The teams assigned to them will have orders not to shoot unless shot at," Talley said firmly, the statement aimed at Unknown rather than Dia.

Unknown's mouth pursed in disgust. "All right, if that's the way you want it. I don't much care for this special treatment business, though."

"What if they were your parents, John?" murmured Dia. "They're Patrollers."

"Stop it!" said Talley. "We owe her that much. *I* do, anyway." There was a shadow in his eyes when he looked at her, and she knew he was remembering his own home, his own family when he said, "I don't want to be responsible for killing your parents."

She bent forward, brushing his cheek with her nose. "All right, I'm with you." Into his ear, she whispered, "You should have confessed to them earlier . . . so that I could sample what I'll be risking my life for."

His arms slid around her. "I had to make it look like a real breakdown."

"Was your capture part of the plan?"

"It was a recognized possibility, but I didn't go out of my way to help it along."

She sighed. "I wish we were in that deep, dark cavern right now."

"We'll get there. Afterward." Softly, he kissed her neck.

Unknown jostled the bed as he slid off his stool. "We have things to do if we're going to strike immediately."

Talley released Dia from his embrace. "Tomorrow night," he suggested. "At about 0300, Citadel time. That's a pretty quiet hour, isn't it?"

"The quietest," she replied. "Can we be ready so fast?"

"We've been ready for months," said Unknown. "Just waiting for the proper moment."

"We never had a better chance than now," Talley said. "Broadcast the ultimatum." He gave Dia's hand a last squeeze. "Go with him. I have to get some sleep."

FOUR

The recorded ultimatum, Unknown explained, awaited transmission from a remote automated microwave station. The signal would bounce off the Patrol's own satellite relay system and be picked up almost simultaneously everywhere on Amphora; civilians and Patrollers alike would see and hear the commander of the Avdotyan fleet request the surrender of the planet.

"And who is the commander of the Avdotyan fleet?" inquired Dia.

"You may recognize him," replied Unknown.

They walked among single-story buildings toward one edge of the village, on a curving street well-lit by pearly lamps. People passed them—humans and burrowers alike—moving purposefully, offering only the curtest of salutations to Unknown and he to them. He strode too quickly for Dia's taste, and she kept trying to lag behind. She wanted to examine the buildings more closely. She realized now that their proportions were suited to Strux's people, the verticals too short for humans; only the hospital was built to human dimensions. She wanted to touch those dark doors in their arched entranceways, those doors that looked so much like wood but had to be something else, for such a damp environment would make wood rot quickly. . . . Plastic, she thought, perhaps courtesy of Talley's grandfather. And she wanted to pluck a few of those fragile-looking fungus blooms, whose thimble-sized caps she now saw were colored scarlet, like fresh-spilled blood. But Unknown wanted to walk fast, and he jogged her elbow frequently.

"Is this village old?" she asked him.

"I wouldn't know," he said brusquely. "I wasn't here when they built it."

"And if you did know," she murmured, "you wouldn't tell me. Only what's absolutely necessary, with an implication that the information won't do the Patrol any good."

"I'm glad we understand each other."

"You think so?"

"I do. If I had my way, you'd be blindfolded the whole time you were here. Unfortunately, the doctor doesn't agree with me on that."

"Thank goodness," said Dia. "Being blindfolded would be an awful bore."

He jerked her arm. "Come on."

They reached the edge of the village, almost directly opposite the subway entrance. Stone drapery cloaked the cavern wall there, tier after tier of it, like a still picture of water tumbling down a cliffside. As cloth curtains would frame a doorway, the stone draperies parted to either side of a tunnel entrance. At the top of the arching opening, only half a meter above Dia's head, the broken stumps of stalactites showed that the aperture had been artificially enlarged.

"In here," said Unknown, waving Dia ahead of him.

"Don't trust me behind your back, hmm?" She stepped into the tunnel. The floor curved upward on either side, leaving only a narrow path flat enough for comfortable progress. It was clean-swept, and here and there she thought she could detect a spot where a stalagmite had been chipped away to make passage easier. Lights smaller than those in the cavern were bolted to the walls, and Dia, letting her hand brush by one sconce, determined by the tap of her fingers that they must be plastic.

The tunnel angled upward gradually and branched several times, and each branch was upward-slanted, and well-lit—obviously, Dia thought, frequently used. She asked Unknown if they led to other caverns and other villages, but she hardly expected an answer and did not receive one. She stopped at each new tunnel mouth and leaned inside, but she saw nothing beyond rock and more rock. And always, Unknown was close behind, crowding her forward.

"Memorizing the layout, are you?" he said when she stopped for the fifth time. "Aim to do for the Patrol what you've done for us?"

She looked at him coldly. "I think I'll take that as a joke. A poor joke."

"Think about it from my point of view for once, Miss

Catlin. You'll want to be valuable. You'll want to be able to say that you know everything about this particular rebel stronghold."

"Aside from natural curiosity," she said tightly, "I'm thinking more that if you disappear, I don't want to be lost underground. I don't want you to be able to go back to Talley and say that I took a wrong turn and you couldn't find me again."

"Or you're just looking for a way out, so you can make your report."

She faced him, her hands curling into fists. "You know, I could knock you down. It wouldn't be hard at all, you're such a big target."

"It wouldn't prove anything."

"No, I suppose not. But it would make me feel good."

"Do you want to try? I'm not exactly defenseless, you know."

"And it would give you a great excuse to have me locked up in spite of Talley. Is that what you want? Are you *trying* to provoke me?"

His lips twisted into a parody of a smile. "Just speaking my mind, Miss Catlin. We rebels do that, among ourselves."

Dia opened her fists with an effort. "Well, since I'm a rebel now, I'll speak *my* mind, John X. You grate on me. Bad. For Talley's sake, I am willing to be civil to you. I hope, and perhaps it is a vain hope, that in future you will make a similar effort. It will be better that way, if we're to work together."

"Are we really working together?" he said.

"Damn you!" she muttered, and she turned her back on him, facing in the direction they had been walking. "Do we have much farther to go?"

"Not much." He prodded the small of her back. "Go on."

Grim-faced, she walked, and she heard him follow, heard his boots crunching on the grit of the tunnel floor. After a time, that last sound registered through the haze of anger that made her legs pump stiffly and her heart beat hard at the inside of her chest. Grit. Elsewhere, the cavern and tunnel floors were clean-swept. Only in the last few dozen meters, since the fifth tunnel branch, had there been particulate matter underfoot; she looked down, and she could see the grains, some as large as fine gravel. And some of it was dark, like soil. She sniffed at the air, seeking the

scent of greenery, guessing that the grit had been tracked
in from outside. She thought there must be an entrance
nearby. But the air of the tunnel was only the cool breeze
of the depths, rising from behind her.

The sixth side tunnel was different from the rest. By the
time they reached it, Dia judged they had climbed almost
a hundred meters above the level of the village, and the
detritus was heavier than ever. She stopped at the tunnel
mouth and peered in, and even when Unknown prodded
her, she stayed there, staring. The tunnel was a little wider
than the one in which they stood, and just as high, but all
along one side, limestone blocks had been laid to form a
continuous pavement a meter higher than the floor. This
made two lanes for single-file traffic, the higher one putting the ceiling within reach of a burrower. And on that
ceiling, completely cloaking the hard surface, were masses
of twisted roots, some of them hanging so low that a human
would have to stoop to pass through the tunnel. They were
near the surface indeed, Dia realized, for plants to have
broken through the tunnel roof. Yet *broken* did not seem
an appropriate word, for this tunnel was as well-lit as any
of the others and there was no large debris on the floor to
suggest real damage. It was obviously in use; if the roots
interfered, they would have been cut away. Yet they
seemed to interfere, hanging so low.

"What *is* all of that?" she said at last, as Unknown
gripped her arm to pull her along.

"What does it look like?"

"Plants."

"Very astute. Now come on."

She tried to shake him off. "Camouflage? There's an
entrance around here, isn't there?"

"No."

"You're lying. We're near the surface."

"Obviously. But that doesn't mean there's an entrance
here. Not all caves are a kilometer underground, you
know."

"Then why don't you get rid of the plants? It would
make walking easier. And I know you walk there, or you
wouldn't have lights on the walls."

"Absolutely right. Your powers of observation astonish
me. We don't get rid of the plants because they are why
the tunnel is lit. The burrowers harvest the roots, a diffi-

cult task in the dark, and they eat them. Would you care for a sample?"

She glanced at him narrowly. "Are they edible raw?"

"Some humans say they are. Personally, I don't even like them cooked."

"Then, no thanks, I'll skip them."

"Afraid I might be trying to poison you?"

"I wouldn't put it past you. You could always say I tried them without your permission, and oh what a tragic accident."

"No, I'm too busy for that right now. Maybe later. Now would you mind if we continued? This is *not* a sightseeing tour."

She let him push her onward.

The tunnel dipped suddenly, the floor turning into a short flight of steps, and then the steps penetrated a huge, almost circular room, a great theater. Lights were scattered among a forest of stalactites overhead; the floor curved downward, descending in a series of tiers to a broad dais. The tiers, hewn out of solid rock, were wide enough for human beings to sit on with outstretched legs, and they extended almost around the entire circumference of the room. They could easily accommodate five hundred people or more without crowding. On the far side of the dais, where the tiers ended against a flat wall, was a screen perhaps six meters across, and in front of that was a podium. The room was empty, echoing.

Seating Dia in the first row, Unknown went to the dais and began to speak. He made a simple announcement of the broadcast of the ultimatum, as if the room were full of listeners; within minutes, humans and burrowers began trickling in through entrances along the uppermost tier, and Dia realized that a public address system had carried his voice well beyond this hall.

Burrowers of various sizes took seats in the front rows; scrutinizing them, Dia doubted that she could identify Strux among them, though she did notice slight differences in coloration, head shape, and even whiskers. Their most distinguishing characteristic, though, was color and style of harness—while Strux's had been a plain and unadorned black, some burrowers wore red or green or brown, and some had bits of bright metal hung about them. She wondered if these were merely jewelry or if they had some significance as awards or denotations of rank. There did not seem to be any pattern to the burrowers' seating, neither by size nor ornamentation, nor by grayness of fur. They clustered together in the main, but a number sat interspersed with humans, chattering with great animation. The humans in turn seemed relaxed with their nonhuman allies, draping arms over them and muttering in their ears. Taken together, the two species formed a restless audience, obviously impatient for the show to begin.

The auditorium darkened, and the screen came alive to show: Strux, looking alien and aloof, goggles hiding his eyes, harness gleaming darkly upon his perfectly groomed fur. He sat in a metal chair designed for his plump, bottom-heavy body. His five-fingered paws rested lightly upon the arms of the chair. Behind him was a blank gray wall.

"Good evening, Brigadier Velicher," he said. "This is a recording which will be repeated once each hour for the next four hours. I am Brenli, Commander-in-Chief of the Royal Avdotyan Space Force. We have come here in strength at the request of our allies, the civilian population of Amphora. We require you to surrender your arms, your garrisons, your Citadel, and yourselves by no later than two days after the last of these broadcasts. In the event of your refusal, we shall destroy all military installations on Amphora. At present, our fleet is well beyond your defense perimeter, but we foresee no difficulty in penetrating it. You may broadcast your surrender on this wavelength. Good evening, Brigadier Velicher." He waved languidly, or it might have been a very casual salute, and the screen faded to black.

The audience, which had been silent during the broadcast, broke into applause and whistling, and many people turned to their neighbors to shake hands or even hug enthusiastically. The man behind Dia grabbed her around the shoulders and kissed the top of her head; when she turned to look at him, he had moved on to someone else, a burrower this time, and was thumping the creature's back vigorously.

Unknown came down from the podium and took Dia's arm. "We don't have to stay here." He steered her toward the tunnel that had brought them there.

"They certainly are happy about going to war," she said.

"We've been at war for eighty years," replied Unknown. "They're happy it's going to end soon."

"I hope you're right about that." She glanced back at the blank screen. "That *was* Strux, wasn't it?"

"Yes."

"He's quite an actor—that air of smug self-confidence was perfect. Velicher will be furious."

"So I would assume."

"Of course, he won't surrender, not to an unknown and untried enemy."

"We wouldn't expect him to. We expect him to watch the sky very, very carefully." They stepped into the tunnel, away from the commotion of the auditorium. Unknown eyed Dia sidelong as they climbed the steps. "You look like you'll want some rest by the time we get back."

"I may. At least it's downhill all the way. I'm thinking more in terms of dinner, though."

"We'll stop at the hospital refectory. I could use some food, too."

"Are you also going to *sleep* with me?" she asked.

His lips tightened. "I will sleep in your room," he said, "and the door will be locked from the outside. Other than that, Miss Catlin, you don't tempt me."

"It's going to be pretty crowded in there with another bed. I assume you'll bring in your own bed."

"Yes. Of course."

"Aren't you afraid of sleeping in the same room with a dangerous prisoner?"

"Don't worry—you'll be chained to the bed."

She halted in mid-stride to stare at him. "You're joking."

"Why should I be joking, Miss Catlin? After all, you *are* a prisoner here." He gave her a push. "I thought you were hungry."

He changed his mind later, deciding that she wouldn't be fresh for the next day's work if she spent the night in chains. Instead, after moving a cot into her room and shifting a wall to make enough space to walk around it, he arranged for a pair of burrowers to stand guard over the two of them while they slept, and to wake him if she woke. They were quiet creatures, sitting in a corner of the dim-lit chamber; it was not any noise on their part that kept Dia awake that night, but only her own worries.

She slept at last, fitfully, and dreamed she was flying the trainer once more, looking down on the Citadel. She could see her mother leaning out the tower window, and somehow her father was there, too, and Sydney, and Paul. She waved, but none of them waved back, only stared and stared, and their eyes were huge and blank. And then she flew away, and the Citadel was shrinking, shrinking to doll-size and beyond, till it dwindled to a dot and disappeared.

She woke feeling refreshed, feeling free of the past as never before, and she sat up and stretched and grinned at her guards. Even as they bent over the still-slumbering Unknown, she tossed a pillow toward him and was gratified at its perfect landing on his face; he surged out of sleep, flailing at air, and when he realized that his adversary was a pillow, he threw it angrily to the floor. Without a word, he stamped into the toilet cubicle—the only place where either of them had found any privacy in the last twenty hours.

At breakfast, he spoke to several burrowers and then said to Dia, "No reply to the ultimatum yet."

She scooped the heart out of a melon and nibbled at it delicately. "Are you surprised?"

"No, I suppose not."

"He's playing for time. He'll wait till just before the deadline, and then he'll want to parley, to stall till his own ships arrive."

"That's all right," said Unknown. "We'll be in the Citadel long before that."

"When does my trusty band of pseudo-Patrollers meet for its final briefing?"

"At 2200."

"Is that Citadel time or local?"

"We keep Citadel time here."

"Would you care to tell me where here is?"

"No."

"I didn't think you would." She tossed the melon rind aside. "Let's go, John—I'm impatient to see myself as a blonde."

FIVE

She was startled by the bleaching results—even her eyebrows and lashes came out white-blond. A dentist then took impressions for the dentures Talley had suggested and assured her they would be ready by evening.

"I'll wear my own uniform," Dia said to Unknown, "but if you have no objections, I'd rather use captain's insignia."

He nodded. "You can be a major if you like, or a colonel. We have them all."

"Let's not be ridiculous, John—I couldn't pass for any age matching those ranks. But captain . . . that's reasonable. How many people will be with me, and what ranks will they show?"

"We were thinking that seven would go for Velicher—one officer and the rest noncommissioned."

"And what do we do when we find him?"

Unknown showed his teeth in a ghoulish smile. "We take very good care of him."

Talley looked as strange with dark hair as she did with light. At 2200 he still lay in bed, but fully dressed in Patrol uniform, sergeant's chevrons on his sleeves. The name on his breast pocket was "Barden." Gathered about him were fifty or sixty fraudulent Patrollers—the leaders of the invasion force. Dia inspected them, admonishing those "officers" that didn't stand up straight enough.

"You older ones can slouch all you like, but young Patrollers tend to be overly aware of their military identity—they'are very spit-and-polish." But she had to admit they looked authentic. "Except that too many of you are wearing obvious weapons." Almost all had heavyweight stunners, adjustable all the way to lethal charge. *They have a factory source,* she thought; *rebels on the assembly line. Of course.* "Only police and officers bound for new assign-

ments or flight in hostile territory wear sidearms in the
Citadel, so I'd suggest that most of you take off your
holsters and put them on *under* your tunics. Or else dis-
card them entirely and put the weapons in your pants
pockets. They won't show if your hips are fairly narrow."
She cocked an eye at Unknown. "I don't suppose *I* get a
gun . . ."

"Sorry," he said. "I don't want to have to watch your
mouth *and* your hands."

"Carry an extra one, then, in case you decide you can
trust me. I don't care for the idea of being trapped in a
gun battle without being able to shoot back."

"At whom?" inquired Unknown.

"At whoever's shooting at me, mister. If you don't shoot
at me, I certainly won't shoot back."

"I'll carry an extra gun for you," said Talley.

Dia ruled that out. "You're going to have enough trouble
carrying yourself. Are you *sure* you can make it?"

"I'll be hyped on stimulants—don't worry about me."

"All right—that only leaves everything else to worry
about," she muttered.

Dia scanned the various Citadel diagrams projected on
the white walls of Talley's hospital room. The pseudo-
Patrollers had fragmented into small groups, each intent
on its own plan of action, tracing the route to some strategic location, discussing the manner in which they would
capture it. Unknown moved from group to group, one
eye always on Dia.

She stood by the bed, accompanied by her own contin-
gent of uniformed frauds—the team that would go for the
Brigadier: three men, including Talley, and two other wom-
en. Unknown, of course, would also be with them. With a
stylus as pointer, Dia indicated the path from the armory
in the West Tower to Velicher's quarters. "Normally, he's
here at that hour. With the ultimatum hanging over his
head, he might be in his office. The two are a single flight
of stairs apart. And remember—wherever he is, he might
not be alone, so keep your backs to the walls."

Unknown slipped between two of the listeners. He looked
uncomfortable in his uniform, as if it were too tight, though
to Dia's eyes it seemed to fit well enough. The name on his
breast pocket was "O'Neill." Dia was sure it was just as
false as the "Rocha" she wore.

"I shall be right beside you, Captain," he said. He

touched the first sergeant's insignia on his arm, tentatively, as if stroking an animal only half-tamed. "Consider me your aide-de-camp."

"Captains don't have aides-de-camp."

"Well, you're not a captain, are you?"

She glanced from him to Talley. "Who's the boss on this mission?"

Talley pointed at Unknown. "He's our expert in guerrilla warfare."

"After twenty years of it," said Unknown.

"All right, Sergeant O'Neill, tell me—how are we going to distinguish our troops from the regular Patrollers?"

"I'm glad you asked that, Captain." With the pressure of two fingers, he stuck a tiny pip to the cuff of her left sleeve. "You were the only one of us not wearing the new improved version of the Patrol uniform . . . and we wouldn't want you shot by mistake."

"Only on purpose," she muttered. She bent her arm to examine the speck, which glittered with self-generated fire. "It isn't very conspicuous."

"That's the idea. We wouldn't want the enemy to get suspicious, after all. Knowing exactly where to look, you'll notice it."

A glance at his left wrist confirmed the statement—his rebel mark was plain, a tiny spark of light. About the room, wherever a sleeve presented the proper angle, there the point gleamed, like a fleck of metallic dust.

Gradually, the chamber emptied, as "officers" left to join their teams, to make the journey to the tunnel. Dia watched their grim faces, their determined stride, the jaunty lift of their shoulders as they wished each other luck. Her own teammates were going over and over plans she already knew by heart, their confidence soaring as they became more familiar with the diagrammatic version of the territory they were about to invade.

"When do we leave?" she said at last.

Unknown looked at his chronometer. "Soon. Four teams will go first and secure the armory. After that, the rest of us will have about six hours before the next shift comes on duty."

"Right."

He removed a handful of pills from his breast pocket and distributed them among his companions. "Stimulants," he explained, "in case things take longer than we expect. They're chewable."

"I have my own already," said Talley.

Dia dropped hers into the right side pocket of her tunic, where they clattered unexpectedly against something already there. She had presumed that pocket empty and, curious, she dipped three fingers in, encountered rustling chain among the pills. Even as she drew the pendant forth, she recalled wearing it the night of the escape, recalled that she had not discarded it with her dress uniform. It had been removed with her clothing during that first sleep in the cavern, probably tucked into the pocket at that time. She held the pendant up to the light, watching the black opal sparkle its multicolored flames, and she remembered the commitment it represented, the days and the nights. . . . And then she reached for the corner post of Talley's bed, to hang it there and leave it behind. But Talley's hand stopped her, captured the pendant like a diving bird of prey.

"Where did you get this?" he asked.

"Velicher gave it to me . . . as a love gift."

He turned the pendant over, cradled it in his palm while he scrutinized its flat reverse. His thumb rubbed at the maker's mark. "My father made this," he said softly. "That's his symbol." He looked up at Dia, and his fingers closed around the pendant, hiding it completely. "He was famous, you know. Not just here on Amphora, but all along the interstellar trade routes. On Quixote they knew his work. On Daphne, on Blandford, on Terre du Soleil. He commanded the highest prices, and we were quite wealthy, back in the old days." His gaze lowered to his fist, the knuckles white, and Dia thought the horns of the demon must be biting into his flesh, but he showed no pain. "It seems strange that Velicher should own a piece of my father." His eyes squeezed shut, and now there was pain in his face. "When I came home, the house was gutted, the workshop, his tools, everything smashed and burned beyond recognition. I had never been the kind of person who keeps souvenirs, so I had nothing to remind me of the past." His eyes opened, and his searching gaze lit on Unknown. "Except people."

Dia covered his fist with her hands. "Keep it," she said.

Talley sighed. "I want it and I don't." He opened his

fingers and stared and stared at the demon head, at the glinting opal. "He tried to teach me, but I had other interests. Strux and I—we were going to be doctors, each to his own people, with a little cross-over someday. He tried to teach me, but I didn't have his artistic imagination." Abruptly, he handed her the pendant. "Hang it on the post. We'll come back for it later." He swung his legs over the side of the bed and stood, swaying only slightly. "Let's get out of here."

Dia offered her arm, and he took it firmly, leaning on her. "I know you can take my weight," he said. "And I'd better do this now, because I won't be able to once we're inside the Citadel."

Unknown took his other arm, and the three of them walked out of the room and out of the hospital, trailing the remaining members of their team.

Strux was waiting for them at the entrance to the subway. He carried a hand flash. "I will accompany you, if I may," he said, "at least as far as the end of the tunnel."

Talley gripped his paw. "Of course." And all four of them climbed into the third of a long line of cylindrical cars, while their companions and the pressing uniformed horde behind them was divided among the rest. Unknown programmed their destination, and as soon as the vehicle ahead had sped out of sight, they felt the drag of acceleration on their own.

Strux snapped off his flash, and darkness closed in like an old friend. The car held four comfortably—they sat cross-legged, watching each other by the faint green lights of the instrument panel. For the first time, Dia saw Strux take off his goggles and his lustrous eyes reflected green pinpoints in the dimness.

"I wish that my role were not finished," he said quietly. "I wish I could go with you into the Citadel."

"I know," said Talley.

"I will stand by the telegraph. You need fear no mistake."

"Good. I'm glad it will be you." In the blackness, he caught Dia's hand. "We have our own form of communication that the Patrol doesn't know about. The wires are strung all through these tunnels, with a sending set at every station. I could have telegraphed in before you and I took the subway from station 8, but I was afraid they'd think it was a trick, that the Patrol had found out about it from me.

"Sergeant O'Neill will be playing a single filament wire out of his heel at every step—it will adhere to the floor undetectably. He has to send an all-clear signal back to our base in the final tunnel every fifteen minutes, or they blow up the Citadel."

Dia felt all her muscles go rigid. "Blow it up? With us inside?"

"If I don't send the signal," said Unknown, "it means we're dead—or as good as dead."

"It means *you're* dead. The rest of us might be perfectly all right."

"The others of our team know where the apparatus is hidden on my body, and how to use it in case something happens to me."

"The others . . . except for *me*. Oh, great. Wonderful." She ran stiff fingers through her hair. "What about all those other rebels who'll be running around the place? How do they feel about being blown up?"

"They know about it. They're willing to take their chances."

Talley said, "With Strux at the telegraph, there won't be any accidents. As for us—I'd rather be blown to bits than taken apart slowly by Velicher."

Dia sagged against him. "I won't think about it. I just hope the sergeant's chronometer doesn't stop."

"I'll be replying to a signal from the other end," said Unknown. "I won't forget."

"What other jolly details haven't you told me about?" Dia muttered, half to herself, but in the silent tunnel, even a whisper seemed loud and demanding. "Is Sergeant O'Neill, perhaps, going to shoot me when we've taken Velicher, just to make sure I don't have an attack of sympathy for him?"

"No!" cried Talley, and he clutched her fiercely. "I'll kill the man who tries to harm you!"

She held him tightly, and her voice was muffled against his chest. "At least someone is on my side. . . ."

"You are in the minority in this vehicle, Sergeant O'Neill," came Strux's childlike voice. "I, too, believe in Captain Rocha's sincerity."

Dia had to laugh, though weakly. "Captain Rocha. Sgt. O'Neill. I feel like we're not talking about us at all. Sgt.

O'Neill, for the sake of my curiosity, in case we're all killed—what is your name?"

"I'll tell you," said Unknown. "Afterward."

She burrowed closer to Talley. "Everything in my whole life, somehow, is . . . afterward."

He kissed the top of her head. "There will be an afterward, my love. There has to be."

SIX

Their vehicle halted at a section of the tunnel that seemed no different from any other and sank out of sight after they had disembarked. Unknown palmed the wall, and a narrow, stepped passage opened before them, leading to a second tunnel and another vehicle. The new journey was briefer, ending at a blank wall. Once again, Unknown caused an aperture to materialize.

"From here we walk." He led the way. Overhead lights made Strux's flash unnecessary. After half a kilometer, they began passing false Patrollers lined up along either wall. A little farther on was a flight of stone steps leading upward; they sat down on the bottom one.

"I watched this step being cut," Strux said, patting it.

"Where are we?" asked Dia.

"Outside the Citadel walls still," said Unknown. "These steps rise two hundred meters in the next horizontal three hundred and end under the West Tower."

She looked up the stairwell and saw men sitting on one side of the steps, all the way up. "How in the world did you manage all of this?"

"Well, we did have twenty years," said Talley.

"Even so."

"The burrowers were in charge of the project."

She turned to Strux, who showed his teeth in his own version of a grin. Once more he wore his goggles, and he looked like a furry welder.

"We have always lived in the caverns," he said. "We have always traveled between them, making tunnels where there were no natural junctures. We have tunnels near the surface, too, where we cultivate the roots of green plants whose tops are exposed to sunlight. Before the humans built us motorized vehicles, we moved heavy goods in wheeled

213

carts. That was slow, but adequate for our purposes. It was not adequate, of course, for the massive and rapid movement of personnel and materiel required to combat the Patrol. Nor were any of our tunnel systems properly located for an assault on the Citadel. Motorized vehicles solved one problem, and the other was amenable to our traditional methods." He flexed his fingers against the step, his broad, flat nails making scrabbling sounds on the stone. "In ancient days we dug with our own hands. Our myths say that the Universe was once solid earth in all directions, and that the Creators made the first burrower to hollow out a space so they could kindle a fire to warm themselves. That first burrower performed her task so well that the Creators allowed her to go on and on. She hollowed out the entire sky, which they filled up with the light of their fire; she hollowed out the basins of the ground, which they filled with water to cool their fire-parched throats; and she hollowed out the deep caverns, which they gave to her and to her children for all time as a reward for her labors. And so we have the sun and the seas and our homes." He showed his teeth again. "Some time after this rather pretty if unlikely occurrence, we learned that hands have other, better uses than digging, and we began to breed small animals to make our tunnels for us. Still later, we learned how to fashion tools of metal, but for the common digging, the animals are still best. They are not very intelligent, but they dig with much enthusiasm. In fact, we must keep them in sturdy cages when we need no digging, or they would be a great nuisance both to us and to our human friends.

"We excavated from the nearest already existing tunnel. For a long time the new passage was very narrow, and the work progressed slowly, but after we short-circuited the Citadel's buried sensors, it speeded up." He pointed up the stairs. "This was the simplest part; above this point, the Citadel rests primarily on a foundation of hard clay, with some pylons sinking to bedrock. Clay does not require the laborious heating and chilling that cause stone to crumble under the claws of a digging creature. We were forced, however, to quarry stone slabs for the higher steps from this portion of the tunnel, and so it is wider than the rest."

"Why steps at all?" wondered Dia. "Why not just a ladder?"

Unknown laughed harshly at that suggestion. "Would you care to climb a two-hundred-meter ladder, Captain?"

"It would be too dangerous," said Talley. "If anyone fell, he'd sweep off everyone below him."

"I suppose we should have arranged a bank of elevators —the high-speed variety that the Patrol—"

Talley nudged him sharply. "What time is it?"

"Still too early," said Unknown.

"Then I suggest we use our remaining free time to pretend we're all friends."

Down the corridor, the double row of rebels waited; some sat on the floor, others leaned against the cool walls, and they whispered to each other occasionally, in voices like wind-rustled leaves. Already, their numbers had increased beyond Dia's range of vision. *Outnumbered twenty to one,* she told herself; *not impossible odds in the middle of the night.*

Talley drew a packet from his breast pocket. "You'd better put these in now." Two semicircles of thin, flexible plastic—the dentures. He helped her fit them over her teeth. "They don't do much for your face."

She ran her fingers over the altered contours of her lips. "It's a little hard to keep my mouth closed."

He grinned. "I recommend oral surgery in the near future."

"Right."

He pulled her to him and kissed her new-shaped mouth. "Different," he murmured against her cheek, "but not unpleasant." He kissed her again, and then he looked over her shoulder, toward Strux. "Strux, if Dia comes back without me, I want you to treat her the way you've always treated me."

"I will respect your wishes."

"Unless she comes at the head of the Patrol counter-offensive," muttered Unknown. "Come on, let's get up those stairs."

The steps were wide; there was plenty of room for them to climb past the line of false Patrollers. They moved slowly, conserving their strength. In two hundred vertical meters, there were some six hundred steps, a long climb for anyone, even in the best of health. Dia knew that Talley could not have made it by himself, but he didn't have to; a pair of men linked arms at the bottom to carry him upward a dozen steps, and then they passed him to another pair and so on. Dia walked behind him, breathing easily, and Unknown was behind her, ever in a hurry, treading almost on her heels.

Over his shoulder, Talley said, "There's only a thin layer of flooring left where the tunnel hits the armory. It's supported from below, in case anyone walks over that spot—we wouldn't want them to hear a hollow ring or, worse, to break through. But we don't expect anyone to be inside at this time of night."

Dia shook her head. "I don't know. In an emergency situation . . ."

"We're ready for anything, of course. I think every one of us is ready for anything."

"I know I am," murmured Dia. Her palms were sweating, and she wiped them on the hem of her tunic. *Combat,* she thought. *I always wanted to see combat.*

They were about ten steps from the top when word came, via the telegraph, that the time to strike had arrived. Dia could see the braces that held a two-meter square section of the armory floor up. Just below them crouched the five-member lead attack team. As Dia watched, they pulled the bracing away and lunged upward. She heard a soft *crump* as the floor gave, and even softer footfalls as the lead team scrambled through the hole and scattered. Then there was silence.

Unknown held his own team back and motioned sharply for the next group on the stairs to follow the first. And the next and the next. By the time the fourth was through the hole, a member of the first was returning to report the armory secured. Only then did Unknown take his team through.

The huge room, with its rack on rack of weapons, was quiet in spite of so many occupants. There was no milling about, only a smooth motion away from the hole in the floor, making room for more and more false Patrollers to enter the Citadel. The bodies of the two duty guards, both very young corporals, lay tumbled in a corner. They had been outside the door when a rebel locksmith overrode the alarm and the lock, taken by surprise because they never expected attack from the rear. Dia couldn't help feeling pity for them; much Citadel sentry duty was given to the freshest Patrollers, the inexperienced, because it was so safe, so impossible to foul up. At the armory, their orders had been to challenge all visitors, to check IDs and authorizations and weapons serial numbers, and to salute all higher ranks. It was routine, requiring primarily the ability to stand in one place for long periods of time, especially in the dull, quiet hours of the night. And there they were, limp as rag dolls, two youngsters no older than Dia, who had probably been thinking about getting to sleep before that door opened behind them. *How much pity should I feel*, she wondered, *for my enemies?*

Out in the corridor, the only human beings in sight were two Patrollers guarding the armory—two Patrollers standing at ease, their hands resting lightly on their sidearms, glittering stars on their sleeves. Unknown nodded to them as he led his team through the door. Behind him, waiting only until his group turned a corner, was the next team.

Dia, as ranking officer, assumed the lead, with Unknown at her shoulder, and the band strode briskly to the main artery of the lowest level, turned right, and headed for the nearest scooter stall. Four vehicles were in their niches. Dia scribbled random names on the use roster, requisitioning them all. She spaced her followers out, giving precise instructions for different routes to a rendezvous at the Central Tower. Unknown claimed the seat beside her, and they moved eastward at an easy speed, no rush, no frantic air about them. The key to success, Dia knew, they all knew, was to seem ordinary, so fit in so unobtrusively that no casual observer could suspect that anything unusual was going on.

She had warned all the teams to get out of the corridors as quickly as possible, to take their objectives and close themselves inside, posting guards in the corridors only where such guards were ordinarily found, at least at first. Too many people in the byways at that hour would be a sign that something was wrong; it would unsettle late strollers, who might call their superiors, who would wake their commanders . . . exactly what the rebels could not afford. They needed the Citadel asleep as long as possible.

Dia and Unknown reached the rendezvous first—the elevators at the base of the Central Tower. The others arrived within a few minutes, none reporting any problems. They parked their scooters against the wall; from here on, they could no longer afford the noise or the encumbrance of motorized transport. All seven false Patrollers stepped into the nearest elevator, and Dia punched the floor for Velicher's quarters.

Leaving one of their number standing casually by the elevator, they walked down the corridor. They passed Dia's own door and left another person there, to guard against the Brigadier escaping that way. Dia didn't spare the spot more than a glance; it was the entrance to a stranger's den now, alien, steeped in Patrol past and Patrol future. Velicher's own door was some meters farther on. Nothing marked it as belonging to the Brigadier; it was labeled only by a location code on the wall beside it: c-17. Unknown propelled Dia past it, to the stairway, where they stood close together on the second step down, as if talking. Talley and two others had halted at the door, and now he and one of them faced each other, their bodies shielding the locksmith at work between them.

Without touching the door, the locksmith manipulated the lock electronically for two long, silent minutes; then, making no attempt to slide the panel open, she looked up and nodded. Talley's curt wave brought Dia and Unknown to him. The five of them were to enter. Four took infragoggles from their pockets and slipped them on; Unknown had an extra pair for Dia. Very gently, he eased the door open halfway, nodded each of the team through, Dia last, then followed her with a firm grip on her arm.

To Dia's newly enhanced vision, the darkened living room was aglow with the light of four blazing-white bodies. She gestured toward the open bedroom door, but they did not need her directions, were already moving that way. Their boots made only the softest of sounds on the thickly carpeted floor.

They didn't need to enter the room to see that the bed was rumpled but empty.

They entered anyway, checked all the corners, the closet, the bathroom, without any more noise than they had already made. Dia pointed to the door that linked her old quarters with the Brigadier's, and at Talley's nod she palmed it open. The adjoining apartment was empty, too.

With an upraised thumb, Dia indicated the office above their heads, and they moved out of the Brigadier's apartment. In the corridor, Unknown plucked the loaned goggles from Dia's fingers and pocketed them without a word —all the members of the team had been cautioned about speaking while in the corridors, to avoid any possible eavesdropping. But his tight mouth conveyed a clear message—somehow the Brigadier's not being in his quarters

was *her* fault, or at least she should have known all along
that he wouldn't be there and not wasted precious time
with the search. Dia could only shrug and glance at Talley,
and receive his answering smile. She noted that he appeared
to be holding up well, standing straight, striding easy. She
wondered how many stimulant pills he had already taken.

They left one team member inside the Brigadier's door
and one inside the adjoining apartment, in case he returned
while they were searching elsewhere. The remaining five
climbed the single flight of stairs to the level of his office.

Dia entered the anteroom with Talley and Unknown
close behind her while the other two stayed outside, out of
sight. One of Ramirez's assistants sat at the captain's desk
—as he glanced up, Dia couldn't help wondering if he
would penetrate her disguise. She had just opened her
mouth to give an excuse for their presence when Unknown
leveled his gun over her shoulder and fired, drilling a small,
silent hole in the young man's face. Before Dia could react,
he had pushed her aside and sprung forward to catch the
sagging body before it could strike the desk.

At Talley's signal, the rest of the team came in. By gesture, they reported the corridor quiet. Softly, they shut the
anteroom door. The locksmith knelt at the inner door,
tested it, found it locked, and began to manipulate her
equipment. Unknown took Dia's arm in a crushing grip
and drew her to one side, away from any line of sight from
the inner office. Talley and the other team member stood
over the locksmith, waiting tensely, their guns drawn. At
the locksmith's nod, Unknown slammed his hand over Dia's
mouth and gave his own nod. Dia was too angry to struggle against the sudden restraint as she watched the door
slide open.

The panel halted at fifteen centimeters aperture, too
narrow for any human being to pass through, but quite
wide enough for the muzzles of three guns, one above the
next. The locksmith fired from floor level, Talley crouched
above her, and the third team member leaned over him.
Dia saw their fists clenching again and again on the butts
of their stunners, shot after shot spewing into the inner
room. Lethal charge, she knew.

After a time they stopped.

Talley shoved the door open all the way and gestured
his two near companions inside. Unknown removed his
hand from Dia's face and pulled her in as well. They all

approached the desk cautiously, weapons in every hand but
Dia's, all trained on the figure that slumped forward in
its chair, face down on the viewscreen keyboard. Behind
the desk, the wall that bore the Patrol emblem was heavily
pocked with stray shots.

Talley pressed the muzzle of his gun hard against the
side of the man's neck, and then he raised the sagging body
by its tunic collar. One shot had pierced the left cheek,
another the right eye, three more the upper chest.

Dia had already recognized that head by its sparse hair.
Ramirez.

SEVEN

Unknown turned on Dia. "What the hell is this?" he demanded. "What kind of game are you playing?"

She looked away from Ramirez, her mouth grim. This was not the time to remember that though she had disliked him she had never wished him dead. Or his aide, out in the anteroom. The rebels could have stunned them both, of course, instead of killing them, but dead Patrollers couldn't wake up later and cause trouble. This was war, and people were going to die in it. She had been trained a soldier and she could accept that. But she wasn't a soldier now; whatever her rebel trappings, whatever the star on her sleeve was supposed to mean, she was still a prisoner. Anger was high in her, and she was fighting hard not to strike out at Unknown; she could still feel the pressure of his hand, still taste the salty palm on her lips. She wiped her mouth with a knuckle. "I'm doing my best, Sergeant O'Neill, *Sir*. What the hell do you think *you* were doing out there? Keeping me from screaming a warning, were you? Thinking I wanted to get us all killed. You idiot!"

"I couldn't take any chances, Captain Rocha," he said. "I'm surprised you don't understand that."

She shook her head sharply. "I understand that I've had about enough of you, Sergeant. I've had a dozen opportunities to raise the Citadel since we got here. And I haven't done it."

"I've kept an eye on you." His tone was defensive.

"Sure you have. You only let me stand right next to the kitchen signal in my own apartment. You must have thought I could only order up orange juice that way. Shall I call a few other little oversights to your attention?"

"That's enough, you two," said Talley. "We can't afford—"

221

The viewscreen chimed.

Everyone froze.

"It might be Velicher," whispered Dia.

"Calling his own office?" asked Talley.

"He knows Ramirez is here. He'll wonder why he isn't answering."

"Wait," said Unknown, and he stood very still. His eyes seemed to focus inward for a long moment, and then he said, "No, it's all right. It's our people. Go on, Captain. Answer it." He pointed at the keyboard.

Talley started to pull the body from the chair to make room for her, and the locksmith moved to help him. Dia sat down at the Brigadier's desk and keyed the response, but she leaned far sideways, keeping her face out of range of the viewscreen pickup, just in case Unknown was wrong. She said nothing.

The voice from the screen was small but clearly audible: "We've received an alarm from your office, Sir. Are you there?"

"It's Driebergen," said Unknown, and he bent over the screen. "Confirmed that we have the Brigadier's office," he said to the anxious face. "The telegraph is still safe."

Driebergen smiled. "Just making sure. We were worried about you when the alarm came through. But we've got both Comm Centers now, and it never got past us. Congratulations."

"None in order," said Unknown. "We don't have him yet. Watch for his code and let me know by telegraph where he's calling from. And send me some people to hold this place while we keep looking."

Driebergen nodded, and the screen blanked.

"But he might not call anyone," said Talley.

Unknown looked at Dia. "He might not," he said. "Where do we go next?"

Gazing up at him, a glint of gold tugged at her peripheral vision—the trophy on the wall behind the desk. Where else would he be? "The target range," she said. "Sixth level, this tower."

"What does it look like?"

She sketched it on a piece of flimsy, the semicircular room, the wedge-shaped segments. "One guard," she said. "At the door. Armed. He has a clear view of the corridor on both sides—he'll see us coming. You won't be able to just walk up and shoot him."

"Sure we will," said Unknown, "using you for cover."

She frowned, glancing up at Talley. "Sounds like a good way to get me killed."

"Afraid your fellow Patroller will shoot at you, Captain?" said Unknown.

"Either him or you. I don't know which is more likely."

"I don't like it," said Talley. "If he gets suspicious, all he has to do is step inside the doorway, but we're out in the corridor with nothing to hide behind but each other."

Unknown smiled—a smile that reminded Dia of the Brigadier's own, cold, humorless. "Captain Rocha and I will take him, just the two of us. He won't be suspicious of two apparently unarmed Patrollers. I shall keep my stunner out of sight in my pocket until the very last moment."

"He'll see you drawing it," said Dia. "We can't count on him being like that kid in the outer office, paying attention to something else when we happen by. He'll be alert. Especially if the Brigadier is there."

"Well, you'll just have to see to it that he *doesn't* see me drawing it, Captain," said Unknown.

"I don't like it," Talley said. "There must be a better way. We could come at him from two different directions, half of us circle around to his other side."

Dia said, "So he'll see both groups. That's sure to make him suspicious. He's going to be twitchy enough knowing he's guarding the Brigadier." She shook her head. "Sergeant O'Neill is right. It's got to be just him and me."

"I'm glad you see it that way," said Unknown.

"But only on one condition."

Unknown's eyes narrowed. "We've already given you all the conditions we're going to."

"You want this mission to succeed?"

"Do I really have to answer that?"

"Then you'll abide by the condition."

"Which is?"

"That *you* follow *my* orders. That you let me take the lead and call the play. You'll draw the gun when I say so and not before, and you'll keep your mouth shut."

Talley gripped Unknown's arm. "She's right. She knows these people better than we do. She's got the right reactions."

Unknown's lip curled, as if he had just tasted something unpleasant. "She wants me to be the one killed."

"I'll do my best to keep us both alive."

"Oh, I believe that. Of course I do."

"All right," said Talley. "Don't go with her. I'll do it."

"No," said Unknown. "She doesn't go without me."

"Three is too many," said Dia, "especially if two are noncoms. This is a range for Staff-level officers, and any of us are going to look pretty funny stopping there. A captain has the best chance, and I'd volunteer to do it alone, but I don't know what I'd be up against. Two to be sure, but no more."

"I'll go with you," said Talley.

"If you're sure you feel up to it," she said, looking at his face. He wasn't pale now. If anything, there was too much color in his cheeks. Stimulants or excitement, she wondered. She touched his hand; his skin felt cool and dry.

"No," said Unknown. "I'll go. In case something goes wrong. You're not strong enough."

"I'm all right," said Talley.

"No, you're not. You're my responsibility, and I say you're not." He turned to Dia. "All right, it's your game. Tell me what to do."

"Follow me," she said. "Don't say anything and don't do anything until I give the word."

"And the word is . . . ?"

"What else? *Shoot*."

Reinforcements arrived—four false Patrollers. Unknown ordered three of them to guard the Brigadier's office, one at Ramirez's desk and the other two on either side of the anteroom door, ready to pick off anyone who walked in. The other he took along with his team, raising its strength to six. They split up again, taking two different routes to a rendezvous around the corner from the range. They assembled there without incident and huddled together against a wall. Dia gestured for Unknown to come with her while the others stayed where they were.

The guard was older than she had hoped, a man of some experience, judging from the chevrons on his sleeve and the medals on his chest. He stood easy inside the doorway, one hand on his sidearm, and though he noticed the newcomers as soon as they entered his corridor, he did not shift his stance at their approach.

"Sorry, Patrollers," he said as they stopped in front of him. "This range is reserved for Staff only."

Dia nodded. She could hear the soft and rhythmic chiming of targets being struck inside. He was there. He had to be. "Would you please tell the Brigadier that Captain Rocha is here as ordered?"

The guard reached for the comm unit that hung just within the doorway, and in that moment when his attention was not entirely focused on Dia and Unknown, they had him. Dia clamped one hand on his right wrist, locking the gun in its holster, and with the other she slammed his head against the doorjamb. The sound of skull against metal was surprisingly quiet, she thought, as she gave the word and Unknown stuck his stunner into the guard's ribs and fired. She and Unknown looked at each other tensely as they lowered the limp body to the floor, but the faint chime of targets continued inside uninterrupted.

Unknown signaled the others, and they eased through the doorway, leaving one man on guard in the dead Patroller's place. There was no cover when they entered, no shadow to hide in, no furniture or fixtures to stand behind. The door was at one end of the observation crescent, with only the narrow rail between observers and the wedge-shaped segments of the range. They could see Velicher clearly, his back to them; he stood some meters down the range, firing methodically at moving targets. He heard them enter, half-turned to see who it was, and Unknown raised his gun and fired.

Chaos.

Whether Velicher understood instantly, Dia could not guess. Perhaps it was only reflex, the seasoned soldier reacting to the sight of a gun pointing in his direction. In the split second before Unknown fired, he moved, diving, rolling, his pistol coming up to aim at the rebels.

Maybe Unknown would have missed anyway. He hadn't had enough hours on a target range. *Maybe none,* thought Dia, *the fool,* as she knocked Talley to the floor. Silent shots were crisscrossing the air above their heads, coming from all directions as the team scattered—stunners set on lethal against a target pistol just as deadly. The woman who had been standing nearest Unknown was the first casualty because she didn't hit the floor fast enough; she hit it hard then, face first. Velicher, twisting, dodging, was a target none of the rebels could pinpoint. *They're no match for him,* she thought. A rebel cried out; he hadn't hugged the floor close enough.

There was no immediate cover, not for him and not for them. They were pinned in the observation crescent, scarcely daring to lift their heads, firing wildly, pocking the walls and floor with their shots. He was only ten meters from the line of targets, though—once behind them, he would be proof against every weapon in the room. And he was moving.

Dia scrabbled at Talley's hand, at his stunner; he let it go. She didn't know what setting it was on, but she could guess. Her cheek pressed against the floor, her gun arm extended like a striking snake, she fired once.

EIGHT

The rebels lay still for a long time. Dia was the first to lift her head.

Unknown hissed, "Stay down!"

"I got him," she said. "He's not going to shoot back." Rising to her knees, she looked at the gauge of the stunner in her hand. Lethal. She offered it, butt first, to Talley, but he shook his head.

"You handle it better than I could."

Unknown approached the body warily. Half a meter away, he aimed his stunner and shot the Brigadier again and again, as if he could make his enemy more dead with every discharge. Then he kicked the body over onto its back.

As Dia neared, she saw there was a hole in the forehead just at the hairline—her shot. Blood was beginning to ooze out, half-coagulated from the lethal charge. His face was expressionless in death. As if he had been killed in his sleep. Here was the true end of their relationship, not that day in Talley's cell nor the night of the escape, but here, now. Now the Brigadier was one with Michael, a piece of the past. She felt nothing for him, for either of them, but relief that they were gone. The gun seemed heavy in her hand, dragging her arm down against her thigh. "Sergeant O'Neill," she whispered without looking up at him, "Mission accomplished."

Talley came to stand by her after a time, after he had examined the wounded rebel and the dead one and suggested that Unknown send for help to dispose of the corpses and render first aid. When Unknown turned away to take care of those matters, Talley put his arm around Dia. "I knew we needed you," he said.

She nodded.

"He would have been an impossible prisoner. Too dangerous."

"I don't regret killing him. It was him or us."

He stared down at the corpse another moment and then stooped suddenly and lifted the dead hand. He slid Velicher's heavy gold and jade ring off. He glanced up at Dia but said nothing, only closing his fist around the piece of jewelry, and she knew without asking that it had been made by his father. She understood that he hated the idea of it being buried with his enemy.

When he stood up at last, he turned to her and opened his hand before her face. The gold glinted in the bright light of the target range. The jade was mossy green, with a smooth, subtly mottled surface, like the egg of some strange bird. Velicher had worn it on the little finger of his right hand. Dia slipped the third finger of her left through the band, and Talley pushed it over the knuckle. He closed both of his hands over it. A pledge. A pledge made on the corpse of a man and the corpse of an empire. As long as that ring was on her hand, Dia knew, there would be no forgetting for either of them.

Medics arrived to tend the wounded and dead. Unknown, Talley, and Dia went out into the corridor. The last member of their team was still guarding the door, and from the outside, the target range seemed as quiet and normal as the hour suggested. 0400. The Citadel was still sleeping. They left their last teammate on duty there.

The three of them walked toward the South Tower Communications Center, briskly, as if they had important business waiting. They passed Patrollers in the corridor—six marching in a compact group, glinting stars on their sleeves. Unknown lifted his arm to them, to show his own mark, and they nodded soberly and continued on their way. Looking back a minute later, Dia saw that they had stopped at a door and were clustered about it, as if waiting for something. For their locksmith to get it open, she guessed, for the opportunity to go inside and arrest the occupants. This was a residential area—upper-echelon residences. Who, she wondered, would those officers think was arresting them, and for what crime? She saw the door open and the false Patrollers flow through the opening, and then she and her party turned a corner, and she saw no more.

On the next higher level, they met a real Patroller, a

sleepy-looking lieutenant coming out of her quarters. They surrounded her, and Unknown took her elbow roughly and told her she was under arrest. She gaped at him and demanded to know the charge.

"Treason," he said.

Struck dumb, she looked to Dia, the ranking officer, for confirmation.

Dia nodded. "You'd better come along peacefully."

Patrol discipline overcame the lieutenant's disbelief, and she let them walk her to the entrance of the South Tower Comm Center, where they turned her over to a pair of guards with stars on their sleeves. No real Patrollers were allowed to cross that threshold.

Talley, Unknown, and Dia went in.

Inside, the whole operation had been taken over by the rebels. A telegraph station maintained contact with Strux in the tunnel and with other rebels throughout the Citadel. A subdued murmur suffused the place, as if the people were all humming instead of speaking. Fraudulent Patrollers came and went swiftly, each report of a completed assignment winning a fresh duty. Unknown and Talley hovered over the telegraph, reading dispatches as they came in. Dia read over their shoulders, absorbing the growing number of strategic points captured, corridors secured, officers imprisoned.

Unknown was compiling a master list of captured Patrol personnel. Most of the names bore high ranks, most were familiar to Dia, and many were underlined.

"The underlined ones are dead. They made too much noise or too much trouble. The rest are in detention," said Unknown.

Dia's mother, as a Councillor, had been detained already. Her father's name was not on the list, nor was Sydney's. The latter absence hardly surprised Dia—Sydney's husband was, as usual, absent from the Citadel, and Sydney herself was too low-ranking a reserve officer to warrant prompt attention. Dia was more concerned about her father. "You haven't arrested Oliver Solares yet," she said to Unknown.

Talley replied, "He was assigned a third level priority. The team that drew him probably hasn't gotten to him yet."

"Then I'd like to go to him myself. There's less chance of some accident that way."

"I prefer to stay here," said Unknown. "And where I stay, you stay."

"She saved your damned life," said Talley, "and you still don't trust her?"

Unknown's mouth turned down at the corners. "She saved her own life. He wasn't being very discriminating about who he was shooting at. And he didn't recognize her with the hair and the teeth."

"He would have shot at me anyway. He probably would have made a special effort if he'd recognized me."

"So you say. We can't ask him, can we?"

"That's enough," Talley said. "She's going to be the one to arrest her father, if that's what she wants. I'll go with her."

"You're not going anywhere. You look like you're about to pass out."

Talley popped a stimulant pill into his mouth. "I'm all right."

"Who's running this operation?" demanded Unknown.

"Who, indeed?" answered Talley, smiling at his comrade. "Things seem to be running themselves, and very smoothly. You can afford to take half an hour off for a small errand. You know, if the Brigadier had killed you, you'd be taking a lot more than half an hour off, and the rest of us would manage fine without you."

"I belong here."

"Nonsense. You're just killing time here. Anybody could keep that list current, and any really important news could be telegraphed with your own code attached, to catch your attention."

"I want to hear *all* the news."

"Are you afraid to go out in the halls, Carmelo?"

Unknown flushed, the first time Dia had seen the hot blood rising to his face in all the time they had been together. His voice was almost too low to be heard above the background noise: "You weren't supposed to use my name in front of her."

Talley cocked his head toward Dia. "My dear, the time for formal introductions has come at last. I want you to meet Carmelo Ostberg, gentleman farmer, card shark, and rebel. He owns twenty thousand square kilometers in East Greentree, which makes him, at last reckoning, the third largest landholder on this continent. Don't ever play poker with him."

She stared at the man she had called John X. Unknown. "Ostberg. You." She shook her head slowly. "Oh, he wanted you very much. If he had known who we all were, he would have shot at *you* first."

"I don't doubt it," Ostberg said drily, the color in his face subsiding. "He always suspected me. I know he tapped my communications."

"But he didn't know about the telegraph," said Talley. "Or about the subway station underneath Carmelo's house."

Ostberg looked at him. "And now he'll never know. But *she* does."

"Are you really worried?" asked Talley. "Do you think she's going to engineer a counterrevolution?"

"I'm not so blinded by . . . infatuation that I put it beyond the realm of possibility. Why does she want to be the one to get her father? He's a high-ranking officer. He could make himself the hub of a counterattack. We're still outnumbered, you know. All these damned Patrollers need is a few good leaders and we'll have hand-to-hand combat down the halls. Do you want to risk that?"

"So come along and keep an eye on her yourself, Carmelo—that's an easy solution."

Ostberg shook his head sharply.

Dia said, "I would like to spare my father the experience of waking up to a band of armed troops breaking into his bedroom. That's all, nothing more."

"You'd rather he woke to a traitor," snapped Ostberg. "I can't imagine a good Patroller being very happy about that."

"That's my problem," said Dia. "I'm going up to my father's quarters. You may come along if you wish."

"You're not going anywhere!"

"Don't you want to see him spit molten lava at his sinful child?" asked Talley. "I'd think that would be exactly your sort of show, Carmelo—watching a strong woman break down and weep." He linked his arm with Dia's. "I think I'd like to go up and say hello to the father of the woman I love. And make sure nothing unpleasant happens to him. Don't worry—I won't let them foment anything while we're there."

"Those pills have addled your brain," said Ostberg, and, scowling, he fell into step with them.

Outside the communications center, they strode swiftly, alert to danger, not even whispering among themselves.

There were no scooters available; all were in use as the revolution moved faster and faster. Dia led her companions upward and eastward. At every cross-corridor, every elevator, every stairway, there was a sentry who had to be shown the stars on their sleeves. Elsewhere were knots of false Patrollers consulting over residence rosters, preparing to lock lower-echelon officers into their own quarters instead of removing them to the already crowded detention cells. In their journey, Dia, Ostberg, and Talley encountered only one authentic Patroller, who was accompanied by two frauds; Dia recognized the chief of the south hangar crew. Communications and transportation—by controlling them, the rebels had effectively sealed the Citadel off from the rest of the planet. Three hours had passed since they broke through the West Tower armory floor.

Standing before her father's door, Dia spoke her name. Inside, she knew, the annunciator was chiming by his bedside, and whispering her name in her own voice even as the door slid open to admit her. He was alone, then—his children were welcome at any hour if he had no other companionship.

Talley and Ostberg followed her in. She shut the door, switched on the lights, and gestured for her companions to take seats in the living room; she claimed the couch, and Talley pulled a chair close to her side. At the last moment, she remembered her dentures, and she peeled them out of her mouth and stuck them in a pocket.

Oliver Solares emerged from the bedroom, hair rumpled, mouth agape in a yawn. He cut the yawn short and looked from Talley to Ostberg. Then he turned to Dia, a quizzical expression on his face. His gaze abruptly focused on her shoulder. "When did you become a captain?" he inquired.

"Sit down, Poppa," she said, patting the cushion beside her.

He sat. He recognized the tension in her voice and answered it with some of his own. "What's wrong? Is it Paul? Sydney?"

"No, Poppa. It's me."

His eyes swept over her. "You look all right, except for your hair."

"Haven't you heard about me?"

"Heard what?"

She leaned back, licking her lips. "Brigadier Velicher

didn't make any kind of announcement about me? Public announcement? Or personal communication?"

"No."

She sighed deeply. "I suppose it must have seemed . . . too embarrassing to let out of the inner circle."

"What's wrong, Dia?" His gaze caught on her name tag, and he touched it with light fingers. "What's this? Rocha? You've changed your name?"

"Poppa . . . I've done something that's going to be hard for you to understand. Two nights ago, I set a rebel free. It was the doctor who saved my life, and he was being interrogated, and he didn't have a chance of surviving without my help. I flew him out of the Citadel in the middle of the night, and I went with him to rebel headquarters. I was there until a few hours ago, and I told them everything I knew. Which was quite a lot. I saved his life because I owed him mine, Poppa, and I gave the information because I came to believe that the Patrol is wrong and the rebels are right. Now I'm back as one of them, and at this moment we hold the Citadel. And you . . ." Her voice broke, and she had to swallow heavily to continue. ". . . You are under arrest."

He sat very still, his lips parted slightly, his face frozen, the eyes a trifle wide and still riveted on her name tag.

"Poppa, I know it's hard to accept . . ." She clasped her hands in her lap, to avoid grasping for his, afraid of his reaction to her touch. She had never seen him like this, so at a loss for words, for expression. It was almost as if he hadn't heard her. "It's all over, Poppa," she said quietly. "The rebels have won. After today there won't be any more Patrol. Not the Patrol we knew, anyway. Velicher is dead. A lot of top officers are dead."

His brow furrowed, and his eyes seemed to be focusing on some inner vision. Very slowly, he shook his head, as if to a memory. "Sydney?" he said at last.

"She'll be all right. Mother, too. And you. That was part of my bargain with the rebels."

"And Paul?"

"I don't know what will happen to him, Poppa. If his garrison commander is smart enough to surrender without a fight, nothing."

Oliver Solares surveyed his visitors once more. "I presume then, that these are not . . . real Patrollers that have come with you to arrest me. Is he here—the man you helped escape?"

"Yes," said Talley. "I am."

Dia's father stared at him a moment, and then he said, "You can't possibly be worth it." He pushed himself up from the couch. "You were right," he said to Dia. "This is hard to understand. Too hard, for me. Will you permit me to dress before taking me to prison, Captain Rocha?"

"Of course," Dia whispered.

Ostberg followed Oliver Solares to his bedroom and stood in the doorway to keep watch over his activities, while Dia and Talley remained in the living room.

"That's that," Dia said dully.

Talley took her hand firmly in his own. "You couldn't expect anything else, Dia. He's Patrol, through and through."

"Yes."

"And you're not."

"No." She looked down at the floor. "You know, there was a time when anything I did was all right with him, any decision I made."

"Dia, there are limits . . ."

"Yes. Limits to a parent's love. Yes."

"Maybe later . . . after he's had a chance to think, and to talk to you again . . ."

"Maybe," she said, but all she could think of was how he had looked at Captain Rocha, the stranger. *Gone. Everything. Everything. How often in the years to come will I be reminded of that?* She put her head down in her hands and did not lift it again until she heard footsteps coming out of the bedroom.

Her father had dressed in his uniform, as if he were going to the office on a typical day in the Citadel. Without even glancing at Dia, he went to the door and stood, waiting for his captors to escort him outside. Ostberg edged by him, opened the door, and then he looked past Oliver Solares' shoulder to Dia and Talley. He started to speak, just the merest first syllable passing his lips, meaningless except in tone, but Talley cut him short. "I don't want to hear a word from you," he said. "Not a word."

Ostberg shrugged and waved the prisoner out.

The return journey to the Comm Center was silent and uneventful, but Dia felt exhausted at its finish. She watched two false Patrollers take her father away, watched his figure dwindle down the corridor, waited in vain for just a single backward glance. When he turned a corner and vanished from her sight, she went inside. There were no chairs free, so she sank to the floor against a wall near the telegraph, pulling her legs in close, wrapping her arms around them, to keep out of the way. She put her head down on her knees, letting the hum of the room wash over her like a gentle summer breeze. There were no words in that hum, just sounds all blurred together. She was very glad not to be hearing any words. Talley and Ostberg had left her, to confer with the telegrapher and study the master list, which had grown considerably in their absence. From the corner of her eye she could see the two men, their heads close together, their hands gesturing sharply. She closed her eyes.

Eventually, Talley joined her on the floor, sliding his arms around her and drawing her to him.

"I love you, Dia."

She murmured, "You are apparently the only person who does."

"After the ships get here, and after we've taken the crews prisoner, we might want to send an expedition back to the heart of the Federation. To tell them what happened and to suggest that anyone who wanted one of the decommissioned ships could come and get it. An expedition like that might take eight or nine months. A year maybe. And it might stop at quite a few interesting places along the way. You and I could be on it."

"On it?" She looked up at him. "But the new government —you'll be needed to help run things. You can't leave."

He shook his head. "I've done my share, and I don't even want to be around for the elections."

She inclined her head toward Ostberg, still hovering over the telegraph. "Would he be going on the expedition?"

"Not if I can help it."

She searched his eyes. "And what will we be coming back to?"

He smiled at her. "Peace and quiet. And Strux. Don't forget him." Gently, he kissed her lips. "And if you still want it then, we can find that deep, dark cavern where no one will bother us."

She clung to him. "You are worth it, aren't you?"

"I don't know, my darling," he whispered against her hair. "I don't know if anyone could be."

After a time, the floor began to seem too hard, and they sought out a couch in a far corner. It was already occupied by a pair of pseudo-Patrollers, but Talley invoked his authority and chased them off. He and Dia spent the rest of the first morning of the revolution there, sleeping in each other's arms while the telegraph clicked and the list of captured officers spread to page after page of flimsy Patrol-issue paper.

Even Ostberg left them alone.

ON THE OTHER SIDE OF TIME AND SPACE

Stories of Fantastic, Futuristic Worlds That Illuminate Universes

Pocket Books offers the best in Science Fiction— a genre whose time has come.

170

Fantasy Novels
from
POCKET BOOKS

____83217   THE BOOK OF THE DUN COW
Walter Wangerin, Jr. $2.50
*"Far and away the most literate and intelligent
story of the year."—The New York Times*

____43131   THE WHITE HART
Nancy Springer $2.50
*"It has everything; a believable fantasy world...
a lovely, poignant book."
—Marion Zimmer Bradley*

____82912   BEAUTY Robin McKinley $1.95
*"The most delightful first novel I've read in
years...I was moved and enchanted."—Peter S.
Beagle, author of THE LAST UNICORN*

____83281   CHARMED LIFE $2.25
"An outstanding success."—Andre Norton

____83294   ARIOSTO
Chelsea Quinn Yarbo $2.25
*"Colorful and exciting...a vivid tapestry come
to life...superb!"—Andre Norton*

____82958   THE ORPHAN
Robert Stallman $2.25
*"An exciting blend of love and violence, of
sensitivity and savagery."—Fritz Leiber*
